The
Spy
with a
Clean Face

Russell R. Miller

BeachHouse Books

Chesterfield Missouri

Graphics Credits:

Cover design by Dr. Bud Banis assembled from art in the Hemera Photo Objects 50,000 collection, Hemera Technologies, Inc.

ISBN 978-1-59630-031-6 BeachHouse Books Edition
ISBN 978-1-59630-032-3 MacroPrintBooks Edition

Library of Congress Cataloging-in-Publication Data
Library of Congress Cataloging-in-Publication Data
Miller, Russell R., 1928-
    The spy with a clean face / Russell R. Miller.
        p. cm.
    ISBN 978-1-59630-031-6 (regular print : alk. paper) -- ISBN 978-1-59630-032-3 (large print ed. : alk. paper)
    1. Retired executives--Fiction. 2. International Executive Service Corps--Fiction. 3. Americans--Ukraine--Fiction. 4. Illegal arms transfers--Fiction. 5. Ukraine--Fiction. I. Title.
                                        PS3613.I5528S79 2008
    813'.6--dc22   2008000135

BeachHouse Books

PO Box 7151

Chesterfield, MO 63006

(636) 394-4950

www.beachhousebooks.com

To the Family
Elsie
Cheron, Mike, and Paul
Mark, Margaret, and Cindy
Timothy and Melinda

Contents

People with butter on their heads shouldn't
dance around the sun.

old Yiddish saying

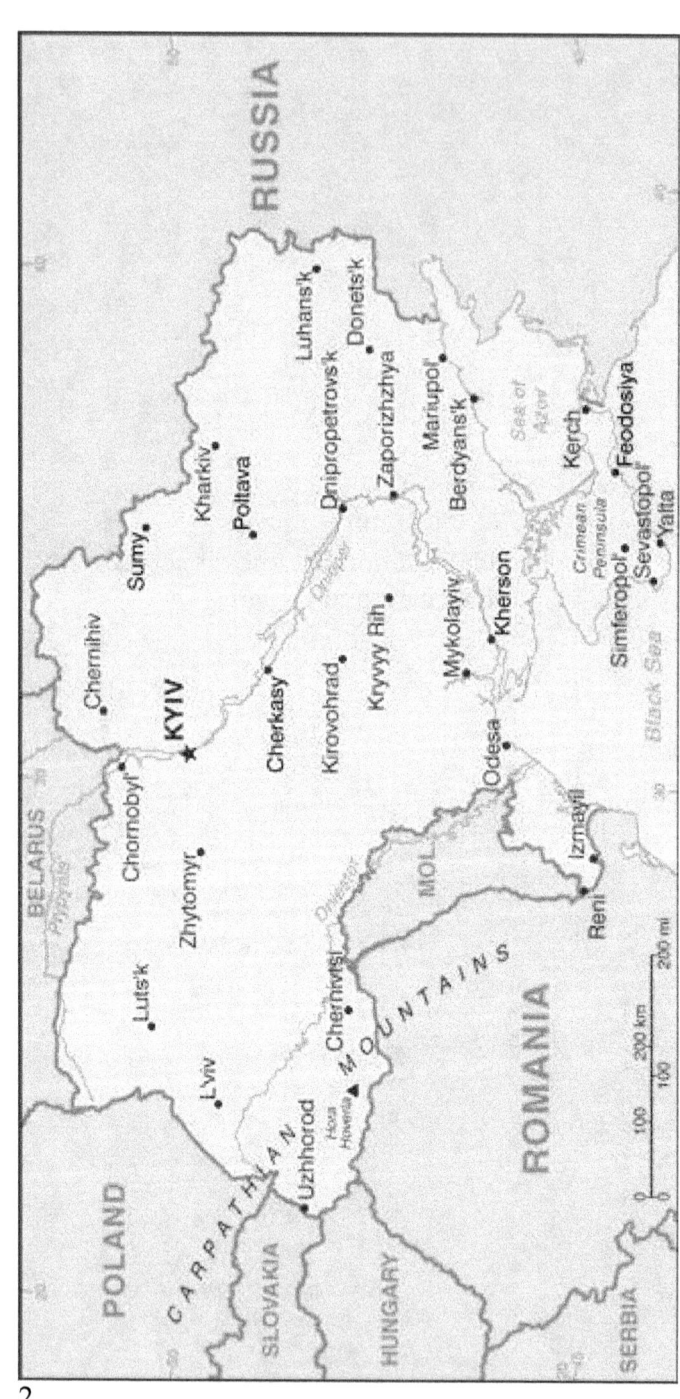

2

Prologue

The wind was gusting out of the Carpathians. It was the type of weather the local people knew well, and had learned to respect. A nearby grove of chalky birches rattled together like shivering skeletons driven by strong breezes, growing stronger then weakening as if directed by a giant metronome.

Two men, one tall one short, approached in the distance trudging through yesterday's snow. Their black felt hats and long black leather coats easily identified them as members of the once dreaded KGB. The peasants living in the Ukrainian countryside had come to fear them as they did the devil himself, and for good reason.

The two seemed guided by the thin trail of smoke rising from the remaining embers of what had once been a prized dacha. An unburned section of roof remained sugar-caked with frosted snow and decorated with newly formed icicles that were starkly outlined by a dreary aluminum sky. Behind the still smoldering remnants of the building stood a steep cliff, which in better days protected the small house from frigid winter winds.

They appeared to be searching for something as they walked. On closer inspection the dwindling importance of their once powerful organization was evident from the frayed collars of their shirts and cuffs protruding from their ill-fitting coats. A few years ago, before the collapse of the Soviet Union, the KGB represented the cream of Russian bureaucracy, with tentacles reaching throughout the world. Now in the new economy, many of the top people had become redundant. Even the organization's name had been changed to the SVR (Russian Foreign Intelligence Service) in an attempt to better represent the times.

"Here is *sukin sya* (that son of a bitch)," the short one called excitedly to his taller companion. Soon both men were staring down at a body partially covered by drifted snow. The man's head lolled grotesquely on his shoulder, his hair providing a dramatic contrast with the fallen snow. Looking closer they could detect a frozen trickle of blood that was barely apparent on his unshaven chin.

The taller of the two kicked the body with his worn shoe. "Well, he is certainly dead alright." Bending over he closed the man's eyes in an act of unlikely compassion.

"Do you think he fell from the cliff," the other asked?

"It's possible; he was always drinking, ever since he came to us. But I would rather think that someone broke his lousy American neck. I wish I had the chance to do it. You can never trust a double agent. Once a spy always a spy."

"Well whoever told us we would find him here was certainly right," the other replied, going through the dead man's pockets.

"Does he have any money?"

"Not anymore" was the answer as he gave half of what he found to his towering companion. "We will take his passport and watch back with us so they will know that we found him. What should we do with the body?"

"Let the wolves take care of him. There are plenty of them in the dead zone. It's better than he deserves. Come on lets get out of here. It could still be contaminated. Anyway it will be dark now before we get back to town. Hurry I need vodka, lots of vodka."

"Only after we call Kiev" counseled the more prudent of the two as they set off in the direction they had recently come.

It began to snow once more as the pallid sun started to set. The descending flakes camouflaged the men's dark

4

clothing, and seeped through the thin soles of their shabby shoes. The stand of white birches they passed just minutes before had become invisible. The chill wind penetrated their bones, as they thought about the call they had to make.

While they walked, the blowing snow quickly covered their tracks. Soon, it was as if the Russians had never been there.

Many miles away in a darkened hotel room another man waited for another telephone call. The room was lighted only by the blinking neon lights outside his window, advertising the dwindling pleasures of the now darkened streets. In the distance, an ambulance raced through town with claxon caroling its eerie two-tone melody familiar to Europeans, but unnerving to Americans.

Gazing through the cloudy pane, he could barely make out the dimly glowing lights of the revolving giant Ferris wheel that had come to symbolize Vienna's past, as well as its future.

The man had been waiting patiently for his call to go through that would announce his long awaited return home. He had kept the room dark out of practice on the theory that the scarcity of light would allow time to pass more swiftly. Now he was beginning to doubt the validity of his rationale.

After a time, he turned stiffly away from the window and his thoughts. Bending over the room's single bed he fumbled with the clasp on his worn suitcase. Tucked discretely among his carefully folded clothes was a still unopened bottle of Stolichnaya he had purchased at Odessa's duty free shop. Certainly the vodka would make the time pass more quickly and, if nothing else, perhaps tonight it would bring a less troubled sleep. He broke the seal and poured an ample amount into the room's only glass, before returning once more to the frosted window.

By now the Ferris wheel had stopped for the night, and only a few faint lights flickered in the distance. He raised his glass in a silent toast to old times and old friends, and his thoughts raced back to that golden day in October when he was first contacted by the Agency. Was that where this all began he wondered, pouring himself another drink.

One:
Washington Recruitment

Fall is a melancholy season in the Midwest. Perhaps, because of a recollection of the summers pleasures that have past, or an omen of winter's rigors to come. This day, however, was the kind that Midwesterners dream of. The midday sun filtered through the large oak trees shading the campus, casting deepening shadows on the concrete walkways. A few leaves had already lost their color and turned brown, but the mild temperatures provided little hint of the harsh weather that would inevitably follow. A lanky young man hurrying across the quadrangle paused to stare at the golden dome of the Old Capital Building glistening in the bright autumn light.

Turning away, he waited impatiently as the University band, on its way to the football stadium, blocked his path. The bright sun caromed off their recently polished instruments, and caused the student musicians to feel uncomfortable in their black and gold woolen uniforms.

On Saturday, Most of his classmates headed for the game. Normally he would join them, but today was different. A late call to his room the night before informed him a representative of an important government agency would be on campus, and asked specifically to see him.

How could he refuse? He was flattered to be so singularly selected. There would be other football games before mid-year graduation, and he had made it a practice to take as many interviews as he could. If nothing else it was good experience, as the Placement Director always advised.

It had been difficult to find a clean shirt in the pile on the floor of his closet. Finally he had found one that looked reasonably presentable, and a sweater that would hide any stains he may have missed. Searching further, he had located a pair of khaki trousers that had not been worn recently, then adding a pair of scruffy loafers and he was ready to go.

The band finally passed. The notes of "Seventy-six Trombones" could be heard fading into the distance. He glanced quickly at his watch as he rushed up the stairs of the Administration Building.

Entering the campus Placement Office he asked the young woman behind the desk if the Director was in. "Not on Saturday" was her curt reply. "You're Charlie? Go to the first office on the right." She immediately returned to the movie magazine lying open on her desk. It was abundantly apparent that the she was not especially pleased to be there on such a beautiful Saturday afternoon.

He was already nervous, and the interview hadn't even begun. Entering the small office he saw a nondescript man in a rumpled suit staring at several files spread before him on the shabby old desk. Charlie wondered which agency the man was with, and why he was interviewing so few people after traveling all the way from Washington.

"Charlie Connelly?" the man asked. Without waiting for an answer he motioned the young man to a chair.

"Look I'm sorry to give such short notice but we only recently learned that we could add more people. I'm with the Central Intelligence Agency. Do you know what that is?" Without pausing for an answer the man began to describe how his group was the recent offspring of the OSS, formed by Wild Bill Donovan during the war. "After it ended," he continued, "the powers that be couldn't decide if they should expand or disband the organization. Harry Truman was an old infantry officer and didn't think that spying in peacetime was a gentlemanly thing to do. Then

8

the Rosenbergs stole our atomic weapon information, and gave it to the Russians.

"Now Senator McCarthy claims that the State Department is full of Communists, and maybe they are. Maybe we are too. Who knows? Finally everyone has decided to continue our organization to keep track of what the bad guys are doing overseas, while the FBI concentrates on looking inside the country. With the Russians backing the North Koreans, they have decided that we need new blood and more people to keep the Reds in place. Are you following me?"

Charlie nodded that he was, although he wasn't sure.

"Well anyway, to come to the point, in the past most of our people have come from the Ivy League schools. Not me and a few others, but most of them are Yalies or damn close by. Some people got the idea, and I agree" he continued, "that we have depended too much on the East Coast and what we need are some Midwestern guys, and nothing can be more Midwestern than Iowa. That's why I'm here to recruit a few smart guys who might be more to the center. You're one of them. One of our "spotters" on the faculty recommended you to us. You're also Catholic, which doesn't hurt. The Pope has been giving the Russians fits in the occupied countries. You have good grades and have been in the service so you're a perfect match. I'm a good judge of talent. That's why I'm in this job, and you're the kind of talent we need right now.

"I see in your records that you already have a secret clearance — right?"

"That's right," Charlie acknowledged. "At least I used to. I was a yeoman with the Naval Air Transport Service. My job was to read and route all the incoming communications for the Commander's staff, but it wasn't too secret. It was more flight schedules, cargo loads, and the names of an occasional VIP and his scheduled arrival."

During the interview the man from Washington nervously shifted his heavy frame from one side of his chair to the other, as if it was uncomfortable to sit still for any length of time.

Charlie continued while he had a chance. "I am curious what kind of a program you have? What do you expect the recruits to do? What kind of training is provided and that sort of thing?" His voice trailed off nervously.

At this point the interviewer rose to his feet and began pacing the room. "That's a good question son." Charlie had thought so too. "By the way do you like to be called Charlie or something else?"

"I prefer Chuck." He had always thought that Chuck sounded manlier, but he was seldom able to convince anyone else.

"Ok, you can call me Marvin—Marvin Brady."

Somehow Marvin didn't sound like the type of name a secret agent should have Charlie thought, but then what did he know.

Returning to the desk the man shuffled through some papers in a file clearly marked "Secret." Extracting a sheet he asked pointedly, "were you ever a member of any of these organizations? Read the list carefully before you reply."

Charlie scanned the single spaced sheet. He had heard of some of the groups, but he was unfamiliar with most of them. A few he couldn't even pronounce. Finishing he grinned, "Marvin, where I come from most people can't even spell Communist much less join any of these crackpot organizations."

Marvin smiled as he retrieved the list. "It might surprise you to learn, young man that I know exactly what you're talking about. As a matter of fact, I used to live there myself. Before the war, I worked for Gilberts, the farm implement dealer. You know them? That was one of the reasons I especially wanted to see you."

Charlie couldn't mask his astonishment. He knew the Gilbert family, and while he thought that he was familiar with most people in town, he certainly didn't remember Marvin. He also wondered if his former job with the equipment dealer explained the missing forefinger on the man's right hand. Charlie had attempted not to stare at his hand since the interview began.

"Now to answer your question," Marvin continued. Charlie had almost forgotten what he had originally asked. "Well, our program is a little different from most others; say Western Electric for example."

Charlie wondered if the man knew he had already received an offer from that company. All through college he had assumed that he would end up with a large corporation. That was his goal and he had worked hard on his grades in the hope that the major companies would consider him. Now they were.

On the other hand, he thought, there was something to what the man from the CIA was saying. He was like most college students. Between his studies, and his social life there wasn't much time left for national or international politics.

He did believe the Russians were posing a considerable threat to the United States, and that at some time in the future he knew they would have to be stopped. It was only when Truman countered their attempt to blockade Berlin with a mammoth airlift that they backed down. Now it was pretty well accepted there was a "Cold War," and most people thought that it would heat up sometime in the near future. Maybe this guy did have the right idea.

He began to think that perhaps spending your life behind a desk might not be as exciting as he had first thought.

"Excuse me," something that Marvin said about the Agency's training program refocused his attention. "Did you say that included parachute training and Ranger training?"

"Yeah that's right. We also throw in some language courses depending on where you might be going. Then later we show you a little, what we call tradecraft, to help you get along."

"And where would I be going?"

"Well, right now there are two curtains. One is the iron curtain and the other we refer to as the bamboo curtain. After training we would probably put you behind one of those to see if you could establish a network of agents that would provide us with the information we need. You would stay there about two years. Then come back to Washington for awhile before we send you somewhere else. Does it sound interesting?"

"Well it doesn't sound dull, I will say that much for it" Charlie replied with certainty.

In the back of his mind he was thinking of Beth. They had been going together for the four years they had been in college. He wondered what she would think of being married to someone with that type of life. Perhaps, it was best not to mention it. Maybe he couldn't ever mention it. Anyway he was sure as hell not convinced that this was what he wanted to do. Or could do for that matter.

Marvin continued. "If you're interested I will arrange for you to come to Washington to meet some of the guys. They can look you over. Tell you a little bit more about us. Then we can both decide if we want to get together. How about it?"

"I am interested, and I guess I would like to do something to contribute. It sounds like a tough haul. I'm not sure I am up to it, but let's see what happens."

"Sounds good to me," Marvin replied, glancing at his watch. "We will be in touch. By the way, don't tell anyone who you were talking with. If someone asks, tell them Quaker Oats or something. OK?"

"I understand. Thanks for seeing me," Charlie said as he went out the door. His mind was reeling. Waiting in the small outer office was someone he had seen frequently around campus.

They both said hello as they passed. "How did it go," he asked Charlie.

"Piece of cake," he replied confidently. "

Following his interview, Charlie expected to hear from the Agency but not, as it turned out, in the middle of the night. Didn't these people ever call in the daytime he wondered? The woman on the other end of the line informed him the Agency would like him to come to Washington. A plane ticket would be waiting for him at the placement office. Could he be there on Friday?

Why not he thought, what's to lose?

The DC-4 was taxiing down the runway, its four propellers cleanly slicing the crisp winter air. Slowly the plane became airborne. Charlie gripped the armrests until his knuckles turned white. Looking around sheepishly, he could tell this was an everyday occurrence for the rest of the passengers. Not for him. It was his first flight.

After completing boot camp he had been assigned to the Pacific Staff of the Naval Air Transport Service in Honolulu, the closest he ever came to flying was watching the large cargo planes land for refueling on their way to the Orient. Each day he dreamed of personally seeing these exotic places, but it was not to be while he was in the Navy.

He had traveled to Hawaii on a lumbering old troop transport, and returned to the mainland aboard an ancient, empty oil tanker that bobbed like a cork on rough seas.

Staring out the plane's small window, Charlie studied the emerging clusters of miniature lights that encircled the small towns along the route. He wondered what the people below were doing. Most of all, staring into the ebony darkness, he tried to decide if he would ever have the guts to parachute out of a plane at this altitude, and then land in an unknown and hostile environment.

The flight attendant arrived with dinner before he could reach a conclusion. After forcing his fears to the furthest corner of his mind he began to eat.

The next morning he took a taxi from his hotel to the address he had been given on the phone. "Twenty-third Street and Constitution Avenue North West," he told the waiting driver, as authoritatively as a young man could.

It was a beautiful day. The air was unusually brisk for Washington. It was the first time he had seen the city, and he was impressed with the beauty of the Capital. A deep sense of patriotism engulfed him as he thought about the city, and what it represented to the world.

This time he was dressed for a serious interview in blue blazer, white buttoned-down shirt, striped tie, and well-polished black shoes. He believed that he was prepared to compete with the best of the Ivy League.

The taxi passed the reflecting pool in front of the Lincoln Memorial and quickly pulled to a stop by one of several decrepit looking wooden buildings that were typical of many scattered around Washington. The old structures were originally intended to serve their purpose only temporarily during the war, but continued to remain in place many years afterward.

Charlie gave a number to the tall Marine guard at the entranceway. Soon, a slender rather severe looking woman appeared inside the gate. "My name is Mary Kool," she said extending her thin hand. "Follow me," she ordered leading the way down a darkened corridor past a long line of closed unnumbered doors.

"The first thing they want for you is an intelligence test, then a physical. Mind and body that's us." The woman didn't appear to be the type that excelled at small talk, and Charlie followed her submissively, her high heels echoing eerily down the empty hallway.

Occasionally, someone would dart out of one of the offices, only to disappear once again further down the hall. Some carried papers, others did not. No one paid any attention to the slender woman and her young companion.

He followed his guide to a cramped office equipped with a single government-issue green metal desk, and two matching metal chairs. A scholarly looking older man entered through another door as Mary Kool abruptly turned and left the room. He peered at Charlie through his thick glasses, while silently handing him a bulging booklet containing the exam.

Apparently, the man's principal function was to pass out a multi-paged test, take out his watch, explain the time constraints, and then occupy the remaining chair while Charlie worked on the answers. Initially, the older man's presence was distracting, but he was soon forgotten as Charlie scanned the questions. The exam was similar to many others he had taken in school and the Navy, with hundreds of multiple choice questions requiring the taker to select the most correct answer from several illogical choices. The test emphasized reading comprehension with only minimum references to math or science. Charlie had expected it to be more difficult, and he finished well within the allotted time.

The physical was also less demanding than many of the others he had been subjected to in the past. The doctor checked his blood pressure, felt his pulse, and had him breathe deeply while placing a stethoscope on his chest. He looked into his eyes and throat, told him to cough, and examined his fingernails, giving the impression to Charlie that he had performed this boring routine many times before, and wished he was doing vastly more important things.

When Charlie finished dressing, Mary Kool reappeared and led him to another office further down the long labyrinth of poorly lighted hallways. Entering, he was pleased to see Marvin's familiar face at the head of a long conference table. Another man was seated to his right.

"How was the flight Charlie?" Marvin inquired pleasantly.

"Routine," Charlie replied with a grin, hoping to give the impression that he had flown many times before.

"I want you to meet my boss, Emmett Valentine. He heads up Clandestine Operations. You've already met Mary Kool. She's our resident shrink, and heads the Personnel Department. I have told them about you and they thought that it would be a good idea to take a look at you themselves. At the same time they can tell you a little more about what you might be doing at the Agency.

The Director was tall, much taller than Charlie's six-foot frame. His seersucker suit was slightly out of season, but looked expertly tailored to match his slender physique. His patrician appearance was in stark contrast to Marvin who was wearing a wrinkled short sleeve white shirt without a coat, topped off by a wide bow tie.

Valentine's commanding presence and his impeccable attire made Charlie uneasy as he sat uncomfortably in his own department store blazer and slacks.

16

"Emmett and I were both in the OSS," Marvin explained. "When the war was over, Bill Donavan asked him to come along with him to help start up the CIA. After he got here, Emmett asked me to join him. We have seen a lot together and it looks like our work has just begun."

"You know Charlie old man, I don't want to hide the facts from you," the director began, "but this is a very tough job, and it takes a different type of person to handle it. The people we hire always work in the shadows. No one can know what it is that you do, or for whom you work.

"One of our more scholarly associates compared his life to working in a house of mirrors. You never know which reflection is real and which is false. After awhile some people lose track of reality and drift into a world of false reflections. They become overly paranoid and lose their effectiveness.

"On top of that," he continued staring intently at Charlie, "when you succeed no one outside of the agency will know it, and when you fail it is often apparent to the entire world. That's why we have to be very careful about the people we hire. We know many of them won't be able to handle the pressure and the anonymity." Emmett paused to sip from a glass of water that was in front of him.

Replacing the glass he continued. "The barbarians are storming the gate, and we are the ones that have to repel them. We are looking for patriots that are willing to work alone and who are able to think for themselves."

"In many cases," he added "the United States will base its foreign policy on our information, and if it proves wrong our country will suffer."

It was a thrilling, but also frightening prospect. Somewhat perversely, the harder the job was made to sound the more interesting it became to the young applicant.

There was a faint knock on the door. A woman entered and handed Valentine several sheets of paper. He scanned them impassively and quickly handed them to Marvin who, after studying them more closely, passed them to Mary Kool.

"It looks like you did very well on your tests," Valentine observed. "Marvin also tells me you played football in high school, and spent your summers as a lifeguard. We expected you would do well on both counts. I do have some questions, however, about your Navy record." Opening one of the files in front of him the director continued, "It says here you were once brought up on Captain's Mast, but the charges were dropped. What was that about?"

"Well," Charlie began nervously "a Captain's Mast is kind of low level court martial."

"I know what it is Charlie. What I actually want to know is why were you there?"

"The enlisted staff in Hawaii was a closely knit group of men who were all about the same age and educational level. We lived together, three or four to a room, with no regard to enlisted rank. Some had been in the Navy longer than others. Never the less, we always took turns, a week at a time, cleaning the room and sweeping the deck.

"One of the men made second-class petty officer. In the Navy scheme of things this would be the same as a sergeant compared to a corporal. When it was his turn to sweep he told me to do it for him. I pointed out that it was his turn, but he ordered me to do it anyway. At that point, I suggested that he perform an anatomical impossibility with the broom."

"What the hell does that mean? Marvin asked.

"Well putting it more crudely," Charlie hesitated and looked apologetically toward Mary Kool. "I told him to put the broom handle where the sun don't shine. But, I am surprised that it is in my record. After hearing the two sides Captain Nation lectured us on how we should conduct ourselves, and said that nothing would go into either of our records."

While he attempted to explain, Charlie began to get a sinking feeling in the pit of his stomach. He was afraid that the long forgotten incident would eliminate him from further consideration.

"The Captain told you the truth. It didn't go in the file. It mentions only that you were brought up on disciplinary charges, and they were dropped," Valentine assured him as he continued paging through the file.

Charlie glanced furtively at Marvin who seemed to be suppressing a grin. Mary Kool continued taking notes.

"It also says here that the Captain later recommended you for Annapolis and you turned him down. What happened there?" Valentine asked.

Charlie was shocked how much information they had. He had no idea that his file was so complete. "Well," he began "it seems that the Navy decided that it would be good to draw on some of their enlisted personnel already in the service rather than relying entirely on congressional appointments. I was told that I had been selected for the program, and if I accepted I would be sent to a preparatory school in the East for a year. If I got through that I would then go on to Annapolis. There was a catch, however. I would have to reenlist for four more years to be considered. If I flunked out at any point I would be back in the fleet to serve out my time as an enlisted man. I thought about it a lot, and decided to turn down the offer. I could go to college on the GI bill when my enlistment was over, and then go into any field I wanted. So I declined."

Clearing his throat Charlie added weakly, "That's just about it."

Emmett Valentine looked down the table toward Mary Kool who nodded ever so slightly. He then turned to Marvin who was also nodding in agreement.

"Look Charlie," the director began. "We are looking for people who are imaginative and who can work alone without direction. We are also looking for people who are analytical as well as physical, and we think you possess the qualities we need. Marvin has told you what the job involves and the training you would receive.

Do you have any questions?"

Charlie had been thinking it over during the interview, but at this point couldn't think of a single thing to ask, so he just shook his head.

"If you join us you would be paid a salary commensurate with what you would earn at a major company," Valentine continued. "You would then receive periodic increases in accordance with the government pay scale. If you are interested in the job there is one problem. You graduate in January, and our training program will not begin until June. How would you handle that?"

Using his Navy credits Charlie was graduating in three and one half years, and still had another semester available on the GI Bill. The June start date was no particular problem. It would also give him an opportunity to take some courses he had to miss in order to graduate on time.

"I could do that without any problem" he replied.

"All right then. Would you like to accept our offer?" Valentine asked.

"Yes I would," he replied confidently.

Back at the University, Charlie was enjoying the spring semester without the pressure of grades, or having to find a job. He had told Beth the truth about the offer from the

Agency, but no one else. She was less than enthusiastic with his decision, but raised no major objection. He also informed Miss Barnes at the Student Placement Office, who had originally set up the interview. To his parents and friends he said that he had taken a job in Washington with the Commerce Department, and everyone seemed satisfied with that explanation.

There were times, however, when he wondered what had possessed a normally rational young man to accept such a job, when all of his mature life he had wanted to work for a major corporation. When his chance finally came he turned the companies down and decided instead to become a cowboy. Perhaps it was patriotism, perhaps it was a sense of adventure, and perhaps it was something that even he didn't fully understand.

Just as the trees were beginning to leaf out again, Charlie got another late night call. This time it was from Marvin.

"Charlie old boy" he began. "I am terribly sorry to have to do this. I know it isn't fair, but Truman has cut our budget and we are not able to take on new recruits as we planned. Now, we're going to have to go with the people we already have. The President is upset over some of the mistakes we made. We didn't know in advance that the North Koreans were going to invade South Korea. We also have had a few other little problems that I can't tell you about now."

Charlie was shocked, and angry. Angry is too mild a word he was furious. Before he accepted the job with the Agency he had been in demand by everyone he had interviewed. Now, all the big recruiters had been to the campus and filled their quotas for new hires. The agency had really screwed him, and there didn't seem to be anything he could do about it.

He first thought about writing his Congressman to complain, but then recalled that Marvin had said they would have to conduct a further background check on him. Perhaps they had found something they didn't like, and this was their way of getting off the hook. On the other hand, Charlie couldn't think of any kind of a problem that might disqualify him.

Finally, he decided to do nothing other than to appeal to Miss Barnes. Charlie had been one of her favorite students. He had good grades and conducted himself well in interviews.

She began immediately calling her corporate contacts and eventually found that AT&T had been unable to find all of the people they needed for their new management-training program. An interview was arranged, and Charlie ultimately was offered a job.

If he had wanted to go with a large corporation this was it. It was the largest in the country.

A month later he and Beth became engaged.

Six months after he started with the Telephone Company Charlie was in Chicago and half way through the training program. One of the secretaries came to his office to tell him that while he was at lunch he had received a telephone call from Washington. It turned out to be from Marvin who was apologetic about what happened, but wanted him to know the Agency had now received increased funding and could hire once more. He and Emmett Valentine would very much like to have him join them.

Charlie asked Marvin if he remembered what he had told the petty officer to do with the broom. Marvin recalled that yes he did. Charlie brusquely told him he could do the same thing with his job, and hung up.

Two:
Maracaibo Meeting

Charlie never regretted his decision to reject the renewed offer from the Central Intelligence Agency. Years went by without any thought of his first experience with Marvin and his clandestine organization. Occasionally, he would see an article in a magazine or a newspaper about the Agency's activities. When he read these accounts, he would sometimes wonder what his life might have been like if he had gone to work for the CIA. Would he have been an entirely different person than he was now? He could never decide. One thing was certain; his life with Beth would be completely different. It was hard to imagine how they could have remained married as long as they had under the conditions Marvin described during the interviews.

Of course, corporate life had not been entirely as he expected either. When he first joined AT&T, he planned to stay until he either died or retired. Times were changing and corporate culture was responding to the rapidly moving demands of new technology, and increased foreign competition.

Charlie was determined to never again be in a position to be taken advantage of by an employer as he was by the CIA. It was embarrassing to be fired from a job before it began, and Charlie resolved to never be that naïve and dependent.

As the years passed, Charlie became expert at adjusting to the corporate fox trot—two steps forward—then one back. If you danced long enough, and with a little luck, you could eventually make progress across the crowded floor. It had also meant that he and Beth, and later the three children, moved from company to company and town to town whenever it seemed necessary to maintain a semblance of upward momentum.

Eventually, it had worked out all right. Beth seemed happy. The kids were doing well in school, and now he was head of international marketing for Apex Electronics. It was a challenging job that gave him an opportunity to travel, and hopefully to save enough money to put the kids through college.

"Welcome to Venezuela Mr. Connelly." The customs agent energetic stamping of his passport abruptly returned Charlie from his reverie to the stuffy Maracaibo airport. He had been here many times over the last few years. Taxiing in on the tarmac he noticed that the same army tank was positioned next to the hangars, and the same armed militiamen were standing outside the terminal. Such consistency gave Charlie a feeling of continuity, if not a great deal of confidence.

The 707's luggage bins were crammed with large plastic wrapped stuffed animals the returning Venezuelan families had purchased at Disney World. The slowly revolving luggage conveyer with its unwitting toy menagerie gave him the impression of a silently sad carousel.

Grabbing his bags before some stranger could, Charlie dashed to Customs ahead of the luggage laden Venezuelans. He was waved through without problems, and headed for the nearest taxi. The scorching outside air hit him like a powerful blow. His travel-wrinkled clothes immediately began to cling to his sweaty body.

"Hotel Del Lago *por favor*" he ordered the driver. The name was almost unnecessary. There was only one hotel in Maracaibo where foreigners stayed. The taxi took a familiar route past the harbor with its tankers and cargo ships lashed tightly to the docks. Leaving the waterfront the ancient cab passed many small, brightly painted houses partly shaded by giant palms. The modest homes formed an attractive

24

reminder of the country's colonial past, but they were rapidly being replaced to accommodate Maracaibo's oil rich expansion.

As the cab careened through the narrow streets a slight breeze came through its open windows. The most over utilized accessory on South American cars is the horn. The driver made liberal use of his to get to the Hotel Del Lago. The air-conditioned hotel lobby came as a welcome relief to the sweaty American traveler.

After a hurried swim in the naturally heated hotel pool, Charlie called the room of Luis Falcon. Luis was the Caracas attorney that Apex used for their affairs in Venezuela. He was resting, and they agreed to meet later for dinner.

Apex had long held a one-third interest in a local television assembly company. Charlie was on the Board of Directors, and Luis was his legal advisor. They met at least once a quarter. More often if there were problems, which there frequently were.

The hotel restaurant was crowded as usual. Stale tobacco smoke hung like a heavy cloud. The oil business was booming, and Maracaibo was the principal center of Venezuela's production. Most of the men at the bar worked in the fields, and were from either Oklahoma or Texas. Many of them were engineers, but a few were the drillers and roustabouts who had taken off for an evening in town.

"*Como esta Luis*," Charlie shouted across the room.

"Hey amigo, how is the family?" the attorney replied in his cultured English. The two had become close friends over the years.

Catching a passing waiter's attention Charlie shouted "*dos Polars por favor*. The waiter quickly returned with two bottles picturing a large white polar bear on their poorly painted labels. The local beer was frosty cold and disappeared quickly.

"Dos mas amigo, muy rapido," Luis ordered a passing waiter.

The man scurried away to get two more bottles. It was a busy night the waiter thought. All the Yankees in the world must have decided to come to the Del Lago. Anyway, they tipped well, better than the tight fisted Venezuelans.

Over dinner, Charlie and Luis discussed their plan for the next day. Both men had ordered thick steaks. Maracaibo is located in Zulia Province, and the local residents consider it to be the Texas of Venezuela because of the large cattle ranches and seemingly inexhaustible supply of high-grade crude. In such an environment it is socially unacceptable to order anything in Zulia other than rare beef, and the two men were more than happy to conform to local custom.

They were scheduled to meet with the Gorman brothers, who owned the remaining two-third interest in the local company. The family had originally come to Venezuela during one of the frequent purges in Russia.

Then, Venezuela was eager to attract accomplished Europeans to enhance its less educated population. After the death of the parents, the older brother Adolpho took responsibility for his much younger sibling, Jacob. Now the two were more like father and son than brothers.

Adolpho established an appliance business in Maracaibo and sent his brother to boarding school in the United States to further his education and improve his fluency in English. The two men eventually added a television production company after licensing the Apex brand and technology.

Jacob ran the company, with Adolpho's son Rene' as assistant manager. The business had done well, but now with color transmission being introduced to the country there was increased opportunity for even greater expansion.

It was a mystery to the people at Apex why the Maracaibo Company never had enough capital to take advantage of their expanding market. As a result, it was losing significant market share, and might not be able to recover.

Something was wrong, and Charlie couldn't figure out what it might be. The purpose of tomorrow's meeting was to introduce a new outside auditor he had insisted they hire. The auditor represented an American accounting company in Caracas, and both Charlie and Luis believed it was desirable to have someone take a fresh look at the books.

"Are you sure he will be there tomorrow?" Charlie asked.

"He assured me he would," answered Luis, "but this is South America, and you can never be certain that someone will show up when he says; even if he does work for an American company."

The oilmen were still at the bar when the two men finished their coffee. Drilling is dirty thirsty work, even when the rig is in the middle of Lake Maracaibo.

He was awakened early the next morning by the bedside telephone. "Hi traveler. How goes the battle?" It was his secretary Linda who had worked for Charlie for many years. She was very familiar with the business, as well as the company's disparate collection of international customers.

"It hasn't started yet, but I will let you know. What's happening?" He knew that it was important. She didn't call often. It was too difficult to get a line to some of the more remote locations he visited, and Maracaibo was one of them.

"His highness wants to make sure that you will be back in time for the Staff Meeting on Friday. He wants to go over forecasts for next year. He says it is important that you be there."

His highness in this case, Charlie knew, was his boss Norman Baines, who was head of all the company's marketing organizations. Norman had never understood the international business and really had no desire to learn. He thought the foreign customers were all a little bit peculiar, to say the least. Not at all like his solid domestic people.

All Norman understood was that the international business sometimes interfered with his U.S. distributors, and he often thought that it was more of problem than it was worth. Even though the international business was increasing rapidly and was highly profitable, Apex was having difficulty with profits. The company had at one time been the most important consumer electronics company in the US. Now it was being badly battered by Japanese imports, and profits were critical.

"Tell him I will be there," Charlie said looking at his watch. "Anything else?"

"Yes, I was pretty sure you would be, but I also got a rather strange call from Washington. The man said he was an old friend of yours, but wouldn't tell me what company he was with?"

"What was his name?

"It was Marvin. Marvin--let me see. Where did I put my notes? Brady — it was Marvin Brady."

There was a good deal of noise on the line and Charlie wasn't sure he heard correctly. "Marvin who?"

"Brady-Brady, Marvin Brady" she shouted. "Do you know him?"

"It was a long time ago. What did he want?"

"He was really anxious that you call him. What shall I tell him?"

"You can tell him to go-" Charlie stopped in time. "Maybe that's not such a great idea," he laughed. Tell him I will call him when I get back in the country."

"Will you?" Linda asked.

"No." Charlie replied.

"Hey," he added quickly before they lost the connection. "Please call Beth. Tell her I am having a good trip, and I will try and call from Bogota."

"OK boss. Stay safe, and don't drink the water."

Charlie hung up, and hurried to check out. He planned to leave for the airport immediately after the meeting, and didn't want to have to return to the hotel.

When he and Luis got to the factory they learned that the auditor from Caracas would be late. His flight had been delayed.

Charlie, Luis Falcon, and the three Gormans were seated around a large conference table. The situation was unusually strained. The Venezuelans resented that the American was bringing in an independent accountant. It would cost the company money, and it implied a lack of trust.

Charlie studied the other men while he sipped the strong thick Venezuelan coffee that the secretary had served in the traditional small cups.

Adolpho, the patriarch of the family, sat at the head of the table in deference to his age, and position as founder of the company. He was an impressive older man. His thick gray hair and pencil thin mustache only added to his already distinguished appearance. He dressed impeccably, and always wore a tailor-made suit and carefully matched tie. Even in the tropical heat of Maracaibo, Charlie had never seen a wrinkle so brazen as to crease Adolpho's expensive clothing.

Over the years, Adolpho had acquired a prominent position in the city's business community. He and Charlie had always gotten along well, and when they differed on a particular position they were always able to settle it amicably.

The two men also shared a fondness for very dry gin martinis. Adolpho always kept a large pitcher of them in his refrigerator. This way they could be adequately chilled without being diluted by ice during the mixing process. Adolpho insisted on using generous amounts of Beefeaters gin, with only a whiff of dry vermouth.

Jacob, or Jake, was the complete opposite of his older brother. He was tightly wired and aggressive. He had proved to be a competent, hard working manager with a fondness for his female "cousins." A term he used with Charlie when referring to his extra marital activities.

Adolpho's son Rene' was Princeton educated and happily married with two growing sons. He had never appeared to be overly ambitious, but was bright and willing to work hard when it was necessary. Rene' shared Charlie's love of reading and the two of them often discussed books while enjoying Adolpho's seeming inexhaustible supply of very dry martinis.

Charlie enjoyed working with all three men, and had developed confidence in their combined management ability, but something was dramatically wrong with the company's finances. He wasn't enough of an accountant to determine what it was, but he had been around long enough to know that things were certainly not adding up.

The entrance of the secretary and the auditor from Caracas abruptly interrupted his thoughts. If appearances are an indication of a person's competency, Luis had done a wonderful job selecting this one. His slight frame and rimless glasses gave the impression he was the personification of the title "Certified Public Accountant." As a matter of fact, Charlie thought, this guy looks like Arthur Anderson himself.

After taking his place at the table, the auditor carefully cleaned his glasses with an immaculate white handkerchief, while the other men fidgeted nervously. The man finally decided that his lenses were sufficiently clean for the task at hand, and then carefully extracted a thick file folder from a black leather brief case.

Clearing his throat, he began to speak in a squeaky high-pitched voice. "I have had an opportunity to examine this organization's quarterly financial statements that Senor Falcon has been kind enough to provide. While I am yet unable to establish the source, I believe that I can state, without fear of contradiction, that there has been a systematic drain of this company's financial resources. I therefore intend to-."

"That won't be necessary," Jake said as he rose from his chair. Every eye in the room focused on the source of the unexpected interruption. "I have been dreading this day for a long time. I hoped it would never come. I thought that I could fix it before anyone found out."

"Good God Jake, what have you done?" cried Adolpho in a pained voice, desperately fearing what he was about to hear.

"I've been siphoning money from the company, and investing it in my cattle ranch. You all knew I had a ranch," Jake said defensively. "I needed more cattle, or I was going to lose the ranch. So, as our sales increased here I took a little money from the company to expand the herd. I planned to sell the excess steers and replace the funds, once I got the spread back on its feet.

"When Charlie was so god-damned determined to hire an outside auditor I knew there would be a problem. Our company accountant agreed to cover up for me and cook the books. If he didn't, he knew I would fire him."

Everyone in the room, with the possible exception of the auditor, was shocked. Charlie didn't know what to say. He felt he should have acted sooner, but what could he have known living so far away.

"Jake how could you after all I have done for you?" moaned Adolpho pounding the table. "Not only have you stolen from the company, you have stolen from both Rene and me. We trusted you implicitly."

Jake was visibly shaken, his defensive resolve broken. "I know, I know," he sobbed. I will pay you back. I'm going to New York tomorrow and sell my stamp collection. It's very valuable, and will bring enough money to pay back the company. I think," he trailed off unconvincingly.

"Like hell you will," shouted Charlie unable to suppress his anger. "You can do whatever you want with your damn stamps, but that won't help this company survive. We trusted you, and we depended on you, and you let us all down."

Charlie's mind was racing wildly. "Here is what you are going to do. Right now! You are going to sign over the ranch to the company. Then you are going to walk out of here and never come back. Adolpho and I are putting Rene' in your place as General Manager. We are going to continue the audit and if more money is required we will seize your house and any other property you have. Then we will freeze your bank account. Do you understand?"

"I won't do that; it's all I've got. What do you want me to do kill myself?" Jake cried, reaching under the table and withdrawing a small Derringer he always carried in his boot. He looked around the room as he pointed the small pistol menacingly at his temple.

"No Jake!" shouted Adolpho.

"Would you want us to leave the room Jake?" Charlie asked coldly. The usual smile had disappeared from his face. He spoke the words softly, but their implication thundered through the silent boardroom. Everyone turned their gaze from Jacob to Charlie, who had had enough of his partner's theatrics. There was little room in his life for dishonesty and betrayal, and Charlie felt only disgust for the man he had trusted for many years.

The chill in Charlie's voice took Jake by surprise. Hesitating, he looked around the room and saw the sorrow in the faces of his brother and nephew, and the total loathing on the face of the Venezuelan attorney. Broken, he sheepishly lowered the gun and laid it on the table.

"Do you agree Adolpho?" Charlie asked, not waiting for an answer. "What about you Rene'?" They both nodded in silent agreement.

Adolpho removed the neatly folded handkerchief from his breast pocket and mournfully blew his nose. The auditor sat in stunned silence. He hadn't expected this when he came to Maracaibo. He was unaccustomed to such drama in his otherwise orderly life of debits and credits.

Charlie pointed to the attorney who was already reaching into his briefcase, "Draw up the papers Luis. I want them signed by all of us before I leave."

Working in international for so many years Charlie had long ago abandoned subtleties and nuance. "Adolpho we depended on you. Chairman of the Board is more than just an honorary position. We expected you to keep close watch on the business, and you didn't do it. Now it's time to get involved or the company is going under. It won't be good for Apex, but it will totally ruin your reputation in Maracaibo."

Charlie turned quickly and stared pointedly at Rene. "Now, Rene, it's time for you to step up to the plate. Do you understand? This is more than just a company it's your inheritance."

The papers were rapidly drawn up and were signed without further discussion. On his way out Charlie dodged into the men's room, and vomited into the toilet. Not only had Jacob betrayed Apex, he had also betrayed his own family. That type of disloyalty made Charlie physically ill.

"Your cab to the airport is waiting outside Senor Connelly." The secretary smiled pleasantly as he passed her desk, wiping his face with a damp paper towel.

Three:
Mayhem in Medellin

Charlie glanced at his watch as the small plane taxied down the narrow runway. He was drained from the confrontation with Jake, and was glad to be on his way to someplace else--anyplace else. Fortunately, the Avensa flight took only forty-five minutes from Maracaibo to the Caracas Maiquetia Airport. He reclined his seat to a more comfortable position, as the plane banked slowly to gain altitude in the heated atmosphere.

Closing his eyes, he searched his mind for anything more he might have done with the Gormans. He finally decided, once it became clear the younger brother had skimmed the company's funds for his own use, there was nothing more that could be done.

But what was the story with Marvin, he wondered. There hadn't been time to think about the unexpected call to his office until now. After all of these years, why now? It couldn't be just to talk about old times. There weren't any old times. Charlie tried to doze, but there was too much on his mind, and the flight was too short.

After claiming his bag, he caught a taxi to the Macuto Sheraton. It was a pleasant seaside hotel, easier to get to than fighting the heavy traffic over the mountains to smoggy downtown Caracas. Safer too. The U.S. Embassy had just issued a Traveler's Alert describing a threat that an increasing number of taxis were being held-up as they traveled between the airport and the city center of Caracas.

His room faced the Caribbean, and he quickly threw open the door to the veranda to clear the musty tropical smell. He stood for a moment inhaling the sea breeze, hoping to rid himself of the lingering stench of Maracaibo. After a quick swim in the hotel pool, he dressed for dinner.

The door to the elevator parted, and he was surprised to see three old friends from Boeing. The men were equally startled to see him, and they quickly tried to catch up on what had happened to each of them since they worked together in Seattle.

Their conversation continued in the lobby until one of the men spotted the heavily gold braided Venezuelan military officers that were to be their guests for the evening. Several brawny civilians, furtively talking into their coat sleeves while anxiously surveying the crowd accompanied the officers. The mixed group quickly dispersed into a waiting chain of long, black American limousines.

Charlie continued toward the dining room alone, stopping briefly at the bar for a martini to take to his table. He noticed three of Jacob's more attractive "cousins" sitting by themselves at a nearby table, and winked playfully as he passed.

That evening he decided on duck a l'orange, accompanied by a little wild rice, washed down with a glass of crisp Chilean white wine. No salad, Charlie was an experienced traveler. He was also a cautious one, and ordered agua mineral con gas, never trusting the local bottled water unless it was processed.

While he ate, he thought about the uncommon likelihood of meeting old friends from Seattle at a seaside hotel in Venezuela. But no more unusual, he thought, than once meeting a former California boss in the Hilton hotel lobby in Tel Aviv.

One of the reasons Charlie didn't fool around on the road was, regardless of how distant he thought the location might be, with his luck he would probably be seated at a table next to one of Beth's many sisters.

He considered a dessert with his coffee. He really shouldn't but, what the hell it had been a hard day.

"*Amigo,*" he snapped his fingers at a passing waiter. "*Para me*" Charlie began in his fractured high school Spanish. "*Un flan lime con Coconut.*" Coconut lime flan was Charlie's favorite desert, but trying to remain trim he rarely indulged. But tonight, he decided, he had earned it.

Returning to his room, he briefly listened to the atonal symphony provided by a chorus of tree frogs lending a high-pitched accompaniment to the deeper base sounds of a booming tropical surf. Soon he fell into an exhausted, but fitful sleep.

In order to catch the Avianca flight to Bogota, Charlie had to rise at four o'clock. The night before he had arranged to be picked up by a hotel taxi. It was still pitch black. It would be an hour before the sun rose above the rocky Venezuelan coast.

As the driver sped through the narrow winding back streets, he thought how vulnerable he would be to an assault. A lone stranger in a foreign land provides an easy mark for a local driver and his accomplices. No problem this time, he thought. He also knew the Colombian licensee's engineers would meet him at the airport in Bogota.

Shortly after takeoff, the attendant served a small breakfast. As is always the case, once food is served the flight became bumpy, and the old 707 was flying over the Andes. When the plane's wheels finally hit the ground the relieved Latinos aboard broke out in a loud round of applause.

The plane rolled slowly to a stop alongside a waiting airport bus, but there was no attempt by the crew to remove the passengers. After several minutes Charlie stopped one of the attendants.

"What's the problem?"

"When we removed the trays a passenger in the rear aisle hid his silverware and won't give them back."

"You mean those little plastic knives and forks?" he asked her incredulously.

"They may look like nothing to you Americans," she caustically replied "but if we let every passenger take them home, the airline would go bankrupt."

Time passed slowly, and sweat began to trickle down the center of Charlie's back. Another, hopefully more amenable, attendant came down the plane's narrow aisle toward him. "Look miss, we all want to get off. It's getting awfully stuffy in here," he pleaded, "and I have people waiting for me in the terminal. Here is ten dollars. That should buy a lot of plastic knives and forks."

There was a quick furtive conference with the other attendants, and finally the door to the outside gangway slowly opened. The first person off was the small South American with his treasured plastic utensils.

After claiming his baggage, Charlie found Luz Estrella, the Colombian company's office manager. They had known each other for many years, and she was the one constant among the continually changing management personnel. He had always been convinced she could manage the entire operation herself, if the owners would let her. Luz, with her jet-black hair and sparkling brown eyes, was also considerably better looking than the other managers.

"*Como esta* Charlie", she called. "How was the trip?"

"A little bumpy, but what's new?" he replied.

"Hey Carlos" Charlie called to one of the men accompanying Luz. "Are you the driver today?" Carlos Muniz was the company's Chief Engineer.

"Si, Mr. Connelly I'm the man. *Vamonos!*" he yelled to the others, grabbing Charlie's bag.

Charlie preferred staying at the Tequendama when he was in Bogota, and Luz always made his reservation there. It was an older hotel in the center of town, with a connected shopping mall. The rooms were airy and clean, and service top-notch. The lobby was large, well appointed, and served as a social center for the city's business and political elite.

An additional attraction for Charlie was the excellent jewelry shop in the hotel lobby. He had bought a very nice emerald ring for Beth on a previous trip, and he hoped that he would have time to pick up a pair of matching earrings before leaving.

Carlos carefully parked his small car, and immediately disconnected the windshield wipers, self-consciously putting them into his briefcase. "Gaminitas," he embarrassedly explained. These, Charlie knew, were roaming bands of young orphan children who lived by stealing anything they could lay their hands on.

After sending his bags to his room, he joined the others already seated at a table in the bar. They wanted to discuss the problems the Colombian Company was experiencing before he went on to Medellin. The technical and sales effort was centered in Bogota, while the factory and executive offices were in Medellin.

Carlos explained they needed an engineer from Chicago to help them with a new TV set they were assembling, while Luz translated.

While they talked, Charlie's mind began to wander. It was hard to concentrate when he had to wait for translation, and he had had similar conversations many times in many different places.

"Hey," he interrupted Luz. "I just noticed all of you wear your watch on your right wrist, but none of you are left handed. Is that the custom here?"

"No, not the custom," she laughed, "but the practice."

"That's right" chimed in Carlos. "Most cars don't have air-conditioning in Bogota, and we usually drive with the window open. If you are waiting for a stop sign, one of the gaminitas will run up and snatch your watch right off your wrist."

"Once I had one pull my earring off," added Luz.

"So now," continued Carlos, "we all wear our watches on our right hand."

"And now," added Luz "when you stop for the light to change the little devils run up with a lighted cigarette and burn your left wrist. Then when you instinctively grab the burn, they grab your watch anyway. You can't win," she laughed.

The next morning the desk clerk called to inform him it was time to get up. He hurriedly braced himself with a quick cup of strong Colombian coffee and a stale croissant before leaving for the airport.

On arriving in Medellin, he immediately went to the desk of the heli-taxi that flew from the main airport to the city center. The local officials had put the new airport thirty miles from the center of town to monitor the traffic between the town and the airport. Medellin is the drug capital of South America and not coincidentally, the murder and kidnapping capital as well.

The road to town was treacherous and winding, and it was not uncommon for cars to be stopped on the way, and held up by bandits. On the other hand, Charlie never had much faith in the maintenance ability of transportation companies in developing countries, and he was very uneasy about helicopter rides in general. This day, however, the coin flip came up helicopter. He knew that the Ortega brothers would have a car waiting for him at the heliport in town.

Flying over the mountains, he had a clear view of the large haciendas, and their equally large swimming pools dotting the countryside beneath him. Drug lords owned most of these sprawling estates, and they were not shy about conspicuously displaying their recent wealth.

The tiny helicopter landed safely in the center of Medellin. The Ortega's driver and a hulking bodyguard with a short shotgun partially concealed under a long coat greeted Charlie. At first, it had been unsettling to be accompanied by so much artillery, but now it had become routine.

The Ortega brothers were in their early thirties, and identical twins. They were handsome young men, and very aggressive businessmen. Their family had recently purchased the television assembly company from the Palenzuelas, who had been unable to make a successful business out of the complicated television assembly process.

Once Charlie agreed to transfer the Apex license to the new owners, the size of the factory doubled, and it was soon operating as a highly successful company.

The purpose of his trip was to discuss new orders. Apex provided extended credit terms for the purchase of components used in producing the finished sets, but required their customers to open letters of credit guaranteed by an American bank. It was a complicated process, and the Ortegas were having trouble finding a US bank that would assure payment originating in Colombia.

The two brothers spoke little English, and Charlie could barely handle restaurant Spanish, so the boys had enlisted the services of one of their cousins (a real one) who was capably weaving her way through a verbal minefield of financial and technical terminology. She was an attractive young woman, with long legs, and a ready smile. Her parents had sent her to college in Florida, and she welcomed the opportunity of displaying her language skills to her handsome relatives, and their equally attractive American visitor.

At lunchtime, the older brother nonchalantly reached into a desk drawer and removed a matching pair of silver Berettas. Smiling self-consciously, the two young men stuffed the pistols into their belts.

"Don't worry amigo, we'll take care of you," Pablo grinned.

"I'm counting on it," Charlie replied with a half-hearted laugh.

The translator expressionlessly provided the necessary interpretation. Apparently, she had lived in Medellin so long that she saw nothing unusual in the precautions of her relatives.

At lunch Charlie, the two brothers, and Alba the translator sat at one table. Nearby, the Ortega's driver and bodyguard sipped bottles of mineral water, while alternately watching the door and the other diners. Looking around the expensive restaurant, Charlie could easily identify several other similarly disjointed groups of businessmen and their armed escorts.

"So you don't like to stay overnight in Medellin?" one of the Ortegas teased him. It was a sore point with the two brothers. They considered it somewhat insulting that Charlie always flew back to Bogota after their meeting. They knew their city was dangerous, but disliked being reminded of it.

"Well you guys know how it is, I have a little *chica* on the side, and I want to see her before I go back to the cold, passionless north."

The boys didn't believe him, but it was an explanation they could accept.

Alba, on the other hand, looked at Charlie with renewed interest.

Returning to the Ortega's office, the men finished their conversations and Charlie was packing his briefcase to leave. Alba's work was finished and, aware of the visitor's proximity, she automatically began repairing her makeup by carefully tracing the lines of her lips with red lipstick.

Charlie studied her more closely. She had translated for the Ortegas on several previous visits, but he had never paid much attention to her. In addition to being a competent translator, the Latin woman was also very attractive. She was obviously fond of short skirts, and tight blouses, and understood the complexities of a business conversation. She saw him watching her, and smiled engagingly.

Alba and the two Ortegas followed him down the stairs to the waiting car. As soon as he stepped outside he heard tires screeching, followed almost simultaneously with a deafening explosion coming from a hurtling red Ford. Glancing quickly to his side, Charlie saw the bodyguard level his shotgun at the open window of the passing car, and release both barrels. At the same time, the Ortegas began shooting wildly at the intruders with their Berettas.

Reacting quickly, Alba violently shoved Charlie through the open door of the Ortega's waiting car, shrilly screaming "Go-Go, kidnappers, Go!" His driver had started the engine immediately on seeing the approaching auto, and was already putting the car into motion, while Charlie clung to the armrest of the backseat-halfway in and halfway out-of the speeding Mercedes.

"Jesus Christ!" he yelled to no one as he pulled himself into the weaving automobile, now careening almost uncontrollably through the narrow Medellin streets. He strained to pull himself to a position where he could see the violent scene unfolding behind him. Staring through the rear window he was shocked to see Alba crumple slowly to her knees then fall face forward on the concrete.

Three bodies were now sprawled on the ground. Two of them seemed to be from the other car, and one was Alba's. The Ortegas, positioned behind their bodyguard, were firing furiously at the retreating red Ford, while the bodyguard reloaded. Two other men came running out of the office building joining the melee.

The driver turned to Charlie shouting "*Camino, camino.*" while stomping heavily on his accelerator. It was clear he intended taking the road to the airport instead of going into town for the helicopter. That was all right with Charlie. He agreed that was the safest route, although he realized that he was probably not the target, just an innocent bystander. But hell, he thought, innocent bystanders often get killed. Then he felt something trickling down his cheek.

Finding his handkerchief, Charlie dabbed at the blood. The cut wasn't deep, just a scratch. He thought a small sliver of brick must have caused it.

On the winding road through the mountains, Charlie was gripped with sadness thinking how Alba died, and wondering if the Ortegas survived the assault.

The plane to Bogota was just boarding and he quickly climbed aboard. While he searched for his assigned seat, several of the passengers stared at his ashen complexion accentuated by an ever so slight trace of crimson on his cheek.

44

Back in the city, Charlie checked into a small hotel in the Miraflores district, and called Luz Estrella.

"Hi Luz, what's new?"

"Not a thing Charlie. Same old, same old," she replied, immediately recognizing his voice.

"Look *mi amour*, I have decided to stay at a different hotel tonight. I am at the El Presidente in Miraflores." Charlie thought that a smaller, less expensive hotel than the Tequendama might be safer if someone was looking for him. "Would you call Linda and tell her I am on schedule, and to tell Beth to pick me up at the airport tomorrow." Luz and his secretary Linda frequently talked setting up Charlie's travel schedule and reservations.

"*Claro* Charlie. *Buena suerte*." She smiled as she hung up. Carlos Muniz was passing by her desk, "I think old Charlie may have found a new friend," she informed him. "You men are all alike. I'm very lucky my Ramon is different."

Carlos chuckled as he returned to his desk.

That night Charlie had difficulty sleeping. He kept recalling the picture, playing over in his mind like a bad movie, of poor Alba slowly dropping to the street. Finally he was able to lock the disturbing image in a mental closet next to the picture of Jacob pointing a pistol to his head.

The Avianca flight to Chicago was on time, and Beth was there to meet him. "How did it go Charlie?" she asked as he climbed into the waiting station wagon.

"Same old stuff. One of the Gormans is stealing the company blind, and the Ortegas got in a fight."

"That's nice dear. Do you plan on going to our boy's swim meet tonight? You will just have time to see the opening event." She was the type of woman who won the West. Nothing interfered with the best interests of her family, which she ran like a captain commanding a very tight ship.

"Beth I'm dead tired," her husband moaned.

"I know dear, but you won't have to time the events. They already have enough fathers for that. I checked. You can get a nice shower and a clean shirt before we go. What happened to your cheek?"

Charlie had found a Band-Aid in his shaving kit, and thought it would conceal the cut.

"Nothing really. Strange hotel room, and I was going to the bathroom in the middle of the night."

Four:
King of Prussia

It was a bitter November day in Chicago. Charlie stared out of his window watching the company plow clearing the remains of an early morning snow. He had been attempting to make some progress with the stacks of correspondence and unanswered calls that piled-up during his absence, but he had become distracted by a call from Luz Estrella.

She tearfully described how the Ortega brothers had gone underground immediately after the failed kidnapping attempt and no one had heard from them since. According to Luz, neither of the brothers had even attended their cousin Alba's funeral.

His mood was bleak before the call from Luz, but now it was dismal. Earlier that morning he had a meeting with Norman Baines. His boss was eager to go over the international forecast for the coming year. These discussions were always difficult, but they were becoming increasingly strained as the company's financial position continued to deteriorate.

He had struggled to project an optimistic ten percent increase in sales for the next twelve months. Norman unreasonably insisted on fifteen percent, and Charlie was trying to find an answer to his dilemma in the stack of figures his staff had worked weeks to prepare.

Further complicating matters, the international distributor in Puerto Rico had recently opened a large warehouse in Miami, and was reportedly selling to customers who were coming up from Panama. Smugglers operating out of the Canal Zone would then resell the sets all over South America. The domestic distributor in Miami believed that these people were his customers, and wanted the warehouse shut down.

Norman was furious, siding with his Miami distributor. Charlie had to admit he had a point, but he didn't know how to tell the Puerto Rican that he had to close his new Miami operation.

"Sorry to interrupt," Linda called quietly from the doorway. "The receptionist just phoned, a couple of people from the Commerce Department are in the lobby and want to see you."

"OK, have them sent up, and would you please meet them at the elevator," he replied. This was not a good time, but the Commerce people had been helpful in the past, and he was willing to return the favor.

Soon Linda reappeared. "Mr. Brady and Ms. Kincaid from the Commerce Department," she announced, winking as she left his office.

At first, he didn't recognize his visitors, although the man did look somewhat familiar.

"Hello Charlie old boy. Remember me? I'm your old friend Marvin Brady from the Central Intelligence Agency, and this is my partner in crime, Karen Kincaid."

Tall and tan and young and lovely.

The opening line of Carlos Jobim's "Girl from Ipanema" ran through his head as he watched Marvin's companion purposefully enter the room. The willowy young woman wore an expensively tailored blue suit, along with a short string of pearls. She was exquisite, but there was an air of aloofness about her as she stared directly at him. She sat down and straightened her skirt, and mindfully gazed at Charlie. He had the feeling she was calculatingly sizing up the person with whom she would be dealing.

Marvin appeared to be wearing the same rumpled suit, but it now appeared a little too tight for his burly frame. The closely cropped hair was slightly more gray, Charlie observed, and there was the slight beginning of a roll around his waist. Aside from that, old Marvin looked pretty much as he had, many years before, when they first met at the University. As they shook hands Charlie was reminded once more that the man from the Agency was missing his right forefinger.

"I suppose you are wondering why we are here," Marvin began self-consciously clearing his throat.

"You're very perceptive," was the caustic reply.

"Well to be candid, we would like your help. Not in a clandestine way mind you. Just in--well let's say--in an advisory position." Karen continued to study Charlie while Marvin talked.

"You recall the problem we had with our budgets and our staffing? Of course you do," Marvin laughed nervously answering his own question.

"I was very sorry what happened to you, but I had nothing to do with it. It was just the government. Now we're in almost the same position. You probably read how we screwed up the Bay of Pigs invasion? Every one has, but it wasn't all our fault. Kennedy promised air cover and then backed out at the last minute. He blamed it on us, but hey that's what we're here for. We did tell him about the Russians putting missiles in Cuba to begin with. So it all evened out--I guess," he added his voice trailing off.

"Well," he continued disgustedly, "now we have this fellow in the White House who doesn't care for us at all. He believes we should all hold hands and sing Kumbaya, then everyone will love us, and we can all get along. Recently, he put a former Admiral in as Director of Intelligence. This guy doesn't like us anymore than the President does. He wants to rely only on satellite information. He calls it SIGINT for signal intelligence," Marvin added conspiratorially. "Then he can cut back our assets on the ground."

"You mean spooks?"

"We prefer to refer to them as agents in play, Charlie."

Karen hastily took over: "We know this will pass eventually. It always does. The problem is that it takes years to build up HUMINT. Sorry, now they have me doing it," she apologized. "I meant to say a human intelligence network.

"Human contributions are the most important component of intelligence gathering," she continued with obvious sincerity. "It's not something you build up overnight, and it could be too late when they realize what we don't have. Then there will be hell to pay. If there is one thing Washington excels at it is finger pointing.

"In the meantime, we have a responsibility to do the best we can with what we have. One of the answers we came up with is to rely on people like you to-"

Marvin interrupted impatiently. "I see you are a Vice President now Charlie. Very nice. We know your job takes you many places."

"It does Marvin," he conceded. "I'm building up a hell of a lot of frequent flyer points, and the salary will help put the kids through college."

"How many kids do you have?" Marvin asked.

"Three. Our daughter is in Japan as an exchange student, and the two boys are in high school. It looks like we'll end up paying for three of them in College, all at the same time."

"That's heavy," Marvin sympathized.

"Planned Parenthood run amok. How many kids to do you have Marvin?"

"None, I've had three wives, and no children. This job doesn't exactly lend itself to domesticity."

"What have you been doing all of these years?" Charlie asked curiously.

"Well I quit recruiting when the Agency didn't have any money to hire more people. After that, I ran some agents in Berlin. I was doing great until someone burned me. After that I couldn't breathe without some Russkie tailing me. After awhile they rolled up all my agents, and I was cooked.

"The Agency brought me back to Washington, and sent me down to Huntsville to spend some time with Werner Von Braun and his boys that we brought over from Germany before the Russians got their hands on them.

"Now I'm just hanging around and filling in here and there until I get a new assignment."

"What about Miss Bryn Mawr here?" Charlie asked looking toward Karen, who had continued to observe him closely as Marvin talked.

"Actually, I attended Radcliffe not Bryn Mawr," she replied defensively, languidly uncrossing her long legs. "Got a Ph.D. in Political Science, but don't judge me by where I went to school. My family changed their name from Kaminsky to Kincaid when they came to the United States from Poland. They worked their tails off to get me a good education. Since I joined the Agency, I've been working undercover in Central Europe trying to help them build up a democratic structure they can use someday."

As Karen spoke, Charlie recognized the scent of Allure emanating from her direction then mingling valiantly but ultimately losing to the stronger odor of Marvin's Old Spice after-shave lotion. Since he had given up his two pack a day habit, his sense of smell was gradually returning. Karen's perfume reminded him of a long ago summer's night with a former girl friend. The scent is appropriate Charlie thought. The woman is alluring.

"Here is our problem Charlie," Marvin broke in on his reminiscences. "We can't hire new people, and we don't have enough agents under cover to keep us informed on what we need to know. We've been working principally out of our overseas embassies, and it is pretty easy to spot our guys. Once they are identified they are usually tailed. Their apartments are bugged and they become no good to us at all. Most of our embassies are penetrated as well.

"Now we don't have enough agents to put in most of the developing countries. That's where the action is going to be in the future, and that's where you come in.

"All we want from you," Karen added persuasively "is to give us a heads-up on what the economic and political conditions are in these funny places you seem to travel. For example, we heard that you were recently in quite a dust-up in Medellin. Why did you go there?"

"It wasn't for the waters," Charlie shot back, unconsciously mimicking Bogart in Casablanca. "Apex has a customer there who buys a lot of components from us, and every few months I go to Colombia to meet with him to jack him up. How did you hear about it? They don't even know about that here in the office."

"We do have a guy in Bogota who is the commercial attaché' at our Embassy," Marvin answered. "He tries to keep us informed, but Colombia is so dangerous none of the Embassy people are permitted to leave Bogota. We don't want them kidnapped, and then have to get into a messy ransom scenario.

"Are your guys in Medellin in the *trade*?" Marvin asked. Our fellow in Bogota wanted us to ask you."

Charlie paused before answering. "You know what Marvin, I don't know. I really don't know. I have often wondered that myself. I didn't think so when I gave them the license. If I had, I wouldn't have given it to them.

"Since then I'm less sure. I have no evidence they are connected to the drug trade. But, they are in Medellin, and you kind of get the feeling that everyone there is involved with the cartel in some way or another. It's not true of course-but you do get that feeling"

Charlie paused again and stared out the window as if he could find the answer to Marvin's question buried somewhere in the snowy parking lot.

"Then," he began again "one time they took me to see their ranch. It's a little way outside the city. We rode in two cars. I was in one with the boys, and the other car carried two armed bodyguards.

"Their hacienda was like a walled compound. The guards at the gate let us through and we drove to the house along a narrow paved road. They had stables with thoroughbred horses, pens for game birds they use in hunting, a stocked fishing pond, a swimming pool and tennis courts, and several guesthouses where the boys offered Beth and I could come and stay anytime we would want.

"With that kind of a set-up you have to get suspicious," he continued "but as I said, I have nothing other than a gut feel about their other enterprises. They invested a lot of money in the business, and I can't be disloyal and jerk their license just because of a bellyache."

"Look my friend, your country really needs your help. The CIA needs your help," Marvin offered compellingly. "We're concentrating all our resources on the Sovs, and we're losing the hearts and minds of the rest of the world.

"We wouldn't even have to create a myth for you. Everyone knows what you are as soon as they look at you.

You walk, talk, eat, dress, and drink like an American businessman. So your cover is exactly what you are.

"All we ask is that we would occasionally like to meet with you when you return from a trip, and get your opinion on what was going on where you were. OK?"

Charlie realized professionals were manipulating him, but he had no objection to being taken where they wanted him to go. Marvin had always been persuasive, old Marvin the manipulator he thought, and of course being accompanied by a very attractive young woman didn't hurt. "I don't mind helping you people when I can," he began. "Actually, I am still sympathetic with what you do. I know we're both on the same side, but it has to be abundantly clear that I will not do anything to jeopardize my company here in the U.S., or any other place for that matter. Is that clear?"

"Absolutely Charlie."

"Definitely," Karen added.

"OK it's agreed. Now Charlie where are you traveling next?" Marvin asked, eager to get on with his business.

"King of Prussia."

"Pennsylvania?" Karen asked surprised.

"What the hell are you doing there?" Marvin asked annoyed. "I thought you were international."

"Well if things work out alright, it could lead to China."

"That would be great." Karen leaned forward intently, her perfume wafting toward him. "We don't have any idea about what's happening there. It was closed to the world so long we have never had a chance to establish covert agents. Those people we do have are all tied to the Embassy so tightly they can't provide us with much information.

"Since Nixon was able to pry open the country," she continued "we've tried to put people under cover, but the

54

country is so big, and our budget is so small, we haven't been very successful. Why are you going there?"

Charlie looked at the two people across from him, trying to decide how much to tell them about his company's problems. "We may not go, but about a year ago Apex, in its infinite wisdom, decided to buy a picture tube factory in King of Prussia. It had been owned by one of the other television companies that went out of business. After buying the plant, we compounded our error by adding a hell of a lot more new equipment.

"Our Engineering Department was working on the development of what they thought was a revolutionary new tube. We called it the Zebra tube, and they thought it would be superior to any others on the market. Management agreed, and then decided we needed more production capacity to take advantage of our new opportunities.

"Well the damned thing never worked, so now the company doesn't need the factory. We don't know what to do with it, but some people have contacted us saying they know some Red Chinese who would buy the equipment. A couple of us are flying to King of Prussia to show them the factory, and then see where we go from there."

"Your trip to China could give us just the kind of information we need," Karen told Charlie. "We would really like to get a feel for their technical ability . The DOD is putting a lot of pressure on us to provide them with a strategic analysis of Chinese technical capability.

"Obviously," she added quickly, "we know they have one of the largest armies in the world, but we don't have any feel for them as a technical threat. We don't have people over there, and if we did they wouldn't have enough industry experience to give us an accurate opinion.

"It would also be very helpful if we could have someone from Washington traveling with your group," she added seemingly as an afterthought.

"You mean a plant?" Charlie asked.

"Well that's not the term I would use," Karen replied engagingly. "It would just be someone who would travel along as part of your delegation. That way they could get a first-hand look at how well the Chinese run their factories."

"Forget it Karen." "We're not going to be running any on the job training program for your people."

"OK, OK, forget I asked, but we would also like to know if you meet anyone over there whom you think might be willing to work with us."

"Good to see you again Charlie. We'll be in touch," Marvin said heaving his stocky frame from the chair and shaking hands. Karen languidly uncoiled her long legs and trailed after her companion. Coquettishly glancing back over her shoulder she waved good-by, leaving Charlie alone with his thoughts.

After his visitors left, he tried to get back to work, but it was hard to concentrate on the dry columns of figures spread out on his desk. He kept thinking about the surprising reappearance of Marvin and his striking associate, and worried about what he might be getting himself into.

Was he getting in over his head, he wondered? It wasn't as if he didn't have enough problems already, working for a failing company, and not getting along with his boss. Why would he want to take on the CIA's problems too? But, then he thought their problems were his country's problems, and it wasn't as if he could just walk away and tell them to go to hell. He did have some responsibility to his country. Oh well, he rationalized, I probably will never hear from them again.

He looked out the window, and could see that the sun had almost set. Winter in Chicago, he thought. Who needs it?

A week after the meeting, a guard at the vacant King of Prussia picture tube factory checked the credentials of Charlie and Paul Murphy. Paul was the son of one of Apex's original founders, and he was now Vice President of Administration. His weatherworn face resembled a map of Ireland, and his penetrating blue eyes hinted at a wry sense of humor that he tried to conceal with an air of mock seriousness. The old executive's responsibilities included the company's facilities, but his influence in the organization was greater than his job description implied.

Paul had also acted like a mentor to Charlie and his advice about how to deal with the corporation's bureaucracy and management's intrigue was frequently provided, and almost as frequently accepted.

"Your people are already here," the guard told them. "I put them in the conference room. I'll show you where it is. After you meet them, if you want, I'll tour the group around the place."

"Good morning gentlemen, glad to meet you," called a grotesquely fat man seated at the head of small conference table. His heavy jowls flowed over a tight shirt collar, and he breathed noisily as he talked. "Pardon me for not getting up. I am Mr. Svetts, and my associate here is Mr. Simms." Simms, a diminutive man wearing horned rimmed glasses rose to greet Charlie and Paul as they entered the cold conference room.

After they were seated, the corpulent Svetts proceeded to explain how he had cleverly managed to maintain his previous contacts in Mainland China, even after the military takeover by Chairman Mao. "I was helpful to them in many ways, here in the United States, which they greatly appreciated. My good friends have recently contacted me and Mr. Simms." With this acknowledgement the small man rose quickly, as if on command, to light his partner's ever-present cigarette.

"Now they've lifted their skirts so to speak," he giggled convulsively, "what they would like us to do is to contact reputable companies in the United States, such as yours, and explore the purchase of your technology. We heard you have a tube factory you may not be using, and my friends in Tianjin would like to help take it off your hands.

"Of course," he added quickly, "my partner and I would expect to receive a small honorarium from you for our efforts. A finder's fee you might call it, say five percent of the purchase price if the arrangement is consummated."

Knowing full well that the Chinese would also compensate the strange pair if the deal went through Charlie quickly countered, "Only on receipt of full payment from your principal, and then just three percent."

Svetts shrugged his agreement.

Arrangements were made for a tour of the plant during a break in the discussions. The facilities were so extensive that it would have been impossible to see it all on foot. The only available alternative was the bicycles the guards used to make their lonely rounds.

The uniformed watchman led the tour, followed by Svetts and Simms with Charlie bringing up the rear. Murphy had decided to remain in the relative comfort of the cool conference room.

As the strange group wobbled and weaved its way through the vacant factory, Charlie watched with amusement as his two visitors struggled to master their unwieldy vehicles.

If it were operational, the abandoned factory would have employed thousands of highly paid workers. Now, as the sound of the bizarre procession echoed through the cavernous corridors it was as if the vacant aisles were haunted by specters of the jobs that might have been.

Five:
The Middle Kingdom

Since landing at the Beijing airport, Charlie had the impression he had unwittingly walked through Alice's looking glass and entered a world where time stood still. China was decades behind anything he had seen in his travels. It was shocking that the Chinese people with their rich cultural history were living in such abject poverty. Certainly, there had been tremendous inequality between the classes before the Maoist Revolution, but from what he could see through the window of his car, everyone was now equally destitute.

It had been two years since President Nixon had made his historic trip to China, and the country was slowly attempting to become more open and attract the interest of the rest of the world. Foreigners were still a rarity, even in Beijing, and the peasants standing along the road were as interested in the passing "long noses," as the tired travelers were in them.

Charlie had to admit that it was fascinating to see the complex country at this point in history, but he would rather have been almost anywhere but China. He was having a great deal of difficulty attempting to meet the increased forecast Norman Baines had insisted he accept, and the picture tube project that brought him to the Orient was only a distraction from his main responsibilities.

On the other hand, he understood that the corporation obviously needed the additional revenue that would result from the sale of the picture tube plant.

Charlie was also becoming increasingly concerned with the attention the CIA was showing in his business activities.

He knew their job was to protect the interests of the Untied States, and he was totally sympathetic with their objectives. He would have quickly rejected the term patriot but he would also admit to a deep and abiding love for his country that was re-enforced every time he traveled overseas. Still there was enough to worry about without their interference, and he sometimes felt that he was inexorably becoming drawn into a life he had no interest in leading.

He had tried to make it clear when he talked to Marvin and Karen, that there were limits to his cooperation with the Agency. He was more than willing to provide them with his opinion and observations on places he visited, but he had refused to take an active role in gathering clandestine information for them.

He was astonished then, when his group checked in at the American Embassy in Beijing, to find a previously decrypted message from Karen repeating her request for a member of the Beijing embassy staff to join the Apex contingent under cover as a company employee. A pink cheeked cultural attaché passed the message to him unnoticed by other members of his group. Charlie read the message slowly, and then angrily scribbled No Dice across the top before returning it to the visibly disappointed young man.

"You can transmit that without encryption," he stage-whispered to the startled civil servant."

During Charlie's brief meeting with the attaché the other travelers were listening intently to the American Ambassador dutifully describing how the Cultural Revolution devastated China during that period, and explaining how students led by the Red Guard created chaos throughout the country. The marauders had directed their hatred primarily toward the better-educated members of the Chinese population, killing many of them and imprisoning millions of others. The ultimate result was that the country was set back even further than before. Their rampage eliminated an entire generation of the most educated Chinese who were now sorely missed as the country attempted to develop modern technologies and advanced management techniques. This was one of the major reasons the country was now compelled to rely on outside interests to bring their industry up to global standards.

Following their meeting at the embassy, the group made a brief tour of the city before departing by train for Tianjin. Driving through Tiananmen Square they passed heavily clothed Chinese peasants on bicycles closely watched over by a mammoth portrait of Chairman Mao tse Sung smiling benignly at the passing masses. The Great Helmsman was ably assisted in his scrutiny of the people by the ever-present green uniformed militia posted in strategic locations around the square, and throughout the city.

Charlie stared from his lace-curtained train window at the passing Chinese countryside. A thin cloud of steam rose from the stack of the ancient locomotive then quickly dissolved into the falling snow that was rapidly covering the barren fields. The train's mournful whistle would periodically pierce the frigid air. Occasionally an isolated farm family, huddled together in their heavily loaded ox cart, was seen plodding slowly along the dirt road beside the tracks.

The man seated next to Charlie smiled disarmingly as he lit his hundredth cigarette, or so it seemed, since leaving Beijing. A gray clad train attendant proceeded, with some difficulty, through the swaying car stopping to dispense cups of boiling hot tea from her battered tin kettle to eagerly awaiting passengers.

Looking around the train, Charlie tried to locate the rest of his group. They had been unable to find seats together in the crowded coach, but were easy to pick out among the almond-eyed Chinese dressed in their gray high collared Mao jackets.

He eventually spotted the sleeping Paul Murphy who had accompanied him to the idle King of Prussia picture tube plant. Paul's gray head bobbed in perfect synchronization with the gentle rolling of the train. Further back, Charlie could identify the baldheaded Ted Barry, the company's picture tube expert, who had come along to provide technical support. He and Jim Parks, the Vice President of Purchasing, were sitting together playing cards to occupy their time during the three-hour train ride.

Seated in the rear row of the smoke filled passenger car, almost lost in the sea of similar Asian faces, was the diminutive Mr. Wu, conscripted by the rotund Mr. Svetts as the group's interpreter. Wu was the owner of a Chinese restaurant in Philadelphia but also, according to Svetts, had important family ties to the city authorities in Tianjin.

In addition to representing the heavyset Mr. Svetts, Charlie believed that Wu's presence was to keep him informed on the progress of the discussions, but more importantly to assure that there would be no shortening of the fat man's anticipated commission.

A large group of Chinese Government officials had come to welcome the weary Americans as they straggled from the train, struggling with their heavy bags. The travelers huddled together in the frigid winter air while the obligatory exchange of cards and limitless introductions took place. Each of the greeters was obviously required to make a welcoming speech emphasizing the newly found need for friendship and cooperation between the two countries. The Americans, on the other hand, wished only to get to some place that would be better sheltered from the icy winds, and as quickly as possible.

Finally, the welcoming protocol ended and the tired travelers were unceremoniously ushered into waiting Russian Lada limousines. Their departure was delayed further while the surprisingly class-conscious Chinese delegation furiously debated which official was to ride in which car; futilely attempting to match the organizational level of the greeters with the presumed rank of their visitors.

Mr. Wu darted wildly back and forth between the two groups vainly attempting to explain the function and rank of one group to the other. It was an impossible task, severely taxing his linguistic ability that was frustratingly rusty from years of limited use in Philadelphia.

The packed cars of the unusual procession wound slowly through the wide streets of the gritty old Chinese City.

Tianjin's initial expansion began at the end of the Opium Wars. As a convenient gateway to inland Beijing, the city grew rapidly from waves of newly arriving Europeans who built ornate banks, tall office buildings, and their elaborate homes in the concession districts. The tide of foreigners threatened to engulf a budding metropolis that was rapidly becoming northern China's belated commercial answer to Shanghai.

The growing city also became a hotbed of political intrigue as Manchurian ministers, and Chinese warlords formed tentative alliances with Western businessmen. Tianjin eventually became a target of the bloody Boxer Rebellion. The Communist revolution in 1949 dramatically terminated the city's rapid expansion, and it entered a period of enforced dormancy.

As Charlie's procession proceeded along Jiefang Dao or "Liberation Road," it passed dusty shells of once powerful financial institutions and crumbling musty mansions that had been subdivided, and were now in an advanced state of neglect.

In 1976, a powerful earthquake had devastated Tianjin, and the effect was still evident years later in the piles of rubble along the dusty roadway. As they rode in their unheated cars, Charlie could occasionally detect an inquisitive face peering through broken windowpanes in buildings scarred by deep crevices running from foundation to rooftop.

The lobby of the Friendship Hotel was large and uninviting, almost as cold inside as it was outside its heavy leather shielded doors. The dark hallways were filled with conflicting odors, and the small rooms were coated with dust and grime.

That evening the welcoming banquet followed a strict protocol formulated years before by a forgotten Communist functionary. It was repeated on many nights during the remainder of the visit. Each table was amply supplied with numerous bottles of overly sweet Chinese plumb wine, excellent beer, and far too many bottles of *maotai*, which proved to be an extremely potent, foul tasting and throat searing rice liquor greatly preferred by the hosts.

The evening typically would begin with a lengthy translated speech presented by that evening's leading local dignitary. Protocol demanded that this greeting was reciprocated by that night's designated head of the American delegation. Each speech was followed by a toast of *maotai,* and ended by ringing shouts of *gambai,* or bottoms up that echoed through the smoky banquet room. As the night dragged on, the speeches became longer and the toasts more raucous.

The Americans eyed each one of the many dishes with considerable suspicion. The food, however, proved palatable with the occasional exception of such presumed oriental delicacies as jellyfish, seaweed, tripe, boiled ells, and squid. During the meal, the travelers struggled with the unfamiliar use of chopsticks, while attempting to maintain a semblance of cordiality toward their local hosts.

Charlie had difficulty sleeping his first night in Tianjin. In the middle of the night, he found himself in his cold room, looking out the frosty window watching phantom figures, bundled in heavy coats, silently riding their bicycles through a heavy winter snow. Where on earth, he wondered are these pitiful people going in the middle of the freezing night? What unknown puppet master pulls the strings that requires them to be there?

Watching the swirling flakes, his thoughts drifted to his family and his comfortable suburban home. When, he wondered, would he be back with them again?

Mr. Wu joined the Americans at breakfast the next morning. It had quickly become apparent Wu was having difficulty with his English when speaking to them, and his Chinese when conversing with the Chinese. The previous night at dinner, Charlie had asked the name of the dish he had been offered.

"Dug," Wu explained.

Charlie had thought he might not be able to eat dog, but decided if he was to be there for some time he had better get used to it. "This tastes like duck," he suggested to Wu after sampling a small piece.

"That's right Dug," Wu replied to Charlie's considerable relief.

"My nephew join us today," Mr. Wu informed his cold traveling companions over their weak coffee. "He is Engineer with China Import Export Company and will be much help to me." Zhang Zheng, Wu's nephew, arrived that afternoon by train from Beijing. Apparently, his Uncle had called the day before and asked for his assistance, and his Chinese company was eager to temporarily release him in hopes of learning more about the American's plans.

The negotiations for the picture tube factory followed a repeatable pattern. The Chinese were initially eager to meet and discuss the technical aspects of the picture tube plant. Then they would adjourn to take the American delegation on tours of the many heavy equipment factories in Tianjin.

The hosts considered these factories to represent the pinnacle of manufacturing sophistication, and were eager for the visitors to appreciate their advanced level of industrialization. The Americans, on the other hand, considered the cold dirty plants to be a meager step above the invention of the wheel.

It also soon was apparent to the Americans that any documents they left unattended in their rooms were examined and copied during their absence. Zhang Zheng also warned them that their rooms were filled with listening devices, and their phones tapped to obtain any possible negotiating advantage. After learning this, the Americans would leave inflated figures in their rooms, and hide misleading messages in their outgoing calls.

Zhang Zheng proved to be a considerable improvement over Mr. Wu, and he and Charlie became close friends. Charlie was used to talking through interpreters, and would speak slowly and as clearly as possible during the lengthy discussions. This helped Zhang who was still unsure of his English ability.

One evening, Zhang confided to Charlie the problems his family had experienced at the hands of the marauding Red Guard during the Cultural Revolution. "My father was an educated man, a teacher and a prominent man in our community," Zhang proudly related. "Because he had learned English from the missionaries they dragged him from his class room and forced him to wear a dunce hat while they ridiculed him in front of his students. Later my family was sent to Manchuria to work in the frozen fields. My father was slight of build, and the bitter cold and manual labor took its toll on his health. He died, but before that he warned me never to let people know I could speak English. Now I am working as an interpreter, and I worry if the Red Guard would ever take power again they would do away with me as they did my Father. But, I have a wife and small son, and I need the money Mr. Wu is paying me to help you Americans get the tube contract," he confided in a restrained voice.

Charlie didn't know what to advise his newfound friend. He felt sorry for him, but knew they would soon be leaving China, and there was no way he could protect Zhang after he left.

Earlier, when Charlie was talking to the Commercial attaché in Beijing, he had been given a very small Minox camera built into a normal appearing, but slightly larger watch. "Karen also sent me a message," the young attaché whispered cautiously, "that she would like you to get pictures of the Chinese factories that she can use in her report to the Defense Department."

Initially Charlie resented her request, and decided to leave the hi-tech device hidden in his luggage. After hearing Zhang's story about the hardships that his family experienced, Charlie changed his mind.

The watch was too small to create any unusual interest among his American associates. He usually wore a large Movado chronograph so there was no discernable difference in size. Charlie used the CIA's watch on factory tours to photograph some of the more antiquated techniques that the Chinese were using, as well as getting pictures of the more important officials that they met.

Photographing the factories, particularly the R&D Labs, made him very nervous. He clearly understood what would happen to him, and perhaps the rest of his delegation, if the Chinese detected what he was doing.

At first, his palms became sweaty, even in the cold factories, and his hands trembled as he awkwardly tried to point the camera at the desired subject.

As careful as he tried to be, his covert photography would occasionally attract the attention of his hosts who wore only the most basic wind-up Russian timepieces, and were fascinated by the blinking digital display. When that occurred, Charlie would laugh and tell them it was actually a camera and to smile while he took their picture. The Chinese would grin obediently, but they fortunately didn't believe him.

Soon, he began taking additional pictures whenever the contract negotiations involved higher-ranking government officials. In order to supplement the photos, Charlie would list the names of the men on a notepad to match them later with the film.

In those evenings when there were no banquets to attend, the Americans would relax in the small hotel bar. Their hotel rooms rarely had heat, and the men were forced to sleep in their overcoats to keep warm. The poorly stocked bar was no warmer, but at least the conversation helped pass the time. Parks, the purchasing manager, had enough foresight to bring along a couple bottles of Bourbon that he and Ted Barry were attempting to stretch to the end of their visit.

Charlie and Murphy, not being bourbon drinkers, located a dusty bottle of Boodle's English Gin hidden behind the bar among the more exotic Chinese liquors.

"Do you think it's smart to be helping these guys improve their operations?" Barry would frequently ask during the night sessions. "You know they are gonna become like the Japanese and eventually bite us in the ass. I think we'll live to regret it."

"You may be right," Murphy agreed, "but if we don't, someone else will and the only thing lost is the revenue we would get from the sale of our plant."

Murphy was right, Charlie thought. His only interest was in getting the job done, and getting the hell out of there as soon as possible. The sale was certainly ethical, and if they didn't make the deal someone else would.

During these sessions, Zhang Zheng would be fascinated with the stories the travelers told describing their lives in the United States. His frequent questions about living conditions in America would sometimes irritate the men, but Zhang had become invaluable to their faltering attempts to explain the intricate equipment they were trying to sell.

During each day's sessions the Americans were becoming increasingly frustrated. The Chinese would frequently change their personnel, and it was often necessary to repeat the information that had been discussed the previous day. It was even difficult for the Americans to determine who was in charge of the negotiators and who would be making the ultimate decision. Even Mr. Wu couldn't keep the Chinese negotiators straight, and some of them were his relatives.

Further adding to the American's frustration the Chinese constantly kept them under observation. If any of men decided to brave the frigid Manchurian winds whipping outside the hotel they quickly discovered that they were followed. The Chinese didn't attempt to hide their actions and seemed not to care that the Americans knew they were watched.

There was the occasional curiosity seeker wanting to personally observe the tall blond-headed men with fair skin and blue eyes, but liberally mingled among them were always the same flinty eyed security people whose job was to keep a close eye on the visiting Americans.

"They don't even try and hide what they are doing," Jim Parks observed. If you turn quickly you can bump into them. Every time you pick up the phone you hear a clicking noise in the background. Sometimes it gets so loud you can't hear what is being said. Even their listening devices are lousy."

Barry didn't care about the phones. He never made any calls. "What makes me mad," he told the group "is that every time I leave the room someone goes through all my papers. If they asked I would give them whatever documents they want, but after they get through rifling my files I can't find where I have put what I'm looking for."

Murphy's bronchitis had grown progressively worse, and he had to return home. The men later learned this often happened to western visitors who were unable to adapt to the highly polluted Chinese air.

The negotiations continued without him. To push things along more rapidly Charlie began calling his Chicago office on the tapped phone to tell them that they soon would be leaving for home, regardless of the outcome of the discussions. This had the desired effect, and the contract was suddenly signed by the Chinese.

Charlie was back in Chicago a week before he heard from Karen Kincaid. The call came late at night to his home, rather than his office.

"Hey Charlie, welcome back," she cheerfully began. Can we get together? How about Saturday morning at our Chicago office? That way you won't have to take off work. OK? I'll have some other people with me that are interested to hear what you learned on your Asian adventure."

"Where is your office located Karen?"

"It's in the telephone book Charlie."

And there it was, listed in the blue government pages at the front of the directory under Central Intelligence Agency. Not too damned covert Charlie thought.

A cold rain, driven by a strong wind off Lake Michigan, buffeted him as he parked his car near the Agency's Dearborn Street office. The normally busy thoroughfare was deserted. The regular office workers had left long ago for the weekend warmth and comfort of their suburban homes. An elevated train rumbled in the distance, as Charlie gladly ducked into the welcoming protection of the old office building.

The vacant information desk in the cramped lobby was unmanned, but the Central Intelligence Agency was prominently listed in the glass enclosed office directory.

Leaving the elevator, a familiar voice floated through an open office door. "Thanks for coming in on the weekend Charlie." Following the sound of Karen's voice, he found four men sitting ramrod erect around an old gunmetal gray government-issue conference table inside an already smoke filled room.

The scent of Karen's perfume successfully mingled with the stronger less pleasant tobacco odor. Charlie tried to recall the name of her scent. It returned to him quickly. It was *Allure*. The perfume always brought back pleasant recollections of a youthful evening by a Minnesota lake, and the seductive charms of a long-legged young woman.

Concentrating, he erased the pleasant memory from his mind and forced himself to focus on the stern men seated around the conference table. They wore well-tailored civilian suits, but their academy rings testified to their shared military background.

The group must have been there for some time before he arrived. The tabletop was littered with empty cans of Classic Coke, and crumpled Styrofoam coffee cups. Idle hands had unconsciously formed the empty packets of artificial sweetener into a perfect square in the center of the table, alongside a single ashtray filled with stale cigarette butts.

Karen intentionally skipped the introductions, and Charlie spent the next two hours going over the details of his trip. The men questioned every aspect of his meetings with the Chinese, and were particularly interested in his opinion regarding the current and potential industrial capability of his former foreign hosts.

"I thought Marvin would be here," Charlie commented to Karen after the others left for O'Hare Airport

"He couldn't get away. The Maestro is retiring soon, and Marvin has hopes of getting his job."

"The Maestro, am I supposed to know who that is?"

"No Charlie you wouldn't, although I think you met him in Washington a long time ago. I noticed in your file that he was one of the people who interviewed you when you first came to Washington from the University. His name is Emmett Valentine. We call him the Maestro because of his love for classical music. It's playing in his office all the time, and it's often difficult to talk over the sound. Sometimes he seems to become more interested in the melody than in what you are telling him.

"Emmett trained to be violinist before he was drafted into the Army. They soon found that he had an uncanny ability to break codes, and asked him to volunteer for the OSS. After he got there he developed a more important talent for coordinating complicated clandestine operations. He has been in intelligence ever since--a very sensitive man in a very violent job.

"He was actually one of the men," Karen told Charlie proudly, "who worked with the British to set-up the CIA on their already developed ethos of intelligence. But now," she continued, pouring the last of a warm can of Coke into her cup, "the Maestro tells us he is planning to shed his cloak and sheathe his dagger before going quietly into the night. That's when Marvin hopes to replace him. Our old friend Marvin has been a GS-14 for ages, and he believes that he now deserves a chance to move up."

"Will he?" Charlie asked.

"Will he get the job? I don't know. He should, but you know how a bureaucracy works. The best don't always do the best at getting advancements, and the CIA has become a huge bureaucracy.

"By the way," she added quickly, "can I get our watch back? Were you able to get any pictures of their factories?"

"I don't know if they are any good," he told her. "It was the first time I've used a camera in my watch, and I can't guarantee the results." While they talked he gave Karen back the watch and half a dozen rolls of film he had taken, along with the list of names he had collected. After shooting the first roll he had become absorbed in what he was doing, and took pictures whenever he thought he could without being observed by the Chinese. In the process he had accumulated a considerable amount of exposed film.

"We will just have to take our chances," Karen replied. Those people you met today are really anxious to see what you got. Many of them feel that China is going to be our next major enemy and they want to be prepared. They have really been very critical of what little information we have been able to provide about the Middle Kingdom, and your information should be a big help in getting them off our backs."

Karen was gathering her things, and trying to clean up the conference room. "By the way Charlie, I was told that you should have a cryptonym," she informed him as an afterthought.

"Is a code name really necessary? It just seems it would draw me more deeply into something I'm not comfortable with, and I really don't want that. Let's just forget it."

"We really appreciate your help, and it's for your own protection. If someone should call, you could be sure they are with the Agency when they use your special name. It's Pinstripes, for obvious reasons."

Charlie decided not to pursue that, but instead asked, "What's your name Karen?"

"It's Snowflake, but I don't know where I got it. It just evolved — kind of"

He decided to leave that alone as well.

"What do they call Marvin?"

"They call him the Machinist, but I could never figure out how they came up with that either. I guess it was long before my time."

"One more thing," Karen added as she finished stuffing her files and the watch into her bulging Gucci briefcase. "Before you left, I mentioned that we could really use the names of anyone you met in China who you thought might be willing to provide us with information."

"I remember," he hesitated before continuing. He was still not sure he should be doing this. "There was one fellow I met who might be willing to work with you, but you would have to make certain he wouldn't get hurt. His name is Zhang Zheng. He is a nice guy with a family. He speaks English, and works for the China Electronics Import Export Corporation so he knows a lot about what is going on over there. He also has good contacts with some of his friends who work on highly classified projects"

"Sounds good Charlie, but why do you think he might be willing to help us?"

"I don't know that he would, but he really dislikes the Communist Government. They harmed his family, and he needs money badly. Also, he came from an educated family, which means he has no chance to ever get ahead under this regime."

"Those are pretty good reasons. Disillusionment and dollars are the two main reasons people betray their country. We'll make a soft contact with him, and feel him out."

"Ok Karen, but the guy is awfully vulnerable, and would require a lot of shepherding. I wouldn't want to see him get hurt," Charlie cautioned unsure if he should be doing this.

"Understood. We'll be very careful," she assured him. I've handled a lot of agents, and I know how careful you have to be. You want to make sure they can rely on you because they take awful chances. I won't be his Case Officer, but I'll be certain to tell whoever handles him that they need to be gentle with your Mr. Zhang Zheng."

"We really need people like him over there who would be sympathetic to our interests. The Agency has never been able to adapt to the concept of multiple adversaries. We are a little like the guy that can't chew gum and walk at the same time. We built up a large bureaucracy with a singular focus concentrating all our assets on the Soviets. Trying to change it is like — you know you were in the Navy Charlie — it's like trying to change course on a battleship. It just doesn't happen quickly regardless how important it is."

Locking up the vacant office Karen turned, "Hey Charlie, I almost forgot, congratulations on getting the contract. How much was it for?"

"Twenty-five million, but Apex turned it down."

"After all that work, why?"

Riding down in the ancient elevator he tried to explain. "The Chinese would have even been willing to send their

76

own workers to dismantle the King of Prussia plant, as well as providing ships to transport the equipment back to Tianjin. But, part of the contract called for us to guarantee that they would be able to meet their production targets once the equipment was installed, or we didn't get paid.

"Corporate management decided there was too much risk. They didn't believe that the Chinese could ever learn to make the tubes, so they rejected the contract. There's no other buyer, so I guess they will just cannibalize the parts that can be salvaged for our tube production lines here, and swallow the rest of the loss."

"That's hard to understand. It must mean a big write-off for Apex."

"It will be Karen, but like you said--you can never figure out bureaucracies, and ours is almost as unfathomable as the CIA's."

Six:
Following the Shining Path

Joseph Conrad once wrote that Lima was "the saddest city on earth." It hadn't changed much since; it's just as dirty as ever Charlie thought riding into town from Jorge Chavez International Airport.

Everything in the country was topsy-turvy. Most of the other South American countries were moving toward becoming democracies. Even China was abandoning their strict Communist dogma. "Communism with a capitalistic face" the Chinese hypocritically preferred to call it, while in reality rushing to open their markets to private investment. At he same time, Peru was paralyzed by radicals advocating the failed policies of Chairman Mao.

The terrorist movement in Peru called themselves *Sendero Luminosa* or shining path, because of the lightening-like speed with which they would descend on a mountain village, wiping out any government troops that had the great misfortune of getting in their devastating path.

Abie Guzman, a former university professor of philosophy, led the radicals. Their movement began as a political party in the central Andean town of Ayacucho, then gradually morphed into a more militaristic style guerilla army.

The road into the city center was littered with trash. Discarded paper wrappings and empty plastic bags swirled in the air, buffeting the speeding auto like avenging apparitions. Perspiration trickled down Charlie's back causing his white shirt to stick to the ancient taxi's worn black fabric seat. He tried to loosen his tie as the cab bounced over the rough road.

There was increasing evidence of the terrorist's transition from the countryside to the city. The cab was passing through a neighborhood of well-kept homes. A formidable six-foot concrete fence, with broken glass bottles embedded in their top surrounded each house. Many owners had also invested in private uniformed guards stationed inside imposing wrought-iron gates.

The last time Charlie was in Lima, the streets running in front of police stations were usually blockaded to reduce the incidence of frequent car bombings. As the cab drove closer to the city center it was apparent that the conditions had not improved.

Lima had never been one of his favorite places, but it had been several months since his last trip. The wasted time in China had interfered with his regular schedule, and he had to catch up on stacks of paperwork before he could start traveling again.

In addition, Paul Murphy and he had begun meeting with Mexican Government officials. Apex had moved much of its production facilities south of the American border in order to reduce manufacturing costs. Now, the company was the third largest employer in Mexico, but it was still not permitted to sell its Mexican-made products inside the country.

Murphy and he had sat patiently through many tedious meetings with the Mexican officials, but were making scant headway in obtaining their approval to sell products inside of the Federal District.

The company's consultants suggested they might try to offer financial incentives to the officials to speed-up the negotiations. Paul and he considered it, but decided against it.

If Apex had been a European company such payments could be deducted from income taxes as an operating expense. In an American company, such actions were discouraged, and anyone participating in under-the-table payments could be subject to firing, fines, or prison.

The taxi, belching toxic fumes from its broken exhaust system, finally pulled to a jerky stop in front of the Lima Sheraton. Charlie planned to meet with the American commercial attaché to get a feel for how his licensee was performing in the local market, and the US Embassy was close to the hotel.

A message was waiting for him when he checked in. Curiously there was no name, only a telephone number. Before stuffing the note in his pocket he recognized the confidential number Karen gave him during their last meeting in Chicago. It had been a long time since he had heard from her, and he was curious why she was calling him here.

Usually, Charlie would have dinner with the local representative, but he had decided to come in unannounced to get a better feel for how the business was doing. Since he would be eating alone he decided to go to his favorite Peruvian restaurant. In spite of all of its political problems and poverty, Lima had the best restaurants in South America.

"La Rosa Nautica," Charlie directed the taxi driver. The restaurant was on the beach outside the central district. Leaning forward he cautioned the driver to avoid the neighborhoods of Monterico and San Borja. During his last visit he had learned that bandits had recently taken to placing railroad spikes in manhole cover holes to puncture the tires of unsuspecting vehicles. When the cars became disabled, the robbers attacked the passengers. His warning was unnecessary. The driver indicated he had no intention of risking himself or his cab by going through those areas.

The setting of the restaurant was as appealing as its food. The dining room was built on a rocky jetty at the end of a wooden pier. It was a long walk from the road to the restaurant, and it was a warm night. Charlie headed immediately to the bar.

"Pisco Sour, por favor," he ordered the bartender. There were few local drinks that Charlie cared for. They were usually too sweet, but this Peruvian favorite with its subtle tartness was different. The bartender expertly poured the grape brandy into a shaker, then added a little orange liquor and egg white powder, a dash of lime juice was thrown in before the drink was finally chilled in a whirring blender. With a professional flourish, the bartender added a dash of bitters before placing it on the mahogany bar in front of his thirsty customer.

Charlie savored it slowly, while looking out the stained glass window at the evening surfers attempting to stay erect on the diminishing waves.

The smoky dining room soon filled with elegantly attired women accompanied by their male partners in expensive designer suits, drinking imported wines and eating elegantly prepared French dishes. Leaving the bar, Charlie was led to a table by a large window where he watched the setting sun, and relaxed over a dinner of Peruvian sea bass and a glass of chilled Chilean sauvignon blanc.

Back in his hotel room, Charlie emptied his pockets and found the forgotten note from Karen. He was tired. It had been a long trip, and Aero Peru was not his favorite airline, but tomorrow would be a busy day. It was late in Washington, but he could at least leave a message. There was a ring at the other end of the line, but no response. An hour later the phone awakened him.

"Charlie?"

He recognized Karen's husky voice. "You certainly aren't at your office this late," he mumbled sleepily.

"I'm not. This is a special line. It connects me wherever I am. It's also secure. Look, I wish I had known you were going to Peru. We really need your help there." She quickly continued without giving Charlie a chance to reply.

Are you familiar with the Sendero Luminoso?"

"I know about them Karen but I'm not familiar with them," he replied drowsily.

"Don't parse words with me Charlie." Her voice sounded cold and brittle, and Charlie was far too tired to play word games with a Ph.D.

"Well, as you apparently know," she continued "their hero is Chairman Mao and they want to turn Peru into a Chinese Communist country. People here don't want that to happen. The Peruvian government is having a hard time with the rebels, and it's not certain they can beat them.

"When we found out you were down there, we arranged to have a military flight deliver an important envelope to the embassy for you. We have Air Force people going down there all of the time to train Peruvian pilots how to fly the high altitude Sikorsky choppers, so it was not a problem.

"When you get the envelope we want you to deliver it to some people in Lima that are not with the government, but are against the radicals."

Karen had been talking so fast Charlie hadn't had an opportunity to object. "Why me?" he quickly interjected.

"The only people we have there is the commercial guy at the embassy."

"And?"

"I can tell you've never met him. He's what we call a legacy. His father was in the OSS with some important people here. We're still pretty much an old boys club, so after he was hired no one could find a place for him. The guy finally ended up in Peru. They thought Lima was such a backwater he could do no harm.

"Now the country has turned into a political hot spot, and we don't have anyone there we can depend on. You remember we told you we were too short-handed to have agents in most of the developing countries. Now it's too late to do anything about it.

"Also, Charlie, if we use someone like you, with no apparent connection to us-in the unlikely event that your cover is blown-we retain plausible deniability."

Karen's comments were less than reassuring.

"So now that I have filled you in, here is what we would like you to do to help us." Before ending the conversation, Karen gave Charlie detailed instructions on what she expected him to do, without ever giving him a chance to object.

That night he had difficulty sleeping. He dreamed he was in a whirlpool, dragged gasping and flaying ever more deeply into its powerful center. He woke sweaty and unrested, with a feeling of profound apprehension.

Rosa Rincon escorted Charlie from the embassy lobby to the office of Stacy Loosetree, the commercial attaché. "Mr. Loosetree is expecting you," she said casually motioning to the open door behind her desk. As he strolled past her she called after him, "Mr. Connelly, I have a package for you in the embassy safe. It arrived yesterday. You can pick it up when you leave."

With her immediate responsibilities completed, the pert secretary resumed sipping from a bottle of Inca Cola she had left unattended.

Terrible tasting stuff Charlie recalled as he entered the adjoining office. The room was like many similar offices he had visited during his travels. It was cramped but well appointed, with over-stuffed chairs and a large leather couch framing a coffee table that held stacks of Department of Commerce bulletins.

Looking out the large office window Charlie could see the broad Plaza de la Republica with the Monument of the Farm Worker in the center. Beyond the Plaza stood the towering Sheraton Hotel where he was staying.

Behind the desk was an astonishing figure. Stacy Loosetree was obese. There was no other way to say it. He was as short as he was fat. His small porcine eyes were hidden behind thick glasses. His thinning hair was carefully combed to hide as much of his baldness as possible. Most startling, however, was a scraggly black mustache draped around the corners of his mouth and running to the bottom of his plump chin, making him a truly comic figure.

Charlie fought to restrain the laughter bubbling up inside, as he was reminded of a giant frog blinking at him atop a large desk. How in the world, he wondered, would the CIA hire such a man and then assign him to such a critical position in an American Embassy?

Stacy seemed pleased to have a visitor, and provided Charlie with a halting appraisal of the current economic conditions in Peru. He began with an oblique reference to a country of contrasts, and ended with a description of a nation in conflict that was mineral rich and people poor.

Before Stacey could continue, Rosa discretely entered the office and served coffee to the two men. She was an attractive young woman with a skirt slightly shorter than long enough. Charlie glanced admiringly at the departing figure.

Returning his attention to the commercial officer, he was dismayed to see that he had fallen fast asleep. Shifting uncomfortably in his chair, Charlie waited impatiently for his rotund host to wake. He noisily cleared his throat, then tried dropping his pen. Aside from the too obvious clatter, there was no visible response from the slumbering attaché. Eventually Charlie gave up his efforts, and left the office to seek help from the secretary.

"Mr. Loosetree seems very tired and has dropped off to sleep. I haven't been able to wake him. I don't want to shake him. I really don't know what to do," he complained embarrassedly."

"Don't worry Senior Connelly; he does this all the time. Mr. Loosetree has some type of illness and can't control it. The embassy doctor says he has narc ah--narco ah," she stammered.

"Narcolepsy?"

"Yes, that's right Mr. Connelly," she confirmed, visually appraising her tall guest as only Latin women can. "We were instructed to leave him alone when that happens. Some times he sleeps a few minutes, other times a few hours. I'll get your package," she added nonchalantly. Come back later if you wish. He may be awake by then."

Rosa returned with a bulging manila envelope. Charlie looked around while nervously stuffing the package into his briefcase. The secretary seemed unconcerned with her errand, and returned to her cluttered desk and nearly empty bottle of tepid Cola.

The night before, Karen had told him that after picking up the envelope he should immediately go to the Cathedral beside the Plaza de Armas. The old church was in the center of Lima and only a few blocks from the embassy. It was too early for the midday heat to settle in, and he decided it would be better to walk than take a taxi. He was new at the game, but thought he could better see if he was being followed walking than sitting in a cab.

85

The unlikely spy walked briskly toward his directed destination, realizing he was in a strange and troubled city, carrying an envelope bulging with bills. He thought he could feel eyes staring at his back, and wondered if it was getting warmer or was it nervousness causing him to perspire so much. Perhaps it was just the smog that forced his breath to come more quickly and his heart beat faster he rationalized as he walked along the dirty sidewalk.

He furtively glanced at the street vendors wearing their Bogart style felt hats as they hopefully displayed their sorry wares on faded blankets spread across the concrete walkway. Were they looking at him too intently? He stopped abruptly and peered into a cloudy store window to see if he could detect an ominous face in the distorted reflection, but all the faces he saw were indistinguishable from one another.

Had Charlie been schooled in the arcane techniques of tradecraft he might have noticed that on leaving the protective confines of the embassy a tall young woman carrying a grocery bag swung into position a few yards behind him. She maintained a discrete distance allowing her to keep her target in sight without drawing his attention.

She was dressed more sedately than most women her age to avoid the gaze of the man she was following, as well as the young men that typically lounged around the statues in the Plaza de la Republica across the street from the embassy. She noticed Charlie glancing behind him as he walked along Constitution Avenue, and alertly darted into a doorway.

He was relieved to enter the cool tranquility of the dimly lighted Cathedral. There was only a scattering of old people piously offering their prayerful petitions to their favorite saints. Concentrating on their well-worn rosaries, none of the worshippers noticed the hesitant figure of a tall American.

Approaching the altar, he was distracted momentarily by an ornate glass coffin containing the remains of Francisco Pizarro, the great conquistador who founded the city and was brutally murdered just six years later. Not a good omen Charlie thought glancing inside the transparent enclosure.

The stand holding the votive candles was positioned at the side of an elaborate baroque gilded altar. Looking more closely, he could identify a series of previously lighted candles in the design of a T that Karen told him would be the sign.

Finding a match in the almost empty dispenser, he carefully lighted three more candles in a vertical row at the top of the pattern. When the small wicks flickered to life in their crimson colored cups they formed the figure of a flaming cross.

His task completed, Charlie blessed himself and turned to leave. Pausing, he fumbled nervously in his pocket and took out a five-dollar bill, which he carefully inserted into the narrow slot at the base of the votive stand.

Leaving the Cathedral he quickly turned to see if anyone was behind him. He was relieved that there was only the solitary guard with his black boots, blue trousers, and red tunic standing stiffly at attention in front of the heavy Cathedral door.

Karen's instructions were to go to the center of the Plaza de Armas and wait. Charlie found an unoccupied bench where he could watch the entrance to the Cathedral. The sun was beginning to burn through the pewter colored sky, causing his white button-down shirt to cling to the back of his gray pinstripe suit. His sweaty hand tightly held the bulging manila envelope wrapped, according to his instructions, in a copy of the weekly English language Lima Times.

He recalled Emmett Valentine once telling him that working at the CIA was sometimes like living in a house of mirrors where a person can become unsure of what is real and what is unreal. He wondered, sitting in the large Peruvian plaza, if he was already becoming paranoid, and tried unsuccessfully to relax.

Seated unnoticed behind him on a nearby bench was the same young woman carrying a grocery bag that had followed him from the embassy.

At exactly noon, a faint ruffle of drums diverted his attention from the Cathedral to the white Palacio de Gobierno, the official residence of El Presidente. Red and black uniformed guards with gleaming Roman style gold helmets began their ritual slow goose-step around the Palace courtyard. The colorful scene seemed out of place in the drab center of the shabby city.

Absorbed by the soldiers performing their daily routine he was surprised at a slight brush against his hand, and instinctively jerked away while even more tightly clutching his precious envelope.

Turning quickly, he saw a nun seated beside him cloaked in a full length black habit adorned with a veil, scapular collar, rosary, and a narrow rope with five knots, which Charlie knew from his catechism classes were for the five wounds of Christ. There was a copy of the Wall Street Journal lying between them. A nun for God's sake, with a Wall Street Journal. He had expected anyone but a nun.

The tall, highly starched, white collar obscured his companion's features, but he could detect a slight nodding in the direction of the paper lying between them. The Journal was the sign Karen said would identify the person meant to receive his envelope.

Charlie placed his paper beside the Journal. In an instant it was retrieved, and he curiously watched the departing black clad figure gliding on hidden feet heading toward a narrow street leading away from the Plaza.

The woman and her groceries stood and unnoticed departed in the opposite direction.

Casually picking up the discarded Journal, Charlie pretended to studiously examine the recent market fluctuations. It would have appeared to a casual observer that two strangers sat briefly together enjoying the daily changing of the Guard.

Charlie spent the remainder of the afternoon visiting local *bodegas* that sold consumer electronics. It was difficult to concentrate on business after his mysterious encounter, but he forced himself to focus on his commercial responsibilities.

Eventually, he worked his way back to the Sheraton. He was too nervous to be hungry, but he decided to stop in the hotel coffee shop for a quick ham sandwich and a cold beer before returning to his room. Finishing quickly he was tempted to order another bottle. Instead he stretched tiredly, and motioned to the waiter for his check.

Fumbling with his room key, he unlocked the door and stepped into the darkened hotel room, only to be violently driven back against the wall. His eyes quickly adjusted to the darkness and he could make out the tall figure of a man wearing a black woolen balaclava, and he felt the razor-sharp point of a knife pressed against his neck.

"*Envoltura, envoltura*" the man whispered, his lips close to Charlie's ear, as he pressed the blade deeper into Charlie's exposed flesh.

"*No habla espanol,*" Charlie replied in a terrified whisper.

He didn't understand what his assailant was saying. Was envoltura an envelope he wondered? Was he about to die because he didn't understand what the man wanted?

"*Dinero Americano,*" the masked man demanded loudly.

Charlie understood the word for money, feeling a small trickle of blood running down his neck into the collar of his shirt. His eyes became better adjusted to the faint light, and he could see that his belongings had been franticly scattered around the room.

"*Yo no tengo dinero*--God damn it," Charlie whispered hoarsely, praying the man would understand he had no money.

Apparently the robber understood, "*donde? — donde?*" he shouted hysterically, while pressing the knife blade even deeper.

Where? — where? Charlie mentally translated. Where was the money? How did this guy know about the money? Was he going to be killed for something he didn't have? What could he tell him without getting his throat cut?

"Embassy — embassy — it's in the embassy," he blurted.

His loud voice startled the intruder as much as the answer and his hold relaxed ever so slightly. Charlie, the avid swimmer, took advantage of the man's bewilderment and shot both arms directly over his head in a perfect beginning to the breaststroke.

Astonished, the masked man took a step backward just as Charlie forcefully brought both his arms down across the forearms of his masked assailant. The knife clattered on the entryway tiles, while Charlie smashed his knee into the intruder's crotch.

The man let out an anguished groan, and jackknifed in pain.

Charlie grabbed his shoulders, and with all his might drove the bent body into the hotel room wall. The assailant dropped to the floor, but in landing rolled over and kicked savagely at Charlie's legs, knocking them from underneath him. Charlie twisted in pain on the floor. Cursing loudly, the man tore off his mask, retrieved the fallen knife, and dashed out the door.

Charlie struggled to his knees in time to see his visitor fleeing down the hallway, then disappear through the heavy stairwell door.

"What the hell was that all about?" Charlie wondered rubbing his bruised legs. Why did he come here? How did he know I had an envelope filled with money? Will he come back? Why in the name of God did I say embassy? I guess at that point, he thought, I would have said anything that came into my head.

He struggled to his feet, supporting his weight on the nearby bed. Once erect, he inhaled deeply and limped unsteadily to the door. Leaning against the wall Charlie quickly jammed the safety chain into place. Feeling more secure, he hobbled to the mini-bar and wrapped all of the available ice in a bathroom towel. Pressing the moist towel against his punctured neck, he stumbled to the bed. Sitting down he gingerly applied the improvised ice pack to his aching shins.

He might have killed me, Charlie thought. If I could have got my hand on that knife I would have killed him myself he suddenly realized; even more surprised at himself than the actions of his assailant.

The pain eventually began to ease and he fell into an exhausted sleep.

A loud explosion violently shook the hotel. Startled, Charlie leapt from his bed and stumbled to the window. Peering into the black night he could see flames begin to flicker in the downstairs window of the nearby American Embassy.

Fearing another attack, and frightened for his own safety, Charlie quickly gathered his scattered belongings and hastily stuffed them into his bag. He didn't know where he was going but he wanted out of where he was--and as fast as possible.

After paying his hotel bill from a startled clerk, he leapt into a parked taxi. "*Aeropuerto muy rapido,*" Charlie shouted to the drowsy driver. The car ground into gear, lurching out of the driveway in a burst of blue smoke. The driver started toward the airport as rapidly as his ancient engine would allow, but abruptly skidded to a stop when he was forced to wait for a chain of speeding police cars, fire trucks, and ancient ambulances racing toward the American Embassy. The eerie screams of their assorted sirens splintered the smoky blackness of the violent Peruvian night. Charlie watched in horror.

Drawing closer to the airport he thought about what to do next. He had left the hotel driven by fear. His singular thought was to get as far away from the scene of his attack as rapidly as possible. The airport was the first thing that came to mind. But, his plane wasn't scheduled to leave for Miami until late that afternoon, and the first faint sliver of light was only now becoming apparent in the eastern sky.

The dimly lighted airport lobby seemed abandoned, with the exception of a few weary workers pushing their wide brooms over tiled floors. A scratchy recording of "El Condor Pasa" played plaintively on the airport audio system. The sound of the Peruvian instruments provided an eerie background for the clumsy choreography of the tired janitors.

In a far corner of the old lobby, a group of German backpackers, returning from their trip to Machu Picchu, sprawled exhaustedly on the floor in front of the vacant Lufthansa check-in counter.

Peering intently at the blinking electronic display, Charlie could see that the day's first flight was to Asuncion, Paraguay. The AeroPeru departure to Miami was half a day later. He recalled the lawyer Luis Rincon telling him Asuncion was so far removed from the mainstream the world could come to an end and it would be a week before the people there knew.

Charlie had chuckled at the Venezuelan attorney's observation, but now Asuncion sounded like the perfect place to go—under the circumstances. Besides, he thought, he had a distributor there whom he had never met.

That afternoon Charlie gratefully relaxed on the wide veranda of the Gran Hotel Parana, nursing a sweating gin and tonic. He had managed to lock the problems of the day before in the back of his mind, and was now watching the people in the adjoining plaza go about their post-siesta activities. Sucking pensively on his slice of lime, it occurred to him that the scene looked very much like an amateur stage play concerning a sleepy South American village hours before the revolution. But, Presidente' General Stroessner, Charlie knew, was far too powerful to allow such dissention.

Immediately after checking into the old hotel, he had tried to call Karen's number, but was unable to get a response. He desperately wanted an explanation of what happened after he made the envelope-drop to his mysterious contact.

He also called Beth. "Dear you'll never guess what happened," he laughingly told her. "There was some stormy weather over the Andes, and my flight got diverted to Asuncion. No darling it's in Paraguay," he answered. "That's all right not many people know where it is. I'm not sure everyone here even knows where they are. Anyway, I have a flight out tomorrow. Everyone OK?" he asked.

"Great--love ya--by," he concluded their brief conversation before he lost the connection. After hanging-up, he dressed for his dinner meeting with the local Apex distributor.

Seven:
Israeli Confrontation

Most of the Apex offices were still empty, and only a scattering of cars dotted the large company parking lot. This was Charlie's favorite time to work. The phones had not begun ringing, and it was possible to get through the stacks of correspondence that always piled-up.

He had absently tuned his office TV to one of the early morning shows, but he paid little attention to the perky Katie Couric interviewing a group of experts describing the Y2K calamities soon to befall the country. Instead Charlie relaxed, leaned back in his chair, propped his feet on his large desk and gazed out his window at the distant Chicago skyline.

It had been months since he had heard from anyone at the CIA. After returning home from Peru he tried to contact Karen Kincaid, but no one answered the number she had given him. He then tried to call Marvin, with a similar lack of results.

Eventually he gave up trying, but he couldn't get his experiences in Lima out of his mind. During the first few weeks at home he would often wake in the middle of the night from a dream about the man in the black balaclava. Sometimes it seemed that he could still feel the intruder's cold blade against his throat. Eventually, the too-realistic nightmare faded, and his life continued as it had before the trip to Lima.

There was plenty to do without getting involved in the CIA's problems, but he begrudgingly had to admit that, in a perverse way, he missed the adventure and excitement of working with the Agency. The experience had also given him a sense of patriotic pride, believing that in a small way he was contributing to the security of the nation he loved.

Things were going unusually well for his international organization. In Maracaibo, Rene' was beginning to make considerable progress after getting control of Jake's ranch. Because of high oil prices, land was selling at a premium in Venezuela. The proceeds from Jacob's ranch were then re-invested in the Maracaibo television business that had been previously drained of working capital. With the funds restored, the company began to expand as it had before Jacob decided his ranch could use the money more than his partner's television factory.

The Ortega brothers had come out of hiding after the failed kidnapping attempt. Their new orders were beginning to flow steadily, and their factory was back to its former level of activity.

The Mexican Government had grudgingly agreed to allow Apex to sell ten percent of its Mexican-made products inside Mexico. The new sales were driving the international business to record levels, but they were also raising the anger of the American distributors along the border who had formerly been selling directly to Mexican dealers.

While he had been unable to sell the King of Prussia tube plant to Tianjin, the relationships he made during the trip eventually resulted in a series of large orders for Apex projection sets the Chinese Army intended to use in training its officer corps.

It was a groundbreaking agreement. Because it was early in America's new business relationship with China, the contract was described in the *Congressional Record*.

After the article was published, Charlie received an unsigned one-word note saying "Attaboy." The envelope was postmarked Washington, and he assumed it had come from Karen.

When things seem to be going exceptionally well it usually means they are about to change. Entering the office, Paul Murphy's voice interrupted Charlie's reverie. "Did you get a call from Bob Sackman last night?" he asked, abruptly switching off the TV set. Murphy was obviously upset. His ruddy face was flushed more than usual from the hurried walk to Charlie's office.

Paul and Robbie Sackman were friends long before Charlie came on the international scene. It was Murphy who was instrumental in getting approval of an Apex license for the colorful Tel Aviv businessman.

Sackman had got his start as a gunrunner for the Haganah during the British Mandate. When Israel became an independent nation the government rewarded him for his work in the underground by granting a monopoly for brewing and the distribution of beer in the new country. Israel is in a very warm climate, and the business was extremely successful.

Eventually Sackman desired to branch out into other businesses, and approached Apex for a license to produce their TV sets in his country. Murphy used his family's influence with the board of directors to grant the license, and the two men had stayed close friends ever since.

"What did he want?" Charlie asked, surprised at the late night call.

"He was terribly despondent. You remember him telling us about his son. Robbie is a very proud man. He was proud of his wealth, and he was proud of his business, but he was most proud of his son. The boy had gone to Stanford and he took a job in San Francisco with the Bank of America after graduation. He worked for them for several years, then Robbie gathered funds from other members of his family and they invested in a bank in Switzerland. Once they had gained control they put the boy in as the bank's president.

"According to Robbie the boy wanted to be as financially successful as his father, apparently with less talent. He got involved with the Swiss Mafia speculating on the commodities market. It wasn't long before he lost all of his money and the bank's money as well. The loss forced the bank to close, The Swiss authorities, who take their banking industry very seriously, issued an arrest warrant, and Interpol began looking for him all over Europe. The boy disappeared and no one has heard from him since.

"Robbie is terribly ashamed. Not only did he lose a lot of his own funds, but also his relative's money. I don't know what he is going to do," Murphy said looking at Charlie as if he might be able to provide the answer.

Before he could hazard an answer, the loud ringing of his phone diverted Charlie's attention. Linda hadn't arrived yet so with an apologetic wave to Murphy he reluctantly picked up the receiver. He listened intently for several minutes, then hung up.

"I know what Robbie was going to do," he told Murphy. "That was Michael Wiedra calling from Tel Aviv. He manages the TV factory for Robbie. He thought I should know that early this morning, apparently shortly after he spoke with you, Sackman jumped off the top of one of his office buildings in Tel Aviv and killed himself. He just couldn't live with the shame of his son."

The two men were silent for several minutes. Both of them not only had great respect for Sackman as a businessman, but considered him a close friend as well.

Murphy, his face ashen turned to leave, but before reaching the door he turned back. "By the way" he began apologetically. I probably shouldn't be telling you this, particularly now, but I was in a meeting the other day with some other members of the Board. They were telling me that your boss is very upset with your organization because it is doing so well and his domestic distributors are doing so poorly. They think he is out to get you." After delivering his warning, he turned and went back to his office.

The day that had started so well for Charlie had quickly turned to dust. He had lost a friend, and if Paul Murphy was correct he might be losing his job. He appreciated the warning. Murphy was well connected within the corporation and had always been a close friend. Paul had also been involved in a number of bureaucratic battles of his own, and he was familiar with the intricacies of corporate infighting.

The problem was that Charlie really didn't know what to do about it. He was fiercely loyal to his international associates. He knew that he could shut the water off to some of the offending distributors by canceling their license, or merely delaying their orders past the duration of their letters of credit. But that would be blatantly unfair. They had been loyal to the corporation and had invested a considerable amount of their personal funds in their businesses. He also had a loyalty to Apex, if it weren't for the international business the corporation wouldn't be able to report any profits at all.

Gazing dejectedly out the window Charlie watched the arriving Apex employees trickling in from the parking lot.

The fasten seatbelt announcement roused him from a troubled sleep as the 747 began its descent toward Frankfurt's Rhein Main *flughafen*. The flight attendant brought a hot towel that he used to try and clear the residue of a short night from his eyes.

Soon, the plane's giant tires squealed in protest as they forcefully encountered the rain-drenched runway. The huge airport is a favorite for international passengers and as Charlie made his way through a labyrinth of waiting lounges he passed sprawling travelers wearing kaftans from

Kuwait, dashikis from Africa, saris from India and well-dressed men in their suits and regimental ties from Great Britain. A universal relationship brought on by fatigue and boredom united the disparate collection of travelers.

It sometimes seemed to him that his life consisted of arrivals and departures while other men's were composed of family and friends. But, there was no choice. No one could refuse to meet with a weeping widow who was imploring him to come to Tel Aviv to discuss her late husband's business.

The situation in Israel was particularly complex. After the license was granted to Robbie Sackman the Arab countries had become more aggressive, both militarily and economically. In order to deprive the new country of needed foreign investment, the Arab countries joined together to punish international companies that established a business relationship in Israel. Those companies that did so were placed on a blacklist administered from an office in Damascus, Syria. None of the Arab countries were allowed to trade with any foreign company whose name was on the blacklist.

Few of the Mideastern states had markets large enough to be important, with the exception of Saudi Arabia and Egypt. Those two countries could provide a substantial market for Apex products, if the company did trade with them. The death of Sackman might make it possible for Charlie to cancel the Israeli license and, with an Arab rather than an Israeli partner, significantly increase the company's total volume. Winding his way through the Frankfurt airport Charlie carefully considered his alternatives.

The unsmiling woman behind the Lufthansa counter curtly directed him to the special departure lounge the airline used for their flights to Israel. There had been several attempted hijackings of previous flights, and the German airline wanted to be careful it didn't happen again.

Once in the lounge, Customs thoroughly examined his carryon bag. Each bottle was opened and his electric shaver was plugged into an outlet to make sure there were no explosives or detonators hidden among his personal possessions.

Afterward, he proceeded to the boarding area accompanied by two armed guards. Outside, the traveler's previously checked bags were lined up on the tarmac. Each person was required to identify his own bag to make sure that none were placed on the plane without an accompanying passenger. The travelers were then loaded into a bus that took them to their flight.

The plane to Tel Aviv was parked on an isolated airstrip far from the central terminal, and far from other planes. Armed guards surrounded it, and an armored personnel carrier was strategically positioned on each side of the ancient 707. After all the passengers boarded, the cabin doors were closed, as the plane taxied down the narrow runway it was accompanied by the military vehicles until it was airborne.

Charlie wasn't sure if the security was reassuring or unsettling, and he was glad to arrive safely at Ben-Gurion Airport.

Passing through customs he requested that the agent stamp his passport "on the side." The official agreeable complied and vigorously stamped his seal on a separate piece of paper, which was then placed inside Charlie's passport to be removed when he left the country. Otherwise, he would be unable to travel to countries that refuse entry to travelers with a Jewish stamp in their passport.

The phone was already ringing when he entered his suite at the Hilton. It had been a tiring trip, and the last thing he wanted was to talk to a grieving widow, or anyone else for that matter. He called the desk and told them to hold his calls. Afterwards he took a hot shower, followed by a cold martini poured over ice from a flask he carried in his suitcase, and went to bed.

The repetitive sound of a throbbing aircraft engine woke him early. Charlie ambled to the window, scratching a two-day growth of beard, and watched hypnotically as an Israeli helicopter slowly patrolled the narrow beachfront.

His attention was quickly diverted from the hovering chopper to the gleaming barbed wire fence separating the beach from the hotel grounds. The barrier seemed like a jagged wound on the otherwise tranquil scene of a blue Mediterranean shimmering in the sunlight.

Charlie would have preferred to spend the entire day gazing at the sea, or better yet swimming in it. He dreaded the encounter with Robbie's widow, but she had asked to see him, and he had traveled a long way to accommodate her.

As he shaved he tried to formulate a plan to handle the discussion. Giving up, he sat down to his room-service breakfast of melon, dry toast, and very black coffee. The night before, when he had ordered, he had decided that the usual meal of ham and eggs would not be the best choice to start the day at the Tel Aviv Hilton.

There was a knock on the door just as he began dialing the phone. Expecting the waiter coming to collect the try, he stared in amazement while Mrs. Sackman strode confidently into the room accompanied by her son Bernard. The same Bernard Sackman that Interpol was searching for all over Europe.

"I was very sorry to hear about the sui--death of your husband," Charlie stammered uncomfortably in an awkward attempt to console the widow who was calmly taking a seat on the sofa alongside her son.

"I know you are Charlie," she replied pulling her tight skirt over her plump legs. Mrs. Sackman didn't present the figure of the grieving widow he had previously imagined. She was heavily made-up, with dyed red hair; and her hands were covered with expensive jewelry.

"Robbie and I hadn't been close for some time. I spend most of my time at our house in Lucerne, while he preferred Tel Aviv. Why, I have never been able to figure out. Perhaps he felt freer to have his affairs here when I was out of sight. But, I didn't ask you to come this far to hear about our marital history.

"As soon as we finished sitting Shiva we wanted to talk to you about the Apex license," she offered staring confrontationally directly at Charlie. "You may have heard that there is some minor misunderstanding back in Switzerland about Bernard and his bank. Israel has no extradition agreements with Europe so he can stay here without being bothered by the authorities, until he clears it up of course.

"What I would like Mr. Connelly," as Mrs. Sackman's gaze riveted on Charlie "is your assurance that you will continue the Apex license," she hesitated tearfully dabbing her eyes for the first time. "That way Bernard will have something to do while he attends to his other problems."

"Are you suggesting that we continue the business here with your son in charge?" Charlie asked incredulously.

"Of course, it's the logical thing to do. The Sackman family started this business, and they should be the ones who continue it. I know that the terms of the agreement are such—I have already had our lawyers look into it—they are such that you could cancel it now that poor old Robbie is dead, but I am sure you wouldn't do that to us. Would you?" she asked plaintively while nervously twisting her damp handkerchief around her plump fingers.

While she was imploring Charlie to continue the business, his attention strayed to her son who was engrossed with his expensive silk tie, rolling it up from the tail to its broad knot then allowing it to slowly unroll-only to begin again.

Charlie refocused on what he was to tell the widow Robinson. He had abandoned the use of subtleties long ago. Usually they were misinterpreted, and at this moment it was important to be very clear--even if he wasn't very diplomatic. "Let's face facts Mrs. Sackman," he attempted to explain. "Your husband is dead because of the actions of your son. There is a warrant out for Bernard all over Europe, and you want us to continue doing business here as if nothing has happened."

"Look Mr. Connelly," Bernard broke in. "The whole thing in Switzerland is just a big mistake. The Mafia took advantage of me, I couldn't help it. It's really not my fault, and it won't interfere with the business here. I give you my word."

Charlie hadn't known what to expect when he came to Tel Aviv, but it certainly was not that Mrs. Sackman would want to continue the business with her fugitive son at its helm. He considered telling the boy what a contemptible thing he had done to betray the trust of his father, but if his mother hadn't rebuked the son how could he. There is no accounting for Mother's love, Charlie thought.

The conversation had become extremely tense. The bright sunlight streaming through the hotel window was in stark contrast to the bleak atmosphere inside the room. Charlie had no intention of continuing the license with Bernard, but he didn't know how best to tell the Mother.

The shrill ringing of the phone provided a welcome break. It was Michael Wiedra on the line. He, along with a partner, wanted to see Charlie and discuss the possibility of their getting the license. A meeting was quickly arranged for later in the day.

Returning to the Sackmans and gently leading them toward the door, Charlie told them he would think over their proposition and let them know his decision before returning to Chicago. He already knew what he intended to do, but if he told the Sackmans now it would only lead to an even more protracted discussion.

Later that day Michael Wiedra came to Charlie's room accompanied by his potential partner. Michael was an excellent manager and Robbie always spoke highly of him. He actually ran the business while Robbie provided the interface between the local government agencies and the banks

Michael's partner turned out to be Aaron Greenfield. His Aunt had been a former Prime Minister in the newly established Israeli government. She had died several years before but Aaron and his family remained financially and politically well positioned in the country. The combination of Wiedra's operating experience and Greenfield's financing would provide a formidable business combination that could effectively replace the Sackman family.

Charlie had already decided that he didn't want to be forced out of Israel by the Arab League, as much as he would like to be in the larger markets of Egypt and Saudi. It was a commitment to the country that his company had made years before, and it would be difficult for them to reverse their position as a result of political pressure from Syria.

In the evening he called Paul Murphy to discuss his decision. The next day he informed Michael that Apex would transfer the business to his newly formed company.

His next call was to Mrs. Sackman to tell her that Apex could not afford to be associated with someone wanted by Interpol. She threatened to sue, but he had expected that.

Before leaving Israel, Aaron Greenfield invited Charlie to an impromptu cocktail party to announce the formation of the new company. The only room available was a small banquet room on the second floor of the Hilton. The management had quickly arranged for two open bars and a long table of assorted sandwiches and small appetizers.

Michael was eager to point out the important people in banking and the Israeli Government that had come on short notice. Apparently, many of them were eager to pay their respects to Aaron Greenfield, and wish him good fortune on his new business venture.

Charlie disliked cocktail parties. The idea of spending several hours mingling with strangers and making idle conversation was not to his liking. Earlier in the evening he was asked by the two partners to make a speech describing how pleased Apex was with its new affiliation in Israel, and how his company would provide technical support to the new company. His duties completed, Charlie was spending the rest of the evening leaning on the bar and surveying the crowd. Occasionally, Michael or Aaron would pass and introduce him to one of the guests.

As the night drew on, the room seemed to shrink as the number of attendees increased. Two burly men in blue suits were strategically positioned at the narrow doorway to provide a security filter for those passing by who might try to join the party without an invitation. In spite of their efforts, the growing crowd was challenging the strength of the hotel's air-conditioning system. As the temperature increased, the air became saturated with the powerful stench of European cigarettes and Cuban Cigars.

Charlie motioned the bartender for his second gin and tonic of the evening. Turning away from the bar he found himself staring directly into the lean face of a short man wearing a distinguishing black eye patch. "Mr. Connelly," he began in a raspy whisper. "We are very pleased that your company is staying in Israel, we very badly need your technology."

"You prefer American TV sets to the Europeans?" Charlie asked taking a drink from his sweating glass.

"Well yes. Of course, but it's not that entirely. We need to know how to make the integrated circuits that you use in your products. They are more advanced than any we have here. Just like in the United States, commercial technology is the basis for a great deal of military electronics, and we have to do everything we can to protect ourselves from our many enemies. They are constantly attempting to obtain advanced technology they can use to wipe our tiny country off the map.

"Did you know Mr. Connelly that the entire population of Israel is considerably less than the number of people in your metropolitan Chicago area. You can see that we are very vulnerable, and need all the help we can get to defend ourselves.

"When we heard that Robbie Sackman had come to such an untimely death we were afraid you would close the business down and move the license to Cairo, like many other companies. We appreciate your decision to remain in Israel and if there is ever anything we can do to help, don't hesitate to call on us. Aaron Greenfield would know how to get in touch," he added before dissolving into the crowd.

Charlie noticed, for the first time, that Aaron had been standing behind him. "Do you know who that man was that you were talking to? He is very influential in our government. Some people believe he is the head of the Mossad. He was a close friend of my Aunts. They had known each other for many years and he was always at her parties. He even came to one of my birthdays when I was growing up.

"We don't operate here like the CIA in the United States. We patterned our intelligence organization on the British. Like them, and unlike the CIA, the head of our intelligence agency is never revealed. It's for his own protection. We are such a small country it is far too easy to kidnap someone. It's also very difficult to keep secrets. Anyway, Jews have never been good at keeping secrets," he added wryly. "Hammas and Hezbollah would love to get their hands on the leader of the Mossad, so we do the best we can to keep his identity from them.

"By the way, did you know that before becoming Prime Minister Aunt Golda lived in the United States," he offered changing the subject. "She was born in Kiev, but her family moved to Milwaukee. She lived there many years before moving to Palestine to work on a kibitz."

Finally the crowd began to drift slowly away, and Charlie returned to his room to pack for his early morning flight home.

On his way to the airport, the cab passed the smoldering hulk of an airplane at the edge of the landing field. No one inside the terminal would even acknowledge that it was there, much less had happened.

Hours later his plane taxied to the gate at JFK. Charlie was glad to be home, and hoped that it would be at least several weeks before he had to fly somewhere else. The flight from Tel Aviv to Frankfurt was delayed by bad weather over Germany, and in order to make his connection he had to sprint through the airport maze like an aging O. J. Simpson.

Once on board his Trans-Atlantic flight, the passenger in front of him reclined his seat all the way, cramping Charlie' long legs. Seated behind him was a couple holding a small child who energetically kicked the back of his seat whenever he tried to drop off to sleep. Not even two Remy Martins following his cold airline dinner could induce sleep.

"Welcome home Mr. Connelly," the young custom agent greeted him cheerfully, while slowly paging through the accordion pleated pages of Charlie's bulging passport. "Where are you coming from?" he asked routinely.

"Tel Aviv," Charlie replied, "and glad to be home."

The agent paused, "Could you come with me please Mr. Connelly," he directed, motioning for another person to fill in at his post.

Charlie did as he was asked, wondering what the agent might have discovered in his passport that required closer scrutiny.

Opening the door to a small office the young man announced triumphantly, "here is the Mr. Connelly you have been looking for gentlemen." Satisfied his task had been performed satisfactorily the agent closed the door, and returned to his post.

Puzzled, Charlie looked at the two men in the room. One leaned casually against the faded gray wall, while the other slouched against an old green government desk. Their suit coats hung open ominously, and probably intentionally, revealing large leather shoulder holsters.

The younger of the two was crew cut and towered over his shorter companion--and Charlie as well. The man was powerfully built with broad shoulders and a close cropped head of blond hair. His ham like hands extended past his shirt cuff, as if he had a difficult time buying a ready made suit to fit his lanky frame. He may have been handsome at one time in his life, but now his features were marred by a boxer's nose that appeared to have been broken and poorly set. The opaque lenses of a pair of cheap aviator glasses hid his eyes, as he studied Charlie.

His partner was considerably older and much shorter, with an unlighted cigar clenched tightly between his teeth. His watery eyes gave unwilling evidence to lonely nights spent staring into the bottom of far too many highball glasses. "You're late, we were expecting you to arrive an hour ago," he said accusingly, momentarily removing his cigar and pointing it at Charlie.

"Follow us please Mr. Connelly," the younger of two ordered opening the door behind him. At the same time his partner picked up Charlie's bag that was stored under the desk, while nudging him toward the open doorway.

Charlie had thought that he was going to be asked a few routine questions about his trip, but now it was becoming obvious that this was more serious.

"Who are you? Where are we going? What's the problem?" Charlie demanded. He was not used to being ordered about by anyone, and he didn't like it.

"There are some people in Washington that need to see you right away, and they sent us to bring you to them," the younger man explained, opening the door wider.

At the same time, his companion set down Charlie's bag and reached for his wallet. "We're with NELO, that's the Navy Engineering Logistics Office," he explained flashing an embossed identification card. "The CIA contracts with us to transport people. Are you familiar with the term rendition?" he continued without waiting for a reply. "Well consider yourself renditioned--from New York to Washington," he snickered malevolently. "We have a plane waiting on the runway. Think of it as just a little detour. You'll be home soon," he added unconvincingly

"What if I don't want to be *renditoned?*" Charlie snarled.

"Well Mr. Connelly you really have only two options, and neither one is not going," crewcut said menacingly. "You can walk out of here between us, or you can be dragged out in handcuffs," he added reaching in his coat pocket as he approached Charlie.

"Can I call my wife before we leave-she is expecting me?" Charlie asked convinced the men meant exactly what they said.

"There will be plenty of time for that when we get to Langley. You can even call on the government's dime," snickered the heavyset man, his cigar replanted firmly between his beefy lips.

Charlie walked between them down several flights of stairs, and out a door leading to the airfield. A black Ford LTD was waiting with a Marine in fatigues sitting erectly behind the steering wheel. The car sped across the tarmac to the far side of the field where an unmarked Gulfstream was waiting with its jet engines whining impatiently.

Once on board, the chunky man directed Charlie to a seat in the center of the plane. As he sat down, Charlie noticed that manacles were attached to the armrests and a set of leg irons bolted to the deck underneath each seat.

Removing his cigar, the short man remarked menacingly, "I hope we won't need those."

Charlie thought there was nothing the two men would like better than to cuff him to his seat.

"When do you serve drinks?" he asked wryly as the steeply climbing jet pinned him to the back of his padded seat cushion. A cloud of cheap cigar smoke slowly began to fill the cabin.

Eight:
Return to Langley

A white Buick wagon squealed to a stop alongside the Gulfstream after it landed at Dulles. The plane's hatch opened, and Charlie awkwardly stumbled down the narrow metal ramp leading to the idling auto. As the car's door closed the Marine driver gunned it forward with his three passengers shoehorned uncomfortably in the rear seat.

Cruising past the Lincoln Memorial, Charlie couldn't help but recall when he had come to Washington for his interview with the Agency, many years before. A lot had happened since then, and he wondered what was in store for him now. During the ride his two companions sat rigidly stone-faced, uncommunicative and uninterested in their surroundings.

The Buick turned sharply off Dolly Madison Boulevard, throwing the backseat passengers against each other. After pausing briefly for the Marine guard at the gate, the car plunged down a steep ramp to an underground parking area belonging to the sprawling multi-story office complex.

The men walked from the car to a bank of elevators, with Charlie positioned securely between them. The fat man inserted an identification card into a slot, then tapped a series of numbers into a keypad jutting from the concrete wall. A red light on the small console blinked ominously.

"Shit—-here you try it," he growled to his younger partner. The ID card was reinserted and quickly withdrawn before the numbers were again tapped on the keypad. This time a green light blinked its acceptance, and the elevator door glided silently open. The three men quickly crowded inside before it could close again. The young man punched -

4, and the elevator descended obediently. The door opened silently, and the two men led Charlie down a long narrow hallway leading to a single unmarked door at the end.

The fat man removed his cigar and tapped in a new series of numbers. This time he was more successful. A light blinked and the door swung open. Charlie felt a nudge forward, while the door closed behind him, and he found himself standing alone, abandoned by his former escorts.

The large room was bathed in a diffused amber light that cast everything in a sickly yellowish hue. Charlie strained to identify the tall figure of a man leaning on a cane directly in front of him.

"Come in Pinstripes, I have been looking forward to seeing you again."

The deep voice was vaguely familiar, but it was difficult to identify above the music softly playing in the background. *Madame Butterfly* Charlie thought.

As his eyes became more accustomed to the dim light he saw the commanding figure of an older man. He was impeccably dressed in a well tailored suit that, none the less, hung loosely on the slender frame, as if it was originally made for someone larger—or perhaps younger-than its present owner. A silk handkerchief in the breast pocket matched the regimental tie carefully tucked into the buttoned suitcoat.

The man leaned forward supporting himself on a slender ivory handled ebony cane. He looked, for all the world, like an aging headmaster expecting an errant student.

"Emmett-Emmett Valentine?" Charlie inquired hesitatingly, recalling his first encounter with the Agency.

"Yes Charlie you recall correctly," the man said approvingly. Please, come sit down. We have a lot to talk about. I am sorry about bringing you here this way, but we have a terrible problem at the Agency and it has to be solved in a hurry. You can be of great assistance to us once again."

While he talked, Emmett motioned Charlie to sit in one of the two swivel chairs in front of a large mahogany desk, while lowering himself gingerly into a large leather recliner.

"Do you like Puccini?" he asked turning a dial on the large console behind him. "It's one of my favorites. Poor Madame Butterfly. Lieutenant Pinkerton took advantage of her, and after Cho-Cho San renounced her religion and her culture the callow officer leaves her alone and returns to his own country. How sad.

"Sometimes I think that is what the Agency often does to its agents," he mused quietly leaning back in the recliner staring at the ceiling.

"But, it can't be helped, can it? We are constantly at war with a ruthless enemy that wants to destroy our way of life. Sometime we think we have won our battle, and then a new enemy arises. But that is what keeps the old juices flowing. Isn't it Charlie?"

"Look Emmett, I have had enough of your meandering. I was kidnapped by your goons, and taken away to Washington. My wife doesn't know where I am, and you're talking to me about some god damned opera."

"Spot on old boy. Please forgive an old man's ramblings. Let me tell you why we need your help. Then you can call your wife. Beth--right? Of course you can't tell her exactly where you are, but we will get to that soon.

"Let's start with you," Charlie offered. "I thought you retired long ago."

"I did, but they brought me back. There is nothing more flattering to an old war-horse than to be needed. Perhaps someday you will find that out. Be patient with an old man, and you will see. It will all fit in. Just give me a few minutes more of your valuable time.

114

"Over the last few years the agency has been riddled with defectors. Why that is happening, I don't know. We have had so many moles I wonder sometimes if we have lost sight of how to play the game.

"There was John Walker Jr. He was an ex-Navy man who had his entire family working with him to provide secrets to the Soviets. His son aboard the Nimitz was helped by his uncle Arthur. Together they stole classified information on our submarine operations and manuals. They also gave them technical information on our noise reduction techniques and the knowledge of how to unscramble our secret Navy communications. The FBI eventually picked them up and they were put away.

While Emmett spoke, Charlie became fascinated with his large desk. The highly polished surface was devoid of personal items. There were no family photos, calendars, expensive pen sets, or correspondence to be read and answered; only a blank pad of paper and an old abacus positioned in its exact center. It was as if Emmett could leave at any moment and no one would ever know that he had been there at all.

"Then there was Aldrich Ames," he continued. "Aldrich came to us from some little town in Wisconsin, and was the son of a former CIA officer. We love our own you know. Not only did he give away the name of many of our agents to the Russians, he also provided them with names of their own agent's who we had recruited and were running undercover. They were, of course, assassinated once they were discovered.

"But let's not forgot the super secret National Security Agency that some of our leaders have relied on so greatly. They have their problems too. His name was Ronald Pelton. Ronald made contact with the Russian Embassy here in Washington. Just walked in the door for Christ's sake, and told them he wanted to sell out his country.

"He gave the Russians reams of technical information on a top-secret program we were running called *Ivy Bells*. The Navy had managed to tap an underground communications cable carrying Russian conversations between a classified submarine base and Soviet brass. We spent millions of dollars on the project, and it supplied us with vital information for years. That is until Pelton sold his country out for a few thousand dollars."

Charlie sat transfixed while Emmett spoke. In the background Madame Butterfly had finished her lament and a new selection was providing background to the litany of betrayal. "Mozart G Minor Symphony," Emmett mumbled distractedly.

"Then of course there was Robert Hanssen," he continued. "He was one of your clan I believe," the old man added pointing his cane at Charlie. "Apparently, he proclaimed to be a devout Roman Catholic, even belonging to Opus Dei I am told. The sorry bastard betrayed his country and his wife. He even concealed a closed-circuit videocamera in his bedroom so an old friend of his could watch while old Robert and his wife had sex together. She was a real looker too. Resembled Elizabeth Taylor.

"Mr. Hanssen was an FBI special agent who worked in counter intelligence. One day, he walked into the New York office of a Soviet trade organization and volunteered to spy for them. He worked for them for many years, even after the collapse of the Soviet Union.

"During that time he funneled information worth billions of dollars. He gave them documents revealing American spy satellite technology, the FBI's efforts to recruit double agents and their budget and plans for their counterintelligence programs. He was so trusted by the FBI that he was appointed to a special committee that coordinated technical intelligence projects against Soviet intelligence.

116

"Much of the information he gave up originally came from us here at the CIA, including many of our undercover agents in Russia who were eventually all trotted off to Lubyanka Prison, and summarily executed.

"All of the time he was doing this he was never asked to take a lie detector test. No wonder we have such little confidence in sharing information with our friends down the street."

Charlie had been impatiently staring at his watch wondering what all of this had to do with him. Emmett sensed he was losing his audience and quickly added, "Which brings me to why we are here today.

"I want you to fully understand why we are so paranoid. You see we are the keepers of our country's secrets and one of our key agents has defected. We intend to walk the cat backward to see with whom the agent associated, and how it all began."

"I still don't understand why you brought me here," Charlie exclaimed. "Who the hell is the agent?" Charlie was becoming increasingly irritated and wanted to bring Emmett to the point so he could get on his way.

"Well you see old man; it's your old friend Karen Kincaid. What we plan to do is to form a series of concentric circles composed of people who worked with her. Then we gradually tighten those circles and see what falls off and what remains inside. You Charlie are in one of the outside rings. Some of our people think that you were bent all along, but I never believed that. Never-the-less, we must make sure that you are not involved, so we wanted to determine that immediately."

"I can't believe that Karen would do something like that. She seemed too dedicated to defect."

"Unfortunately my boy, there is no one type. Most defectors, on both sides of the pond, turn against their country for money, others--most I think--do it to solve some kind of a personal problem. Very few turn over for ideology. Those three English toffs, Burgess, Philby, and Maclean were exceptions," Emmett added disgustedly.

"But she's a woman for God's sake," Charlie exclaimed incredulously."

"I appreciate your chauvinism, but defection is proving to be an equal opportunity affliction. You probably never heard of Sharon Scranage. We managed to keep that reasonably quiet. Well, dear old Sharon was a CIA support employee in Ghana. It turns out she was fornicating with a cousin of the Ghanaian Prime Minister. Against CIA regulations, of course.

"We were eventually informed of her ah-indiscretion shall we say. In spite of that, we unwisely left her in place. She proceeded to display her gratitude by providing her lover with the names of all our agents in Ghana.

"Yes, even after that bad experience, I am afraid that we all badly misjudged our dear Karen. We thought that a woman-and a beautiful woman at that-would never be a mole. It has turned out to be misplaced idealism."

"All right—all right I won't argue with you. You must know what you are doing," Charlie grudgingly conceded. "What now?"

"Well all you will have to do is take a little test. Afterwards, I will gladly fill in some of the blanks for you, and then you can get on your way. No harm-no foul," Emmett chuckled dryly.

"First though, I know that you are eager to call Beth so let me set it up for you." Punching a key on a large console he directed, "Mrs. Connelly please."

Beth was on the line by the time Charlie got the phone.

"Hi babe, look I had a little problem and I won't be home for a day or so. My flight got diverted to Dulles so while I was here I decided that I would look up a couple of people I know at Commerce," Charlie lied into the receiver, turning away from the desk and Emmett Valentine.

"OK hon," Beth answered sounding preoccupied. "But I have been trying to get hold of you. I have some bad news. It's Paul Murphy."

"What the hell has he done now?" Charlie demanded.

"It's not that exactly," Beth told him, pausing to figure out how best to break the bad news. "He dropped dead yesterday after work, walking to his car," she blurted. "Apparently he was told his department was being eliminated to cut costs, and he couldn't handle it."

"Oh God. I'm terribly sorry to hear that. He was a great guy, and a good friend. He had spent his life at Apex, and it's a bad way to finish."

Beth and Charlie talked about the funeral arrangements, and Charlie promised to be back in time to attend.

Before they finished, Beth reminded him that their daughter was going to graduate that weekend as well. She was the last of the Connelly children to finish college.

Charlie stood up and placed the receiver back in its cradle on the console.

"Bad news?" Emmett asked.

"I've had better," Charlie replied bleakly. "Look Emmett, I need to get home now."

"I understand. We will finish up here, and see what we can do to help you get there expeditiously."

Turning again to his console, Emmett flipped a switch and a concealed door in the wall behind him silently slid open. A tall, gray haired woman entered, as if she had been patiently waiting on the other side until summoned.

Nodding almost imperceptibly to Emmett, she motioned for Charlie to follow her.

"Perhaps you remember Mary Kool Charlie? Emmett asked as they were leaving. "She has been with me a long time."

With Charlie walking obediently beside her, the tap, tap tapping of her high heels on the tile floor reminded him once again of his initial interview with Emmett Valentine, Mary Kool, and Marvin. Marvin--Marvin Charlie thought, all I need now is to meet old Marvin. He suddenly felt surrounded by ghosts.

As they were passing through a room filled with intense people staring at rows of computer screens Mary turned to explain. "We call these people the *shadows*. They're in-house kabuki dancers who try and organize the fragmented information we get from our field agents and make some sense out of it before sending it up the line to our senior people."

Charlie glanced briefly in the direction of the mostly young people before returning his attention to his guide.

"Have you been here all this time Mary?"

"You think I have been a spinster specter haunting the hallowed halls of the CIA all these years? No Charlie, I retired when Emmett did. I had no interest in hanging around this puzzle palace after he left. We were very close, you see," she added as an afterthought, almost to herself.

"Then I went to live with my widowed sister in Sarasota. We ran a little shop selling stationary. It was a real pain in the ass. Once you've fought the dragon, it's hard to settle down. When the CIA asked Emmett to come back he gave me a call to join him, and I jumped at the chance. End of story."

At the far end of the computer room Mary paused and punched a code into a keypad on the wall. As the door opened Charlie asked,"What's the story on the yellow light in Emmett's office? It makes everything look jaundiced."

"He thinks he may be developing macular degeneration, and his theory is the amber light helps him focus."

"Does it?"

"How would I know?" Mary answered pointing to a chair in the center of the room.

"Now Charlie I get to ask the questions. This is Doctor Fienstein. He runs this little machine—very expertly I might add.

The small scholarly man smiled at the shallow compliment.

"Lie detector? Charlie asked, while being wired to the strange looking device.

"I prefer to think of it as a truth detector," the doctor chuckled.

"It's his little joke," Mary added dryly.

"I thought these things were unreliable," Charlie observed while Mary opened the file folder she had been carrying and began searching for the proper forms.

"Only the people who have something to hide think that," the doctor responded offended. "And by the way, they are called polygraphs. They measure a number of indicators. The cuff I just put around your arm measures blood pressure and heart rate. The pneumographs around your chest calibrate respiration, and the galvanometers on your fingers respond to perspiration."

Charlie had noticed his palms were becoming sweaty. Now he wondered if he was in trouble.

The doctor seemed to be staring at spot on the ceiling while he described the operation of his equipment. "Changes in a person's blood pressure, heart rate, respiration and skin conductivity will reflect the level of stress he is experiencing in response to the questions being asked, and will accurately pick up any physiological changes that result from deceptive answers.

"Some people think they can beat them by taking certain drugs," Fienstein continued, "learning how to constrain their reactions, practicing yoga, and a lot of other things they do to fool us. But when the test is unexpected, and they are not prepared, they can't fool old Mother Nature.

"Did you ever hear of Edward Lee Howard?" the doctor asked Charlie while making some additional adjustments. "He worked here once. They were going to send him to Moscow to work in the embassy in a very sensitive position. Before he left they asked me to give him a "flutter."

"That's CIA speak for polygraph test," Mary explained.

"Anyway," the doctor continued unperturbed, "we found that he was lying about his alcohol problems, and the Agency fired him."

"The problem was," Marry added. "He already knew most of our undercover people in Russia, and gave the Soviets their names. He blew their covers before we could stop him, and he ended up living in Moscow in a flat provided by the KGB."

"So now that we have put you at ease," Mary chuckled. "Let's get on with it." She began with the standard identifying questions. Name, address, married or single, where were you born, parents name, etc.

The doctor adjusted his dials and peered intently at the multiple pens moving in unison, then closely studied the patterns of the thin lines being traced on the paper that was pouring out of his beloved equipment.

Soon Mary was at the heart of her inquiry. "Do you know Karen Kincaid?"

"Of course," Charlie answered.

122

"Answer yes or no" the doctor admonished.

"Did you ever have sex with her?" Mary started again.

That didn't take long Charlie thought. "Never--I mean no."

"Do you know any of her friends?

"No-only Marvin that is."

"Did she ever give you money to deliver?"

"Yes"

"Besides Peru?"

So that's it thought Charlie, I often wondered what that was all about.

"No, only in Peru."

"Did she give you an assignment in China when you were there?"

'Yes."

"Was it to photograph manufacturing facilities?"

"Yes." Jesus he thought they know everything.

"Anything else?" Mary coughed the dry hack of a heavy smoker.

"Yes."

"Well what was it Charlie?"

"I can't answer that yes or no," he replied.

"God damn it Charlie, what was it?" she barked exasperated.

"She wanted the name of someone to contact over there who might be able to provide information on the technological capability of the Chinese. Look Mary," he added "I want to get this over with as much, or probably more than you do. Let me know what you want to know and let's get it over."

"Did you give her any names?"

"Yes."

"What was the name you gave her?"

"Zhang Zheng, but I don't think she ever contacted him."

"How do you know that?"

"I guess I don't know it," Charlie replied. "She never seemed interested."

Mary Kool folded her file and looked at Doctor Fienstein, pouring over his chart. He returned her stare, raising his eyebrows almost imperceptibly. Ripping off a long sheet from his "truth detector" he turned off a switch and handled the results to Mary. "Turn off the lights and lock the door when you leave," he directed. Another sliding door in the back of the room glided open and the doctor disappeared.

As he and Mary walked through the computer room, the same people sat staring into their dimly lighted screens unconcerned with the passing pair.

"Well did I pass?"

"What do you think?" was the curt reply.

"Of course," he answered.

"Of course you did," Mary responded with a faint smile. "If you hadn't passed you would have been categorized as *deemed deceptive*, and possibly aiding and abetting a foreign government--and then handled accordingly," she finished ominously.

Charlie believed her. Trying to change the subject to something more pleasant he asked, "Does Emmett always have that music playing?"

"That's why his cryptoname is Maestro" was the reply, as the door to his office opened once again.

Emmett was in his recliner, bathed in a sickly yellow light. "Rimsky-Korsakoff," he offered. "The Russians always had wonderful poets and composers, but terrible leadership. Ah listen to those violins."

Charlie didn't realize it at the time but, he was sitting across from the type of man who represented the very soul of what the Agency was originally intended to become and who, over the years, had turned out to be the glue that held the disparate Directorates together. The now aging warrior had learned the difficult lesson of placating the demands of a burgeoning government bureaucracy by becoming a very civil Civil Servant, while quietly playing his own "great game" by his individual rules. Now the Maestro was confronted with defections within his own shop and he was determined to correct the situation before he left.

As Charlie watched nervously Emmett and Mary huddled together reviewing the printout from the polygraph. When they finished their analysis, Mary rose to leave. As the door slid open she turned "ta-ta," she called waving absently to the two men.

"Will the curtain now rise on all of this mystery?" Charlie asked, turning his swivel chair toward Emmett.

"Yes it will, but the picture is not going to be pretty," Emmett told him. "Actually I have been trying to decide where to begin. I guess it began with your little Peruvian project that went sideways.

"We were dissatisfied with the way the Peruvian Government was fighting the Sendero Luminosa. We thought that there were many people within their administration that were overly sympathetic to the radicals. We were contacted one day by a very right-wing group down there that was as anxious to get rid of the radicals as we were. The only problem was they didn't have the resources to put up a good fight.

"Well, we wanted to help them, but we didn't want it to get around that the CIA was working with them. If that became common knowledge we would infuriate the Peruvian Government, who was trying to get more money out of us as well. You can see our little dilemma I am sure."

"Karen and Marvin had been working with you, and spoke very highly of you I might add. Karen had the idea that we could get money to the underground group through you. You were a *clean face,* as we say in the trade, and had no apparent connection to us.

"So when she heard you were down there, Karen set up this scheme of getting money for you to pass on to the *Vaqueros.* They like to think of themselves as cowboys. They think they are like John Wayne."

"She got the necessary approval and wrote out an expense appropriation for $200,000 in large bills. We are not without our own bureaucracy, you understand. Then, she arranged to fly down the money for you to pass on to them. You followed your instructions to the letter, and we all sat back and congratulated ourselves on another brilliant scheme. That is until those Peruvian cowboys blew up the goddamned embassy," Emmett exclaimed, waving his arms in mock amazement.

"That was when we began walking back the cat to see where everything went awry. Lo and behold, it began to lead directly to dear Karen. When we wanted to bring her in for a flutter we found she had disappeared. I must tell you, I was shocked."

"There were a lot of red faces here at the Agency, I can assure you. There is only one thing the powers to be hate more than a rogue agent, and that is a rogue agent running off with large amounts of money. We had to take great pains to hide it somewhere in the budget where the Oversight Committee couldn't find our blunder. You have no idea how many dubious debits we had to credit to bury that one," he added somewhat sheepishly.

"I think we finally hid the lost money in our computer procurement budget. No one understands those entries anyway," he added as an afterthought."

Emmett was searching in one of his desk drawers as he talked. Finally he found what he was looking for, and removed a chipped meerschaum pipe. Soon an aromatic cloud of smoke engulfed the old man's head.

"Hope you don't mind," he apologized to Charlie as he continued. "It was also embarrassing to have to turn to our "friends" at the FBI and admit that one of our own was missing, but they have more authority to act here in the United States than we do.

"They eventually found sweet Karen living in Santa Fe, New Mexico along with all the artsy crafty people out there," Emmett related with obvious disdain.

"We told the FBI to just put her under surveillance. We wanted to see who had been helping her. They didn't think that was much of a job. They had bigger things to deal with, so they put some fuzzy-faced youngster in charge of tailing her.

"He got tired of doing that, and decided to make a name for himself so he arrested her in her room at the Santa Fe Hilton. He cuffed her, then called his boss who immediately called us. By the time we got to the hotel we found the young man stripped to his skivvies, all tied up lying on the bed. Needless to say, our dear old Karen had disappeared, and we haven't heard anything about her since.

"One thing though," he added as an afterthought, "you have to admit, we had taught her well. She really put one over on those bright boys at the FBI. And then they want us to share our information with them," Emmett concluded disgustedly.

"Where was Marvin in all this?" Charlie wanted to know.

"Ah yes, poor old Marvin the Machinist. He always figured that he would have my job when I retired. Particularly after all the training we gave him in missile technology. That combined with his experience running clandestine operations gave him-he thought-a clear path to sitting in my chair.

"Unfortunately, it didn't happen that way. After the Vaqueros blew up the embassy in Lima the people here didn't know what to do with the guy we had there. Stacy Loosetree-I believe that you met him.

"Well, when I retired they put Stacy in charge of the department. Poor old Marvin was furious. Who could blame him? He said he wasn't going to work for an imbecile, so he turned in his papers and retired. That's the last we heard of him. There wasn't even a retirement party," Emmett added obviously upset.

"He should have been more patient. It wasn't too long before the Director took Stacy with him to a briefing at the White House. The President was there, lots of National Security Staff members, and the Vice President. Well, during the meeting our friend Stacy fell asleep and that was the end of him.

"I was already gone by then, but the Director tried to find the Machinist and offer him this job. We couldn't locate him. He had just disappeared. We were sending his pension checks to a Swiss bank account.

"That is what prompted them to bring me back. The Agency had all of these defections. They didn't know who might go next, and they were sure of me. And Mary of course. So here we are."

"Good Lord," Charley blurted, unable to think of what else to say.

Emmett turned to shut off his music. "I will walk you out Charlie. We appreciate your coming to see us. I have

128

arranged for one of our planes to take you home so you will get there in time for your daughter's graduation."

As the door to the office silently slid open, Charlie wondered how the Maestro knew about the graduation. Emmett turned to shut off the lights. "The door locks automatically," he told Charlie as they walked down the narrow hallway.

Before the two men reached the elevator Charlie stopped abruptly, "what about China?" Why was Mary asking me about China? Has anything happened to Zhang Zheng? Karen assured me that nothing would happen to him."

"Oh yes, I forgot about that, Emmett added brushing his wrinkled hand across his forehead in a gesture of feigned forgetfulness. "We had managed to build up a very small cadre of Chinese nationals that were willing to cooperate with us. Zhang was one of those. After Karen left, our meager network was rolled up. We heard that Zhang was sent to a work camp in Mongolia, along with the rest of them," he concluded sadly.

"That bitch," Charlie exclaimed vehemently. "It was his worst nightmare, and she promised that nothing would happen."

"We lost the whole dammed network Charlie. I am terribly sorry."

"Can you get him out? After all, it was the Agency's fault he's rotting away in prison, regardless of who turned him over."

"Perhaps," Emmett mused. "I really hadn't thought about that. It has been common practice between us and the Sovs to exchange agents when they were caught spying, but the protocol never extended to locals that didn't have some form of immunity. He wasn't actually one of us you know--but we do have one of theirs that we picked up at Fermi lab. He was a crafty bugger. The Chinese may not be familiar with the rules of the game, let me see what I can do."

Outside, the Buick wagon was waiting to take Charlie to the airport. Before getting in he turned to say good-by. "One other thing Emmett, what about the nun down in Lima? Was she part of the Vaqueros?"

"I am sure my friend Pinstripes, you know it takes more than just a habit to make a nun." Grinning at his cryptic witticism, the old man gingerly settled into the black limousine parked behind the idling wagon. Emmett raised his cane in a jaunty salute, as the big car pulled away from the curb.

Nine:
Retirement

Rumors flew through the hallways of Apex with the speed of forest fires driven by an ill wind, leaving in their wake only the acrid odor of failure. The company's finances continued their precipitous decline, and their principal banks concluded they would no longer provide additional financing. The exodus of employees had begun, and management personnel frequently could be seen huddled together in the Boardroom, whispering for fear that others would learn how desperate the company's circumstances had become.

Groups of prospective investors periodically toured the building furtively glancing into individual offices, while the remaining employees combed the classified ads hoping to locate other jobs before losing the ones they already had.

For Charlie, the suspense ended a month after his return from Israel when Norman Baines summoned him to his office to tell him, with poorly disguised pleasure, that his services were no longer needed at Apex. Norman's plan was to fold the international operation into domestic marketing to reduce operating expenses. This also had the advantage for Norman of removing an irritation to his domestic distributors at a time when expenses had become more critical than profits.

Charlie felt betrayed by his own company. The members of the Board who had previously relished the profits his organization provided were now too fearful for their own position to object to anything that was occurring within the corporation. After Paul Murphy's death there was no one remaining on the Board to aggressively plead his case.

Charlie was also saddened that the reorganization was a betrayal by his company of the overseas customers who had invested in their businesses in the belief they would continue to be supported by Apex. That likelihood was now seriously in doubt.

After notifying his staff, Charlie called each of his foreign customers to inform them of the new organization, and to wish them good fortune with their business. Implicit in his conversation was the advice to find a new source of supply for their technology and parts. He felt an obligation to the people who had worked and risked their future on the continued support of the Apex Corporation, even if the company did not.

The call to Aaron Greenfield in Tel Aviv was especially difficult since his new company was just getting started. Aaron understood that it was not Charlie's doing, and they discussed how the Israeli company might be able to acquire a license from one of the European set manufacturers who were not afraid of the Arab League boycott.

Charlie's own position was less critical. He was nearing the age when people typically thought about retirement. Beth and he had paid off the house, and the three children had completed their education. The boys were working at their careers, and their daughter who had recently graduated was now trying to decide the future course her life should take.

Charlie finished clearing out his desk, and sadly took a last lingering view of the Chicago skyline, before quickly leaving the building.

Retirement is difficult at best. The rapid transition from intense work to extreme leisure can be traumatic. Perhaps the most dramatic changes in a person's life come through graduation from college, marriage, first-time parenthood, and eventually retirement. Charlie had navigated successfully through the other periods of adjustment, and he was confident he could do the same with this.

However, the transition was not easy. He was used to new challenges and new places-even sometimes danger. Life was now more placid and pedantic, and the adjustment was proving difficult. He first tried losing himself in golf, but that grew tiresome. He also tried gardening, but soon found that instead of a green thumb the one given him was black. Everything he planted soon died, and the only things that grew in his garden were weeds.

In desperation Charlie resorted to the thing that gave him the most satisfaction when he was working, which was traveling. One of the few places in the world he had not seen was Burma, so he busied himself with the required arrangements for him and Beth to enter the remote country.

Following WWII, Burma was taken over by a Communist Government and renamed Myanmar. Before, the former British Colony was one of the richest nations in Asia. Since the military took control, government spending was diverted from the country's schools, health care, and infrastructure to merely sustaining the totalitarian government. As a result Burma had become a basket case, and in spite of a wealth of natural resources was turned into one of Asia's poorest nations. To hide its failures the junta discouraged tourism, and it took several weeks before visas could be obtained and travel arrangements completed.

Because of government regulations, Burma remains one of the least traveled and most isolated countries in the world. It is also one of the most picturesque. Charlie and Beth visited the mammoth Shwedagon Pagoda in Rangoon, the ancient temples in Pagan, and traveled by rail from Mandalay back to Rangoon. The antiquated train made frequent stops along the way. Each station looked remarkably like a photograph torn from the pages of an ancient National Geographic.

The trip was a great experience, but the poverty and suppression of the people only enforced Charlie's negative opinion of Communist governments.

On their return trip to Chicago, the exhausted travelers were alarmed by the abrupt decent of their plane. Beth turned ashen, and tightly clutched Charlie's arm for reassurance. The pilot's strained voice on the intercom did little to comfort the passengers when he announced that because of an attack on New York and Washington all planes in the air over the United States were ordered to land immediately.

Once on the ground, Charlie and Beth joined the others in the airport lounge transfixed by the TV monitors. The crowd watched intently while the announcers attempted to describe the tremendous destruction and the rapidly increasing number of deaths at the World Trade Center and Pentagon. Soon the crowd's shock turned to anger at the terrorists, and the way that they planned and implemented their attack while living in the United States.

The earlier bombing of the American Embassies in Kenya and Tanzania had been terrible. So was the deadly attack on the USS Cole, and the first bombing at the World Trade Center. The 9/11 attack was much worse because it had taken so many more lives.

When the couple finally got home, Charlie continued watching the news accounts of the devastation on the East Coast, and the backgrounds of the terrorists repelled him.

Soon afterwards, the Washington finger pointing began directed at the CIA and the FBI and their inability to prevent the attack. The calls for resignations and reorganization intensified, and one day Charlie decided to call the special number Emmett Valentine had once given him.

Several days after placing the call, the phone rang while Charlie prepared for bed. Fumbling for the receiver, he heard a familiar voice, "Hello there Pinstripes, how are you faring during these troubled times?"

"Hanging in there Maestro, but more importantly how are you doing?"

"Appreciate your solicitude my dear Charlie. It has truly been an *annus horibilis* for the Company, but I have learned a few lessons over the years. The Agency has been through hard times before, and we always survive because the country needs us. It does appear, however, that we royally diddled the old dog this time.

"Of course, our politicians first established legislative walls so we couldn't transfer information to the FBI, and now they are criticizing us for not doing what we were originally prohibited from doing. There is plenty of blame to go around, however, and some of our main mandarins should be put out to pasture."

"How did it happen?" Charlie asked. "Why didn't the CIA have a better idea what was going on with Al Qaeda and Bin Laden?"

"I have asked myself the same question a hundred times since 9/11," Emmett replied remorsefully. "I just don't know. Perhaps we were still concentrating on the Russians and ignored the rest of the world. It was more comfortable that way you see.

"There was an odd kind of symmetry that developed during the Cold War. Each side knew the other's roles, and we both played them consistently. We were adversaries so long we learned to look at each other's operations through the same prism. It just became easier to deal with the devil you know than the one you don't know.

"Of course the KGB gave us some reason to keep at them. They are still up to some of their old tricks, only in a more limited way. You know, of course, that one of the former leaders of the KGB is now president of their God-forsaken country. You think the bugger has given up doing what got him to where he is? That's pretty unlikely, don't you think?"

Charlie glanced at his watch. Both hands were straight up. He was surprised to be talking to the Maestro so late at night. Did the old man always work this late he wondered?

"Also Charlie," Emmett continued his lament as the lyrical sounds of Chopin's Polonaise drifted over the secure line, "old Bin Laden is such a scruffy fellow some of our elite Ivy Leaguers never imagined he could pose a major threat. It's funny though in a distorted way. The Agency needs an enemy to prosper, and we had a new barbarian at our gate all along and never realized it. After 9/11 though the ambiguity of the threat has certainly crystallized, and we are going balls-out after him now.

"As you might expect, it's a major turf battle here in Washington now. There are those in Congress that have always wanted to do away with us. NSA and the Defense Intelligence Agency would like to fold us in under their umbrella. The FBI would be after us too if they weren't already up to their collective necks in hot water. It's always the same in dear old Foggy Bottom."

While they talked, Charlie's mind drifted back to the first time that the two had met on that warm fall day in Washington. Emmett seemed far more vigorous then.

Hell, we both did Charlie thought.

Now, not only did the Maestro sound older, but he also seemed less confident and more depressed.

"By the way, old boy how are you doing?" Emmett asked changing the subject. "I heard your valuable services at Apex were rudely done away with. You ought to know by now that one should never expect loyalty from bureaucratic institutions," he added sadly.

"It's a difficult lesson to learn, Emmett," Charlie replied "but I know it now. I'm OK. Retirement is a hard adjustment to make, particularly when it's forced on you, but I'll get along. I always have."

"Was it any satisfaction to you that after you left the company went into bankruptcy? I hear it has now been acquired by a Japanese company."

"Yes they have. It is kind of ironic. I was glad to see that Norman Baines was canned as soon as they took control, but it also means that an awful lot of good people lost their jobs as well. I feel very badly about that."

"I wish I could bring you in here," Emmett mused. You always knew what you were doing and concentrated on getting the job done. We need more like you, but we can't hire anyone right now."

"That's OK Emmett. I wouldn't come even if you asked. I've had enough of your business. I just wanted to let you know I still respect what you are doing.

"Noted gratefully, Charlie."

"Before you hang-up Emmett, have you heard anything about Karen?" Charlie asked hastily.

"Not a blessed thing old boy. She just seemed to dissolve into thin air. We tried to walk back the cat on her, but it led us to a brick wall. We may have taught her too well. She actually graduated first in her training class at The Farm, you know.

"The way things are going now we may never find her. All of our concentration is on al Qaeda, and we can't go chasing after one rogue agent--as much as we would like to.

"One other item of bad news Charlie, I have been reluctant to tell you, but your friend Zhang Zheng is dead. We tried to exchange one of theirs for him. You remember my telling you about that fellow we caught poking around at Fermi lab? We planned on using our Taiwanese "cousins" to make the exchange in Manchuria. When it was scheduled to take place they sent us the poor boy back in a pine box.

Unfortunately, their fellow we were exchanging got our taste of "the People's Justice. You see he was "accidentally" shot during the process so we ended even. Pity, but it's a dirty business.

"We were able to get Zhang's wife and child out of the country and settled them in Vancouver. It was the least we could do."

The melody on the other end of the line ended, and there was a faint click. Charlie sadly hung up the receiver. What a terrible way for his friend to die. He had depended on the Americans he admired, and they had betrayed him.

Afterwards, he couldn't help wondering if he had also been party to the betrayal. He appreciated what Emmett had tried to do but, after all, if he hadn't given Zhang's name to Karen in the first place none of this would have ever happened.

That night, during a fitful sleep, Charlie dreamed of a pine box floating down an ice-choked river, while he stood helplessly alone on a snow-covered bank.

Ten:
NGO Project

A week after the telephone call from Emmett, Charlie received an offer from the Vienna-based Global Bank Corporation for work on a privatization project in Ukraine. The Non Governmental Organization was attempting to help former Soviet countries transform their companies from defense production to commercial products that would be more salable.

Before leaving with Beth for Burma, Charlie had sent his resume to a number of non-profit organizations that might be hiring consultants for overseas assignments. GBC was the only one to answer with a tangible offer.

The European bank was one of several organizations funded by a consortium of Western countries, following the collapse of the Soviet Union. Their collective objective was to help the Newly Independent States make their transition to a more democratic government.

Although he had traveled to many of the former Soviet countries, Charlie had only the barest knowledge of the current situation in Ukraine. He decided that he could get a better understanding of conditions there by renewing the contacts he had formed, over the years, in the Ukrainian Village section of Chicago. The small ethnic community was located on the western edge of the city, providing an island of civility surrounded by a troubled urban area.

Rain had begun to fall as Charlie exited the Eisenhower Expressway on Western, and hung a hard right to Chicago Avenue. He soon passed the Ukrainian Institute of Modern Art, and found an empty parking space in front of the multi-storied Ukrainian Cultural Center.

He reluctantly got out of his warm car as the now drenching rain pounded the Village's vacant sidewalks. The small community had provided a refuge to families seeking better opportunities and a safe-haven from Soviet oppression. The area was gradually becoming "gentrified" as young couples moved out of the central city for less expensive housing; but neither the old nor the new Village residents could be seen on the streets on such a disagreeable day.

Tugging at the turned-up collar of his trench coat, Charlie hurried past the onion-domed Ukrainian Catholic Church, and ducked gratefully into a dimly lit doorway marked, in both Cyrillic and English lettering, the *Ukrainian Village Voice*

The small paper was owned and operated by Natalia Barnych who had taken over the struggling business when her husband died suddenly. Charlie and she had met when they served together on several panels sponsored by the Commerce Department.

At one time, Natalia might have been considered attractive, but the years of hard work had left her furrowed and prematurely gray. A Marlboro cigarette dangled from the corner of her mouth as if it were permanently attached, intentionally giving the impression of a hard-bitten businesswoman. Charlie knew better from past experience. He had always found her intelligent, and quick to provide practical solutions to complex problems.

Charlie relaxed in a dilapidated swivel chair, while Natalie paced nervously about the small office. Over cups of strong Coffee, served on a littered desk, the two discussed their lives since their last meeting. When Natalia learned her friend was going to travel to Kiev she was quick to explain what she believed was going on in her family's former homeland.

140

"Old habits die hard," she told Charlie while lighting still another cigarette. The odor of fresh tobacco smoke mingled unpleasantly with the stale smell of yesterday's butts that were overflowing the ashtray beside her untouched cup.

"When Ukraine gained its independence from the Soviets, the country had no experience in self-government. It had been independent only once before in history. That was after World War I, and then for about only ten minutes. Now that they are on their own they don't have the foggiest idea how to proceed."

A dry hacking cough caused Natalie to pause before she could continue. "Sorry Charlie, I must be catching a cold," she explained lamely.

"Where was I?" she asked brushing an ink-stained palm across her forehead. "Oh yeah, an even bigger problem is that the people who are running the country now were all part of the Communist Party when Ukraine was under Russian control. These bozos were all either bureaucratic *apparatchiks* or part of the elite *nomenklatura* that ran the government agencies for the Russians. Even if they had the brains to change, they wouldn't have the desire. Unfortunately, they have neither. They're just the same old party functionaries wearing new capitalistic suits," she sneered.

"There is some hope the situation may soon change," she told Charlie, lighting another cigarette. "Elections are coming, and one of the candidates--a guy by the name of Viktor Yushchenko claims he will reform the government if he gets elected.

"Maybe he will, and maybe he won't. But it should be easy to be a hell of a lot better than what they have now," she added exhaling a massive cloud of cigarette smoke.

Charlie waved his hand in front of his face in a futile attempt at dispersing the foul smelling fumes.

"His wife grew up here in Chicago," Natalie continued. "She's the daughter of Ukrainian parents. Her name is Kateryna. The Orthodox Church brought her family here years ago. She got her bachelor's degree from Georgetown and an MBA in International Finance from the University of Chicago. I met her several times and she is damned smart, as well as quite good looking.

"God how I hate women like that," Natalie laughed half-heartedly.

"If she and her husband are able to beat Kuchma's cronies they may be able to change things. It's going to be tough. The other fellow is backed by Russian money. Most people think the KGB is also helping him," she added her dark eyes flashing in unconcealed anger.

As Charlie put on his trench coat to leave, Natalie wrote out a short note of introduction to a friend of hers who operated an independent newspaper in Kiev. "Check in with him when you get there. He knows where all the bodies are buried," she said with a wink.

"Watch your back," she added with a wry grin as he went out the door. "They still think all Americans are spies."

The rain had turned to drizzle as Charlie headed his car out of the Village and back on the freeway. Late afternoon traffic was beginning to build, and he had trouble concentrating on the still slippery road. The last thing he needed now was to travel to a place where he had to watch his back. He had enough of that in his previous life.

Returning home, he finished packing while Beth slept. He had an early morning flight, and he tried to make sure that he had everything he might need for a long assignment.

He carefully folded his gray pinstripe suit, and added three shirts-two white and one blue-before selecting three contrasting Rep ties. Reaching into his underwear drawer, he uncovered a forgotten 32 caliber Smith & Wesson revolver he used to pack after his experience in Peru.

He studied the gun for several seconds then wrapped it carefully in an old T shirt before putting it carefully back where he had found it. That was a different time, in another place, during a different life he finally decided, quickly zipping-up his bag. Besides, after 9/11 the airlines had become much fussier about what people carried in their luggage.

There was time to relax before going to bed he decided, and went to his book-lined den for a well-earned martini.

Charlie approached the preparation of a martini with all the precision of a German chemist. He poured a little dry vermouth in the shaker first to better mix with the soon to be added gin. Three ice-cubes were dropped into the vermouth before searching his liquor cabinet for the remaining bottle of Bombay Sapphire Gin. Might as well use the good stuff he thought. It could be a long time between drinks.

The ice and vermouth were liberally bathed with a generous amount of gin. The resulting mixture was stirred slowly to provide a smoother consistency than shaking, while not diluting the final results with melting ice. Two oversized pimento olives were carefully placed in a crystal cocktail glass he had brought from Prague. The now perfect martini was painstakingly poured over the waiting olives to better combine the contrasting tastes. The liquid rose to within a mere millimeter of the rim of the glass.

Winking at the stern-faced British Monarch on the Bombay label he carefully returned "Her Majesty" to a favored position in his liquor cabinet. Long live the Queen he mumbled to himself while turning on his television set to the late-night news.

Taking his customary seat in an old leather recliner he recalled what Natalia had told him earlier that day. Pensively sipping his drink, he decided it didn't sound at all encouraging, and was glad that Beth had decided not to accompany him on this trip.

The anticipation of a long journey to an unfamiliar country always put Charlie in a reflective mood. That night his mind drifted back to other trips, in other times, to other places. He wondered how his friends around the world were doing, and if they had found other companies to provide them with support after Apex deserted them.

The flickering screen of his television set focused on an anchor describing the fall of Kabul, and the rapid defeat of the Taliban forces in Afghanistan. The Safari-jacketed newsman vividly described the death of the first American killed in the war identified as Mike Spann, a former Marine working as a CIA Special Ops Officer.

The scene suddenly switched to a new location and the description of the surprising capture of an American by the name of John Walker Lindh. The young man from California had been found alongside Taliban fighters who were battling US troops for control of an obscure Afghan prison in the same engagement that took the life of the American agent.

What a world we live in he thought, shaking his head in disbelief at the news of an American allied with the enemy. He turned off the set in disgust.

On the way to the bedroom he glanced at himself in the hallway mirror, and was shocked to see a person he barely knew. Over the last few years his hair had become thinner while his waist grew thicker. The small beard that he had grown on the trip to Burma now blended seamlessly with the increasing gray that was sparingly sprinkled through his still wavy hair. What had become of that naïve young fellow he wondered as he turned off the remaining lights and went to bed.

The Austrian Air 747 bounced to a hard landing in Vienna. It had been a bumpy trip over the Atlantic, and Charlie was glad to be on the ground. He quickly joined the other deplaning passengers squeezing together on an airport bus headed toward the terminal. Clearing customs went quickly and the pleasant young woman behind the counter barely glanced at his offered passport.

He quickly retrieved his bag, and was met outside by a car and driver sent by the Global Bank Corp to take him to their offices

The former center of the Hapsburg Empire was veiled in a low-hanging morning fog as the taxi sped through the busy city streets. The Bank's lobby was lined with Italian marble, and Charlie was directed by a stylishly dressed receptionist to the fifth floor office of Helmut Mueller. The highly polished brass plate on his desk identified him as the Bank's Assistant Director of Foreign Affairs.

"Ah Herr Connelly, how good of you to come," the avuncular middle aged man proclaimed with old-world charm, while offering a beefy hand to his visitor. His office was spacious with large windows framing the ancient spires of St. Stephen's Cathedral.

The German Army had preserved much of the City as they made their relatively effortless occupation during WWII. Any damage that had been done was the result of allied bombing and was rapidly repaired following the war. As a result, Vienna's many churches and historical buildings looked much as they had throughout the centuries.

"Let us go to lunch, Mr. Connelly," the Assistant Director suggested with obvious anticipation. "It is a little early I know, but I always thought that it is better to talk of serious subjects over a light meal." Without waiting for an answer he threw a camel colored coat over his shoulders and headed for the door with Charlie trailing obediently behind.

"My car," he ordered his secretary as he passed without a glance in her direction. A black Mercedes was waiting at the building's door by the time the two exited the elevator.

"Drei Husaren," he brusquely ordered the driver. "It is one of my favorites," he told Charlie as the driver deftly navigated the narrow cobblestone streets.

"You would call it the Three Hussars I believe," he informed Charlie while pointing out the Vienna State Opera House as the car turned onto Weiburggasse Avenue. "Vienna has long been one of the cultural crossroads of Europe. That is why it was chosen for the location of the Global Bank Corp. It has also been the center for political intrigue. A fact that has not gone unnoticed by our Board of Directors."

Entering the restaurant it was obvious that Herr Mueller was a frequent customer, and the two were immediately seated by a large window. *"Wiener schnitzel* for our guest" was the order as the waiter offered the menus, "and for me as well," Herr Mueller quickly added.

Between large bites of the thinly sliced breaded veal Herr Mueller described the problems the former Soviet countries were having after leaving the Soviet sphere. Some of the countries like Poland, Hungary, and the Czech Republic were doing very well while others like Belarus preferred to retain their ideological ties to Moscow.

Ukraine was proving pivotal and could tip either way with the eastern part of the country partial to Russia and the western part eager to become independent and align itself with the West.

"The country is about the size of your state of Texas," Herr Mueller explained. "It has the second largest army in

Europe, and the third largest arsenal of nuclear missiles in the world. That is why it is critical to Europe and the United States for Ukraine to remain independent and not revert to Russian control."

Charlie washed down his veal with a pilsner of Austrian beer that, once they were seated, had immediately been brought to their table.

It was obvious that Herr Mueller was not expecting much conversation from his companion, as he continued to describe the problems in Ukraine. That was fine with Charlie, who was still groggy from his overnight flight.

"We know that you are experienced working in difficult countries," Herr Mueller continued, "and Ukraine is a difficult country. Many people running the government were closely associated with the Soviets and would probably like to stay that way. They are trying to maintain control of their industry for their oligarchs, while at the same time attracting foreign investors. Their economic schizophrenia is not working very well for obvious reasons.

"The Bank cannot get directly involved in a political situation. NGO's have to be very careful. President Putin is already putting restrictions on their operation in Russia, and he would like to get rid of them in Ukraine. That is why you must be very careful while you are working there. I think you Americans call it keeping a low profile.

"A very low profile indeed," he added as the waiter cleared away the dishes.

"Coffee, along with two small *Konditorein Sachertortes* when you return my good man," he smiled at the hovering waiter. The man quickly returned carrying two gigantic servings of a chocolate orange cake, liberally covered with chocolate icing.

"A gastronomical masterpiece," he chortled. "Enjoy, Mr. Connelly."

"You have to understand that we Europeans are critically concerned with what transpires in Ukraine, because we are geographically much closer to the country than you are. Many people worry about what they are doing at Chernobyl. When it exploded back in 1986, it was more than a week before anyone realized it, and all of Europe got some of the fall-out. So we have to face the possibility that it might happen again.

"You must recognize my dear Mr. Connelly that we Austrians are more than merely Mozart and marzipan. We want to help Ukraine, but we also don't want to jeopardize the Bank."

"I am sure you don't," Charlie responded.

"That's fine. Our man in Kiev will give you the details of precisely what we want you to do after you get there but, let me emphasize that the Bank will be best served with a low profile.

Herr Mueller dropped Charlie off at the Hotel Imperial on the way back to his office.

"Good luck Mr. Connelly," he shouted through the open car window as his Mercedes sped away from the curb.

GBC was certainly not cheap. He had been told that the hotel had been built in the 1860's as a palace for the Duke of Wurttemberg. During Nazi occupation it served as the German Foreign Ministry. After the Germans surrendered, while the allies jointly controlled the city, the old hotel became Russian headquarters. It was later restored to become one of Europe's premier establishments.

He could never have gotten away with such an expensive room on his expense account while working for Apex he thought, looking at the ornate *Musikverein* concert hall framed majestically in his window.

Back in his office, Herr Mueller quickly placed a call to the United States. "I have just finished a light lunch with your Mr. Connelly," he told the listener on the other end of the overseas line. "As you suggested, I believe he will do a very good job for us. He doesn't talk a lot though does he?" Mueller asked speaking softly into his ornate receiver.

"By the way, is that *The Magic Flute* I hear playing in the background?" he inquired, while using a pudgy finger to reposition his thick glasses on his nose. "That has always been on of our favorites here in Vienna."

Eleven:
Assignment in Kiev

The hotel's breakfast room was beginning to fill with local business people and foreign travelers. The Imperial's chef had attempted to cater to his guest's international tastes by providing a breakfast buffet that included pancakes, eggs, and an assortment of cold cereals for the Americans; bangers and mash for the Brits; cheeses, cold meats and croissants for the Europeans; and a broad array of rice dishes designed to cater to Middle Eastern tastes. Charlie ate sparingly, still full from lunch the day before.

The taxi ride to Schwechat airport went quickly. Airport security had been tightened since 9/11, but none of the passengers complained as they moved briskly through customs to the lilting melody of a Strauss Waltz playing softly over the loudspeaker.

Once on board the Austrian Air flight to Kiev, the attendants moved quickly through the 737's narrow aisles serving strong coffee and sweet strudel to the passengers. It was obvious that only a few people were interested in traveling to Ukraine that day. Or probably any other day Charlie thought. Since 9/11, people were taking a more cautious approach to their lives, and airline travel had declined as a result.

Finishing his coffee, Charlie glanced around the cabin. It had recently become a preoccupation among frequent flyers to try and figure out if any of their fellow passengers were poised to seize control of the plane. He eventually decided that none of the people in the cabin presented an imminent danger. A few seemed to be legitimate business people, but most appeared to be associated with some form of a governmental organization.

Tiring of the game, he wondered which professional category he fit into now he was no longer associated with a corporation. Was an NGO a business, or part of a government? After he left Apex, Charlie had tried to get a consulting assignment that would allow him to continue using the skills he had developed over the years to keep his hand in the game a little while longer. It seemed to him that with his business experience he could be helpful to countries that were trying to peek out from behind their former Soviet seclusion.

He fastened his seat belt in preparation for landing, and decided that wanting to be helpful was in reality only a small part of his personal equation. If the truth were known, the basic reason he was here was that over the last few months he had developed a profound and abiding aversion to boredom, and this project provided him with an escape from monotony.

The lightly loaded 737 bounced to a landing and taxied down the cracked tarmac as it headed toward the old terminal building. Looking out his small window, Charlie could identify the rusting hulks of two abandoned Russian Tupelo bombers converted by the Ukrainians to passenger carriers. His plane finally taxied to a jerking stop, jarring the passengers who had risen to retrieve their carry-on bags from the overhead bins. As the travelers exited the cabin, the smiling flight attendants gave each one a small box of Austrian chocolates, accompanied by a cheerful *Weidersehn*.

Kiev's Boryspil airport was old and rundown. It was apparently getting a much-needed renovation, and the idle construction workers were in the way of the passengers who were attempting to locate the incoming custom's desk.

"First time in Kiev is it?"

Charlie turned to look at the man standing behind him in line. "Yeah," he admitted, "does it show?"

"Not necessarily, but you don't look Ukrainian. Of Course, not many do in the airport. Just the guards," he snickered nodding in the direction of a group of young men in their broad pie-plate hats and poorly fitting cast-off Russian uniforms who were standing in a circle smoking. Their Kalashnikovs rested on the wall behind them, and the soldiers appeared indifferent to the deplaning passengers. "We could be a group of Taliban fighters here to attend an al Qaeda convention" he quipped, "and those sorry fellows would never know it."

The line continued to move sluggishly through the terminal toward customs, while Charlie looked more closely at the man behind him. He was lean and gangly, with thick horned rimmed glasses and wearing a well-worn Harris Tweed jacket that reeked of academia--and pipe smoke. "What brings you here?" Charlie asked, trying to pass the time while the deplaning passengers inched slowly forward.

"I teach physics at Cambridge, and the UN sends me here three times a year to check on the atmosphere. They want to make sure that the radiation from Chernobyl is continuing to dissipate before everyone in Kiev begins to glow in the dark. It was less than 30 years ago that the main reactor blew its bloody top. The explosion threw a hell of a lot more radioactivity into the atmosphere than Hiroshima ever did. We're still not sure what the long-term effect will be. We know it's causing thyroid cancer and other birth defects among children in Ukraine, and we're trying to figure out what else the lingering radiation might be doing.

"So I go traipsing up there in the "dead zone" as they so colorfully call it, and muck around a little. At the UN's expense mind you. It's by far the dodgiest place I have ever been to, and I never stay too long. When I'm finished, I go back to England and write a report. It's not much of a

152

vacation, but it is certainly fascinating. There are still old helicopters, fire trucks, and rescue vehicles that were once used in the cleanup operation that are lying there just like they were left. They look like rusty toys thrown around in a game of jacks.

"Kids play jacks in the US don't they?" the Britisher inquired.

"I guess they do," Charlie conceded, while the professor continued pleased to find someone who would listen to him.

"Yes, yes, I thought so. Some of the locals refer to the area as *the devil's playground*, but there is a certain beauty about it in a weird way. It's a great place to go if you want to get away from it all. A few people still live in the old ghost towns, but mostly wolves and wild boar populate the area.

"Your next," he added politely nudging Charlie forward.

He had been completely absorbed by what the professor was telling him, but he turned quickly to look at the scowling face of a woman customs official. She stared back with practiced bureaucratic disdain, as he slid his entry documents over the soiled counter and under the cloudy glass partition. Her hand shot out from the tattered sleeve of her gray uniform, and Charlie wondered if he would ever see his precious passport again.

It was now clear why the line moved so slowly. The dour faced official looked at each page of his passport, then stared at him intently to verify that he was the same man as the one in the faded photograph.

"I recently grew a beard," Charlie offered feebly. It makes me look a little different."

"Get a new picture before you come back again," she spat at him.

"Next," she shouted at the cowering professor.

Charlie quickly collected his bag from a stalled carousel, and headed toward the line of waiting cabs. "Dnipro Hotel" he ordered settling back in the worn seat while the old Lada automobile jerked away from the curb in a stifling fog of exhaust fumes. After getting on the Karkhiv highway, the driver lighted a foul smelling Russian cigarette as he headed toward the city as fast as the ancient Russian engine would permit.

The Bank had made a reservation for him at a former Russian Intourist hotel near their offices. It was a far cry from the Imperial in Vienna he decided, walking through the large poorly lighted lobby. His room was cramped, and looked like it could use a thorough cleaning. After dropping off his bag, he asked directions to the GBC offices from a sober faced desk clerk.

The address he was given when he was in Vienna was in an old tree-lined section of the city. It looked as if all the buildings on the block were built at the same time, from the same mold, and bore the unmistakable evidence of years of neglect. Their stone fronts were dingy and many had jagged cracks running diagonally through the mortar.

Charlie walked up the well-worn stone steps and entered a dark lobby. Following directions, he took a small elevator that wheezed and jerked its way to the fifth floor. The elevator door opened to a dimly lit office with a small wooden desk and a tall blond secretary.

"Charlie Connelly to see Paul Perriman," he announced softly, fearing he might startle the young woman who was deeply engrossed in her magazine. She looked up briefly, smiled wanly, and flipped a switch on small box on her desk. A dim light flashed above the door behind her, and she jerked her thumb in the general direction of the door. "Go on in," she told him curtly, returning to her reading.

154

Paul was an American who had worked for Citibank before retiring. The two recent retirees quickly exchanged work histories before discussing Charlie's assignment.

"The factory you're going to is located in a place called Ivano Frankivsk," Paul began. It used to be what they now refer to as a "closed city." The town was placed off limits by the Soviets because of the secret ICBM installations they had concealed in the Carpathian Mountains behind the town. There are also a number of highly sensitive factories inside the city that made hi-tech military equipment for the Russians.

"The plant you'll be working with is one of them. It's called Karpaty. They make advanced passive radar systems. Their technology, I have heard, can detect Stealth bombers over 500 miles away. The company did very well and made excellent equipment, but it had only one market and that was the Russian Army. It's like a lot of companies here in Ukraine. They only know how to make products for one customer, and that customer is broke. So what the hell are they supposed to do now?"

"I give up," Charlie admitted. "What?

"I don't know either," Paul replied, shrugging his shoulders.. "But we're supposed to find out and then help them do it. We want you to go down there and see what you can suggest, and teach them how to sell their products on an open market. What they do now is to make what the Ukrainian Government tells them to produce and then deliver it to wherever they are told. The bureaucracy wants to keep them in business to make equipment for them, but they are unable to pay for what they need.

"Will they listen to me?"

"Probably not, but we have to try. I have your train ticket for you. We would have put you on a plane, but the airline here can't afford to pay for fuel on a regular basis and right now they're literally out of gas and grounded."

Charlie didn't mind taking the train. It gave him a chance to see more of the country, and he had enough of taking third world airlines.

"Actually, you need to understand that Putin has the Ukies by the short hairs when it comes to energy. This country gets most of their fuel from Russia and they can be shut off any time he doesn't like what they are doing. It's economic blackmail but that has never stopped our old friend Vladimir before.

"Well anyway enough of that. Your train leaves tomorrow afternoon. When you're finished in Ivano Frankivsk you can come back here. By that time we'll have an apartment you can use while you write your report. Apartments are really scarce, but one of ours should be vacant by then. I also have the forms you'll need for your expense accounts, and the format we prefer you use for the final report."

Charlie took the outstretched papers and stuffed them into his old briefcase. As he rose to leave, Paul offered some final advice. "When you have worked for an NGO as long as I have you'll understand that your report is more important than results. As a matter of fact," he laughed "the report is the result." He waved a cheerful good by as Charlie left his office.

The blond secretary briefly looked up from her magazine. "See ya" she mumbled turning a page.

Charlie decided to stop in the dining room before returning to his hotel room. It was early but the restaurant was already filling up with men in business suits and attractive well-dressed women. Paul had told him that it was a popular place for the movers and shakers of Kiev, and it looked as if he was right.

Studying the menu, he heard the couple at the next table attempting to place their order. Each time they selected a dish, the waitress told them that it was not available. When she came to Charlie's table he decided to try the obvious. Smiling at the young waitress he tried "Chicken Kiev." She made a note in her pad and left for the kitchen.

A brimming bowel of *borsch*, accompanied by a platter of white and brown bread, appeared almost immediately. The beet-based soup was not high on his list of favorites. In fact, it wasn't on his list at all. He had tried borsch before in other Soviet countries, but had never developed a fondness for it.

The bread made up for whatever the borsch lacked. The French writer Balzac once wrote, after living in Ukraine for a number of years, he had counted 77 different ways of preparing bread — and they were all good.

Earlier that day, passing through the airport, he recalled seeing a group of brightly costumed young women waiting to meet an arriving delegation of visiting African dignitaries. They carried small loaves of bread and plates of salt. The taxi driver had told him this was the Ukrainian way of greeting important guests. The Africans, however, seemed more interested in ogling the fair skinned Ukrainian women than they were in what they were carrying.

When his meal arrived, the preparation of the chicken Kiev was different than he expected. The chicken was rolled in a butter and egg mixture then deep fried, and accompanied by small dumplings similar to ravioli filled with cooked cabbage. He was pleased with his order and decided to try and eat here again before he left the country.

The next morning he hailed a cab for the American Embassy. Staring out the window he saw people already idly congregating around corner kiosks or ambling leisurely from store window to store window. Also among the early morning crowd were a few old *babushkas'* wearing their typical long skirts, heavy knit sweaters, and brightly colored headscarves. In contrast to most of the people, these old women were busy setting-up crude sidewalk stands to sell an odd assortment of candy, cigarettes, and chewing gum to the people strolling by.

A tall iron fence separated the embassy from the street. Stationed behind the gate was a young Marine who carefully examined Charlie's passport before waving him through. The embassy was in an old multi-storied Russian-style box building. Inside, a Marine sergeant with three rows of "fruit salad" on the chest of his dress blue tunic stood behind a glass-enclosed desk centered under an official print of President George W. Bush. After showing his passport once again and signing the ledger, Charlie was told by the Marine to wait in the lobby until he could be escorted to the commercial office.

He had just finished paging through a glossy brochure describing the level of sugarcane production in Louisiana when he heard his name called. Looking up, he saw a young woman walking towards him wearing an abbreviated skirt and a tight sweater that strained every one of its polyester fibers.

"Eve St. Ives," she smiled good-naturedly, extending her hand. I'm Barry Durand's secretary. Please follow me."

"Gladly," Charlie blurted before feeling compelled to add lamely "I was afraid I'd have to wait a long time before the commercial officer could see me"

Ignoring his ringing phone, the marine sergeant grinned lecherously at the secretary and her blushing visitor passing his desk. As they walked briskly down a long, poorly lighted hallway the young woman's high-heeled black boots tap-tapped a sprightly cadence on the floor's highly buffed surface. The flickering florescent lights cast eerie shadows down the empty hallway. "Lousy Russian bulbs," she explained. Finally Eve stopped and opened an office door, standing aside to let her visitor squeeze past.

"Ain't she something," the commercial officer offered in greeting, while motioning Charlie to a chair.

"She certainly is," Charlie agreed. "Is she any good?"

"You mean as a secretary? Nah, she's dumb as a rock. Everyone at the Embassy calls her *Twin Peaks* for obvious reasons. You remember that old TV show? No one could understand it, but everyone watched it. That's our Eve. She's civil service. They assigned her here, and I just had to accept her."

"How terrible for you," Charlie laughed.

Barry was a small man with a high pitched voice, probably in his early 50's Charlie decided.

You're the first American I've met from Global Bank, what's your background?" Barry asked arranging the file folders he had been looking at into a more orderly pile on his desk.

Charlie described his work at Apex. It turned out that while he had been involved with the licensee in Maracaibo the commercial officer was working at the American Consulate in Caracas "So you were the guy that uncovered one of your partners skimming the company?" Durand observed. "We heard about that at the Consulate. Your partner came to us trying to sell his stamp collection in the United States. We thought he was crazy. You did right to bounce his ass out of there. All the Americans I knew were glad to see it, and thought it was a good object lesson for the Venezuelans they were working with."

The subject switched to Ukraine. Charlie described what he knew about his project, before asking the commercial officer for his opinion. "It's really a mess here," Durand responded bluntly. "When the Iron Curtain finally rusted and crumbled, the Soviet controlled countries understandably decided to leave their Russian masters and go it alone. The problem was their economies were based entirely on supplying military products to the Kremlin. The economy in Ukraine is like the rest of the former Soviet countries. It has all the characteristics of a giant matryoshka doll. You know what they are don't you?"

Charlie nodded.

"Well you know then how as you take out each doll they get smaller and smaller. Well in Ukraine when you get to the center there is nothing there but corruption, and you can't build a nation on that. Hey, you want some coffee?"

Charlie shook his head, "no-not particularly."

"Aw go ahead," Barry smiled. "It's not too bad, and it's worth it just to see Eve walk around in here. How do you like it?"

"OK, you convinced me. Just black."

Barry flipped a switch on his desk, "Ms. St Ives, do you think you could find a couple of black coffees lurking around your elaborate facilities."

He winked at Charlie, and continued describing the situation in Ukraine. "The problem is that it's important for the United States that Ukraine stays independent. The country has over 5,000 nuclear warheads, and most of the Russian fleet is still stranded in Odessa.

"If Ukraine goes the way of Belarus, and falls back into the Kremlin's orbit, it would re-establish Russia as the regional superpower. On the other hand, if Ukraine can make a success of being an independent democracy it would give the EU and NATO a prosperous and stable eastern neighbor instead of a bankrupt menace.

Both men were startled at the sound of the door kicked open as Eve entered with their coffee. As she was carefully placing the cups on the desk, Barry's pen clattered to the tile floor. Her back was toward Charlie, and as she bent-over to retrieve the pen her sweater crept up, partially revealing the wings of a brilliantly tattooed butterfly straining to escape the elastic constraints of her black panties.

As she turned to go out the door, Barry winked conspiratorially at Charlie

"You did that on purpose?"

"Yup," Barry smirked, "she falls for it every time. Well, where was I? Oh yeah, I was about to tell you about our *oligarchs*. President Kuchma's government's is one of the most corrupt in the world. Whenever he has made any attempt at privatizing some of the industries it has been through sweetheart deals with his friends. Then, these Ukrainian tycoons pay part of the money back to him and his cronies. Now, instead of the government controlling the industries, they're in the hands of a few billionaires. It's just like what's going on in Russia.

"But, we're afraid to get too involved at the embassy for fear of antagonizing the Russkies. So we keep trying to get the Ukrainians half pregnant, and you know how well that works."

The two men eventually finished their conversation. As Charlie was ready to leave, the commercial officer took him by the arm, "enjoyed talking to you. Drop by again, and if I can ever be of help please let me know."

Outside the office, Eve was standing at the filing cabinets. Hearing the door close, she turned to look at Charlie and nonchalantly pointed in the direction of the lobby. "Ciao, Mr. Connelly. Come back again."

Charlie glanced at his watch. There was still time to call on Natalia's newspaper friend before catching the train for Ivano Frankivsk. The marine sergeant signed him out. Outside the embassy he hailed a cab and gave the driver the note with the newspaper's address.

It was a sunny day and Charlie was enjoying the ride. They passed the golden domes of a cathedral with a wedding-cake baroque style bell tower. "St. Sophia," the driver explained. The old cab continued down the now crowded Stalinist style main boulevard. As they passed Kiev's Independence Square the driver pointed "Maydan Nezalezhnosti." Charlie looked in the direction the driver was pointing. In the center of a tree-lined park was a tall statue of Winged Victory. Underneath, a small group of people were marching in circles, carrying banners and bullhorns. A larger group watched from a safe distance.

"Demonstrators," the driver chuckled as he picked-up speed.

The taxi abruptly turned down a narrow brick paved side street and stopped in front of a drab building with a crumbling concrete facade. Inside, an old man wearing an ink-smudged apron stood between two large presses that were loudly spewing out continuous sheets of printed paper. Unnoticed, Charlie looked around the newspaper office until he spotted a closed office door. Tapping tentatively on the window he stepped inside a dimly lit room. A large man sat behind a small desk littered with papers.

"Natalia Barnych sent me," Charlie offered as an introduction.

The man behind the desk rose quickly to shake Charlie's hand.

"We come from the same village in western Ukraine," he offered. "Sit down. Would you like a drink?" Without waiting for an answer the newspaperman reached into a desk drawer and pulled out two small glasses and a tall bottle of Stolichnaya. Charlie quickly motioned "just a little," while his host made a scornful face.

"To independence," the newspaperman lifted his glass in a toast.

"To Independence," Charlie replied. "Before I left Chicago Natalia told me that I should drop by and say hello. I'm here on a Global Bank project and she said that you could fill me in on what is happening here in Ukraine. As a matter of fact," Charlie laughed "she told me you knew where all the bodies are buried." While he was talking he glanced quickly at his note, "Aha--Mr. Ivanov" he added.

"Call me Viktor please Mr. Connelly" the editor replied looking at Charlie's GBC business card. "I am sure that you think she used a funny phrase, but here in Kiev it's not a laughing matter. In fact you could say it is deadly serious. You have to be very careful," he leaned across his desk to emphasize his point, "While you are here never be heard criticizing the government," he advised shaking an ink-stained finger in Charlie's direction.

"They say part of a democracy is a free press," he continued after wiping his lips with the back of his tattered sleeve, but our president Kuchma doesn't believe in one if it prints things that are critical of him. At least 11 journalists have died under suspicious circumstances here in Ukraine over the last ten years.

"Have you heard about Georgi Congadze?" he asked, motioning with the half-full vodka bottle.

Charlie shook his head, taking a sip from his glass.

"Well," Viktor continued, "he was the editor of the Internet news site *Ukrainska Pravda*. He often reported on high level corruption in the country, and wrote very critical news stories about our president and his cronies. One day Georgi just disappeared. No one, not even his wife, knew where he went. A few weeks later a corpse was found buried at a crossroad with one arm sticking out of the ground. Whoever buried it tried to keep it from being identified by burning it with acid, and the corpse's head had been cut off—but the body had been buried along with Congadze's jewelry."

"That's terrible," Charlie recoiled, quickly draining his glass. The raw vodka burned his throat, then seemed to explode in the pit of his stomach. The sound of the presses humming outside the office blended discordantly with the ringing in his ears.

The editor refilled his glass before continuing. "It gets murkier. A security guard by the name of Mykola Melnychenko claimed to have taped over 300 hours of the president's conversations by placing a digital recorder under a couch. He ran away to the Czech Republic a few days before the tapes were released. The tapes are filled with language that would make a sailor blush, but you can hear Kuchma telling someone to get rid of Congadze."

"I would think that would be enough to finish him off," Charlie observed.

"You sure as hell would think so, but Kuchma claims it's his voice all right, but someone doctored the tapes. He implies that it was the CIA, but most people here think that the tapes are real and he is talking to some of his KGB goons when he tells them to get rid of Congadze."

"What about the public? Can't they do anything?" Charlie asked, taking another sip from his glass.

Viktor shook his head, before filling his own glass once again. "I guess not. There were demonstrations for a while. Some got pretty violent, but the oligarchs control the major media, and they all wrote articles throwing doubts on the tapes. The president's men also organized counter demonstrations. Now the whole thing is beginning to fizzle out. There are still some small protests that are continuing—you may have seen them on your way here."

"Yeah I did," Charlie confirmed, "when we passed the *Maydan*. The taxi driver pointed them out."

"Did you see the "black coats" watching?" Viktor asked.

"You mean the KGB? No I didn't notice."

Charlie looked at his watch. "I'm going to have to catch my train to Ivano Frankivsk," he informed Viktor apologetically, getting ready to leave.

"How many are there in your group going to your closed city?" Viktor asked as they walked toward the door.

"It's a low budget project," Charlie grinned weakly. "I'm going alone."

"Give my love to Natalie when you see her again," Viktor called as the cab pulled away from the curb.

Charlie's taxi was about to pull onto the main boulevard when a blinding flash reflected in its rear view mirror. In a blink of an eye a deafening explosion followed the bright glare. The cab pulled to the curb to see what had happened. Charlie leaped out, looking back toward the side street where the newspaper office was now engulfed in flame. Before he could return to help, an old fire truck pulled into view, followed by a police van, and an ambulance. The emergency vehicles arrived so quickly after the explosion it was as if they had been waiting for the tragedy to occur. The police leapt from their van and immediately roped off the entrance to the street while the firemen began playing their hoses on the blazing building.

It was obvious that no one could have survived the explosion, and Charlie sadly returned to his waiting driver.

Twelve:
The Closed City

Inside the depot Charlie searched for his train. He was running late, and it was difficult to read the departure schedule. Once he located the correct track number he began to make his way through the crowded old terminal. It appeared that many of the travelers had been camped there for days. Some had commandeered personal sections of the terminal by spreading threadbare blankets on the soiled tile floor. He carefully wove his way through the complex puzzle-pattern of Ukrainian humanity, trying to avoid stepping into any of their designated boundaries. No one even looked up as he awkwardly hop scotched through the human maze.

The train was beginning to pull away from the station when Charlie finally leapt on-board. Once inside he turned immediately to see if anyone boarded after him. He was reasonably sure he was not the intended target of the explosion, but he knew from his earlier experiences to be cautious when he found himself involved in circumstances that were difficult to understand.

The old passenger car swayed from side to side as the engine picked up speed, making it difficult to maneuver through the train's narrow corridor. A group of young soldiers blocked the aisle as they prepared for their trip by passing around a bottle of cheap vodka. Eventually locating the right compartment he struggled with the warped sliding door.

Once inside, Charlie stowed his bag in the overhead rack, and settled into the upholstered seat. The compartment was in "soft class," which bought two dusty crimson banquettes facing each other, separated by a fold up table supporting a faded green-shaded lamp.

Before relaxing in his seat, Charlie checked the hallway once more to insure that no one had followed him. It was still hard to believe that the explosion was just a tragic accident. More likely it was planned to silence another outspoken Ukrainian editor.

There had been a picture of Viktor's family proudly displayed on top of a metal filing cabinet in the editor's office. He would have to be sure, when he returned to Chicago, to tell Natalie that her friend's last words had been, "give Natalie my love."

The clicking of the rails and the swaying of the passenger car began to fit into a pattern as the train crossed a long bridge over the muddy Dnieper River. Railroads always seem to pass through the least attractive areas of any city, and this train was no exception. The train wormed its way past abandoned factories and empty warehouses, then picked-up speed flashing by never-ending blocks of dreary Stalinist inspired government apartments.

The area outside the train window had a tragic past. During the Second World War, shortly after the German army invaded Kiev, the Nazi troops rounded up the Jewish population and herded them into the Babyn Yar ravine. There they were lined up, forced to undress, and shot. Over 100,000 Jews were murdered in just two days. Later, when the Soviets took control of the city the ravine was covered with concrete and used as the foundation for some of the box-like apartment buildings that the train was rushing past.

The ungainly buildings were becoming a blur as the locomotive picked up speed. They were soon replaced by a view of small communities, then dense forests, and eventually open country. A train compartment is a lonely way to travel. In an airplane, the traveler is surrounded by

167

other passengers and passing flight attendants. On a train, a person is left to their own devices and melancholy thoughts. Charlie's mind became absorbed with memories of Beth and his family, and he wondered what they were doing back in the States.

He searched his briefcase for the sandwich the hotel had made that morning. It contained slices of hard-boiled egg, overlaid with thick wedges of green pickle. The bread was dry, but he managed to wash down his makeshift dinner with a bottle of water that was the most saline he had ever tasted.

By the time he finished the sandwich, the train was passing by seemingly never-ending fields of grain filled with men and women harvesters. This was the area of the country called "Russia's breadbasket," and the rich farmland was still vital to the Ukrainian economy.

In the past, Ukraine's fertile soil and its abundant natural resources had been a benefit as well as a bane to the troubled country's continued sovereignty, often leading to its downfall. The land the train was passing through had been the target of invading armies dating back to the 13th century Mongol hordes. As the generations passed, at any one time, at least a portion of Ukraine's territory was under the control of either Lithuania, Poland, Austria, Hungary, Romania, Czechoslovakia, Germany, or the Russian Army. None of these occupying forces were timid about dispensing their genes among the conquered population, and the evidence of their questionable generosity was evident, to varying degrees, on the various faces occasionally passing Charlie's small compartment.

As critical as this land was to the government, it still was operated by worker cooperatives with little incentives for efficiency. The farm hands laboring in the fields were using long-handled wooden scythes and rakes, rather than the powerful mechanized equipment used on smaller privately held farms in America's Midwest.

Gazing out his grimy window, Charlie had the impression that he was viewing a huge diorama of agricultural history.

As the workers loaded the sheaves of grain on horse drawn wagons the sky began to darken and was soon ripped by jagged shafts of dry lightening. The fury of the summer storm frightened the horses and caused the farm hands to abandon their work and flee for shelter.

The sudden sound of the compartment door banging against its warped frame diverted Charlie's attention to an aging attendant who was unsteadily entering, carrying blankets and pillows to convert one of the banquets into a bed.

That night Charlie fell into a troubled sleep, dreaming of home and wondering what might lie ahead. The stops were infrequent, and when they did occur he was rudely roused by the tinny sound of a woman's voice over an ancient loudspeaker announcing the approaching destination; which would be followed by a ghost-like shuffle of departing passengers squeezing through the narrow poorly lighted corridor.

Shortly after sunup, the train pulled into the Ivano Frankivsk station. Charlie was met by Oleg Shevchuck, Karpaty's marketing director, who was accompanied by Valerie the company librarian who would serve as interpreter. The group quickly piled into the waiting Zil for the ride to the factory. Looking through the window, Charlie was surprised to see tree-lined streets wandering through multi-colored buildings bearing a distinct Mediterranean appearance, oddly incongruous with the surrounding Carpathian Mountain setting.

The town, Charlie learned later, had a conflicting history. It was named after Ivano Franko a famous Ukrainian poet and writer, and it was now considered to be the cultural heart of the Precarpathian Region. During the Second World War, Ivano Frankivsk had also served as the headquarters for fierce and violent partisan activity that was concentrated in the surrounding mountains. The guerilla fighters were responsible for inflicting considerable damage on the invading German army. After the Germans were driven from the region, the partisans fought the Russians who had taken their place. More recently the town had become the center of the area's independence movement.

The company's administration building was imposing and intimidating, sitting on top of a steep hill dominating the town below like a feudal castle overlooking its sprawling fiefdom. Drawing closer, it was evident that very little effort was devoted to building maintenance. Many of the windows were broken or missing. The exterior was cracked, and the paint was badly faded. Inside, stray dogs roamed the dirty hallways, light fixtures were broken, and the elevators seldom functioned properly.

Charlie was led through heavy double wooden doors, on the fifth floor, into a large office with leather-lined walls to meet the king of the castle, company director, Vladimir Ivanov. The director was a large hulking man with ham-like hands and shoulders of a linebacker. Vladimir began by quickly outlining the company's problems and the role he expected Charlie to play during his stay. Leading him to the window, the director pointed to the buildings below. "We have," he explained "an almost completely self-contained industrialized social society. Down there," he pointed "are our production facilities, machine shops, clean rooms, research facilities, cafeteria and administration offices. Around the surrounding areas," he gestured with a broad sweep of his arm, "we have our social structure that includes a bakery, butcher shop, grocery store, medical clinic, kindergarten, fire station, and a cultural center." He thought for a minute then snorted "hell--we even run our own pig farm."

The company was larger than Charlie expected, and he began to understand how dependent the workers were on their continued employment. It is difficult to lose a job, Charlie could appreciate that, but it becomes a tragedy when your entire existence depends on it.

The company director spoke rapidly in Russian while Valerie haltingly translated. He was obviously proud of his enterprise, and he continued his explanation as they returned to his desk. "For years we made advanced radar equipment for the Russian military. At our peak we had 10,000 highly trained workers. Since independence, the Russian's no longer buy from Ukrainian factories, getting what they need for their armed forces from their own companies. Now we make only what the Ukrainian Government can use, and what we can occasionally sell to other countries."

"What other countries?" Charlie asked.

"Anyone we can find that can pay for our equipment," the director responded obliquely. "We would sell to the devil himself if he had money. Whatever we sell is still not enough to keep our workers busy, so they sit idle most of the time. We would try to privatize, but our equipment is too critical for our government to let the company fall into the hands of foreigners. We need new investors, but we don't know how to attract them."

"How can you continue to support your work force if you don't have any business?" Charlie asked.

"We can't," he roared. "Capitalism is cruel. Before independence we were a powerful company. See this phone," he exclaimed pointing to the red phone on his desk.

Charlie nodded. It was hard not to see it. It was bright red, and it was the only thing sitting on the director's desk.

"It is connected to an office in the Kremlin. It used to ring all the time, and if it wasn't for that son of a bitch Gorbachev it would still be ringing. We know, for a fact, that he worked for the CIA. Some day the phone will ring again, and when it does we will be ready."

"You don't really think the Soviet Union will rule Ukraine again do you?" Charlie asked incredulously.

"Of course I do," the director shouted. This time the little librarian jerked in alarm as she continued to translate.

"But I am a realist," he went on lowering his voice. "If it doesn't happen I have to be ready for that too. So you tell me what I need to do, and maybe I will take your advice," the director said rising to his feet. "And maybe I won't," he grinned. It was obvious the meeting was over, and Charlie morosely followed the librarian out of the office. He expected a warmer greeting than he had received, and it didn't auger well for the success of his assignment.

Following the meeting, Charlie was shown his office, which was adjacent to the director's. After looking around, he was taken to the apartment that Karpaty had arranged for his stay. It was located in one of the many large worker complexes surrounding the factory, which reminded him of Cabrini Green in Chicago. His quarters contained a living room, bedroom, kitchen, and bath. The complexes were commonly referred to, as Khrushchev blocks. There were thousands of them identically built throughout the Soviet Union.

This type of housing was conceived originally as way of eliminating class distinctions among the masses. The style was continued through subsequent administrations, as things in a giant bureaucracy have a tendency to do, regardless of how unworkable they prove to be in practice.

While Charlie's apartment was reasonably comfortable it was considerably different from the rest of those in the complex. The hallways reeked of cooking odors and sweat. The individual living units came in three standard sizes, which were one, two, or three rooms. Most of the units were required to share kitchen facilities and bathroom. The single engineers were assigned three to a room, which was part of a four-unit cluster. Each unit shared a kitchen with the other three. The kitchen's cupboards were divided into separate compartments where each residential group had their own dishes, eating utensils, staples, spices and whatever else was needed. Each kitchen was equipped with two stoves and a narrow counter where meals could be prepared. The meals were then eaten in the individual rooms. The engineers also shared communal bathing facilities much like a barracks or a dorm.

When Charlie learned how the other men lived it made his own relatively meager facilities seem more habitable. Arrangements were made for him to eat at the company discotheque located in the cultural center. The discotheque, like most of the cultural center, had been closed because of the company's budget problems, but eating there made it possible for him to take his meals without having to eat in the company cafeteria, or taking a bus into town. That night Charlie, along with Valerie, took their first of many meals in the poorly lighted, formerly abandoned Ukrainian discotheque.

The interpreter was a plain little woman, with a tendency to twist her handkerchief nervously around her fingers when she became the focus of intention. She had been married and divorced, "a common thing in Ukraine," she told Charlie at dinner. "The living quarters here are so cramped that you never have a moment to yourself." Her current lover was a medical doctor, who was able to provide free service to her ailing mother.

"In this country," she told Charlie over coffee, you have to go through the Communist Party to get into medical school. Acceptance has nothing to do with ability. Only those that have influence in the Party get in. That's why our health care is so bad.

"The man I live with is an exception. He is good doctor. The good doctors become well known and they can charge extra for their services. Under-the table—you understand," she added matter-of-factly. "My mother couldn't afford him if it wasn't for me. That's not why I live with him," she explained blushing. "He is also a very nice man."

After dinner, Charlie watched the local news on the TV in his apartment. The only available channel was in Russian. Watching the snowy picture, he felt very much alone and isolated. After a short time he clicked the set off and went to bed.

During the following weeks in Ivano Frankivsk, Charlie met with the individual department directors to get a better idea of the company's business, and the depth of its problems. They were an interesting group of men who had risen to their positions primarily through the structure of the Communist Party. When the Soviet Union collapsed the Party collapsed along with it. As a result, the directors found themselves completely adrift in an unfamiliar type of economy operating under a different form of government. They knew their time was passing, but no one knew how much time was left. They were living in the past, and had no idea or desire to adapt to the future.

The finance manager knew that his accounting system was not responsive to current requirements. The engineering manager was trying to acquire as much power as possible, while the head of manufacturing was trying to take over the marketing department, and the marketing manager was formerly head of the company's union, and

174

had no idea how to operate in a free-market economy. The directors fit together like an organizational cat's cradle with strands that were intertwined but never connected. This resulted in a corporate culture filled with fear and apprehension.

The only one of them who was English speaking was the manufacturing manager who had been the company's most dedicated Communist "They call me Medvid. Medvid the Bear," he told Charlie one day with ill-concealed pride. "Bears may sometimes hibernate, but they always survive." Medvid had been Karpaty's political boss and the Communist Party leader for the area, who reported to the First Secretary of the city's Central Committee before becoming manufacturing manager.

It was he who led the political demonstrations at the plant on holidays or whenever he considered it necessary. "But that was yesterday," he told Charlie one day. "The Karpaty we knew is gone. It is stored away somewhere with the furled communist banners we used to fly at the political rallies. It will never return, but none of these people realize it. They still wait around for the red telephone on the Director's desk to ring and have someone in the Kremlin tell us it is all right again, and we are once more important to them."

"But that's not going to happen," Charlie told him. Once independence comes, you can't turn back the clock. Look how the other countries are advancing. Look at Poland—look at the Czech Republic, and Hungary. They're all moving ahead. Only Ukraine and Belarus are hanging back.'

"You don't understand," Medvid replied slamming his desk with such intensity it startled poor Valerie. "That's because you are an American," Medvid continued with only a slight glance at the frightened interpreter. "In your country everyone is an optimist. Russians have only the past. We don't need your advice. We know what we need to do. It's just that we don't want to do it. You don't know the difficulties that we have. You don't understand us."

Charlie had heard this often before in other countries. The problem was he did understand because he had seen what Communism had done in other places, and how conditions had improved once it was gone. China was becoming an economic powerhouse since it turned to capitalism and opened their markets. The new motto in Beijing was "to become rich is glorious," which was a far cry from their former doctrine.

Never the less, it was hard to convince these men that the system they had spent their lives building rested on a foundation of sand. Charlie knew how he would feel if the situation had been reversed, and he was sitting in his office listening to a Russian Commissar telling him capitalism had failed. He would very likely react in a similar fashion.

One night Charlie was looking over some of his notes while he half paid attention to the Russian language television station. There was a knock on his door and when he answered it there was Medvid staring at him through blood shot eyes. It was obvious he had been drinking, but it was not obvious why he had come to call.

"Connelly," he began gruffly striding into the room and sitting down. "What I want to do is find out how to get into Harvard?"

"You want to go to Harvard?" Charlie replied in amazement.

"No-no you idiot! My son! I want my son to go to Harvard!"

Charlie was stunned. Medvid was quite likely the only one in Ivano Frankivsk who had even heard of Harvard, much less having a desire to have his son attend this center of American capitalism.

176

"You're surprised, huh. You probably thought that no one here had ever heard of Harvard." Which, of course, was exactly what Charlie thought. "Well you are wrong Mr. Connelly. I know that if you graduate from there your future is guaranteed. My son is studying mathematics at the University of Moscow, he is very bright but there is no future in that. I know that the future here is in the free market so I want to know how he can get into Harvard."

Charlie spent the next hour trying to explain to Medvid how he might work with the American Embassy in Kiev to make an application. The boy probably would fit in very well there Charlie decided, and gave him Barry Durand's name at the American Embassy as a point of contact. Wait till old Medvid sees Eve St. Ives he thought. After he gets a look at "Twin Peaks" he'll probably want to go to Harvard with his son.

He was finally able to lead Medvid to the door, and watched as the old party boss, swaying drunkenly from side to side, silently dissolve into the shadowy corridor.

While Medvid was looking ahead, Oleg Shevchuck, the company's marketing manager was looking backward. Up until a few months ago, Oleg had been head of the workers union at Karpaty and he had no idea of what marketing was, much less what it should be. An office in Kiev told Karpaty what to build, how many units to produce, then provided the company with the appropriate production schedule, dictated the prices that they should charge, and when and to whom the products should be delivered.

Before independence, this direction had come from the Kremlin. Since Karpaty and Oleg had no previous experience in acting independently they were floundering when it became necessary to develop new products and market them through their own channels. When Charlie attempted to advise the marketing manager on how things could be done differently his advice was met with profound indifference. Oleg was afraid of shouldering responsibility and preferred to work on improving the document flow through the organization instead of setting up new channels of distribution.

Charlie would occasionally watch from his office window as the workers filed in and out of the factory. The fear of losing their jobs was almost palpable, and he felt badly for them. Having worked at Apex under conditions of uncertainty he could appreciate their concern.

The news coming from Kiev was equally depressing and described a country in turmoil. The current Prime Minister's term was expiring and elections to select his replacement were nearing. Kuchma's chosen successor was Victor Yanukovych, who was backed by the Russians. He was running against a reformist candidate by the name of Yuschenko who Natalie had mentioned when Charlie met with her in the Ukrainian Village. Every night the TV news focused on the expanding political protests. So far these demonstrations had been peaceful, but as each day passed they seemed to grow larger and move ever closer to violence.

One night, however, instead of only Ukrainian news there were pictures of American troops in action in a place other than Afghanistan. The words Shock and Awe were highlighted on the screen in English, and Charlie knew that the invasion of Iraq had begun.

The weather was beginning to change as summer moved into fall. That morning, there was a chilly breeze that carried with it rain-filled clouds from the other side of the Carpathians. The gray sky made it seem colder than it actually was, and Charlie pulled up his coat collar as he made his daily walk to the office. As he drew closer he noticed that the old woman who usually tended her cow on the company lawn was missing, and in her place was a large camouflaged vehicle with several massive antennas. Charlie recognized the equipment as the most recent version of the company's passive radar system that Karpaty had made previously for the Russian military. Some limited production was still taking place for the Ukrainian government, and the company had been desperately seeking additional customers.

Several stocky men with AK-47's slung over their shoulders guarded the area around the truck menacing anyone who, in their opinion, might be coming too close. A crowd milled around the vehicle. Some men were in military uniforms, others were Karpaty technicians, while still others were Mideastern looking men who appeared uncomfortable in their ill-fitting business suits. The strangers were huddled together to shield each other from the chilly wind while they attempted to pay attention to the presentation and furtively work their worry-beads.

Charlie knew from experience that a contract for such complex equipment would require negotiations not only for the hardware, but also for accompanying documentation, and on-site training for operating and maintaining the units before pricing and payment terms would even be discussed. He was also aware that this type of equipment would be critical to any nation planning for war, which would add an additional element of intensity to the developing negotiations.

Following similar demonstrations, it was usual for the visiting groups to continue their discussions in the general director's office. Today was no exception. Charlie's office was next to his, and he could frequently hear the intense wrangling coming through the heavily padded walls. The visitors had apparently left their Islamic piety at home; and the negotiations, fueled by large amounts of vodka, grew more raucous as the day wore on. He could occasionally get a closer look at some of the visitors passing in the hallway on their way to the toilet. When he left that evening the customers were still huddled outside the director's office gesturing and shouting in a heated discussion.

The visitors were gone the next day when Charlie came to work, and he never learned if the meetings had been successful or only a prelude to further discussions. Valerie had served as an interpreter since the customers were more comfortable in English than Russian. When Charlie asked who the men were, she shrugged her shoulders. "Maybe Syrians," was the reply. Then she added, "Or Iranians maybe, we get all kinds. Sometimes Iranians, sometimes Iraqis, sometimes Syrians—who knows. I can't tell them apart."

Time had passed quickly during his stay in Ivano Frankivsk. At first, he was viewed with suspicion by most of the people at the factory and the apartment complex. He couldn't blame them; after all they were conditioned for years to believe that Americans were their enemies and that all of them were spies. Gradually, they came to realize that he was only there to help them adjust to a new economic system that came with the country's independence.

He had tried several times to get in touch with Beth, but had been unable to get through. Direct dialing was impossible, and it was difficult to make the overseas operator understand his English. Twice during his stay Beth had been able to dial his apartment. Once a letter from her had arrived, and occasionally he had been able to send her a fax from the factory.

Now he had done all the work on the project that he could do and it was time to schedule a meeting with the general director to review what he was planning to recommend to GBC on returning to Kiev.

A meeting was set up, and Charlie and Valarie entered the director's office. His first recommendation was, in order to acquire additional operating capital; the company should try and sell their recreational facilities to a foreign tourist group. Karpaty owned desirable land in the nearby mountains where they operated a camp for vacationing workers that would make an excellent year-round resort. In addition, the company had another large recreational facility on the Black Sea. The country, in spite of its political difficulties, was beginning to attract some European tourists because of its scenery and low cost vacation opportunities, and these locations had excellent potential for private development.

Next, Charlie provided an outline for a document that could be prepared to summarize the company's advantages to a potential investor. Karpaty had an educated and well-trained work force as well as the facilities to produce high tech products.

As an alternative to direct foreign investment, Charlie also provided a document detailing how they might obtain a license from a European company to produce their products in Ukraine. The license could then serve as a basis for foreign companies to invest later in a minority interest in Karpaty.

The last subject was the recommendation to reduce employment levels.

The general director had listened patiently, and when Charlie finished his presentation he folded his hands together and leaned forward on his desk. "Mr. Connelly," he began in a hoarse voice. "I appreciate your coming, and the work that you have done. Your recommendations are sound and we will seriously consider them. I am sure from your standpoint they make good sense. When it comes to redundancies, however, we can't lay off our people."

"You're going to have to," Charlie replied calmly. "You can't maintain your payroll the way it is now. Much less the supplemental services you are providing. The vacation camps are just the beginning. And you can't sell them unless you work at it. But you need to close your schools and clinics as well. No one will invest in the company with that type of overhead."

"Look what's happening in Kiev," the director accurately pointed out. "The companies are going to President Kuchma's pals, and the workers are just as bad off as they were before. You have to understand that we Russians are used to sadness," the Director observed. (The managers always referred to themselves as Russians while the workers considered themselves to be Ukrainians.) The director continued his lament while glowering at Charlie "We wallow in sadness. We embrace it. Our music is sad. Our poetry is sad, and we are not happy unless we're sad. That's why we drink so much. Vodka mixes best with melancholy.

"But we are not completely without hope. We have met with group of oil-rich visitors who are interested in purchasing our equipment. They have many interests and it all depends on what they are able to negotiate in Kiev. So don't despair for us. We may yet survive," he told Charlie, standing and holding out his hand.

The meeting was over. The two men understood each other's position and recognized that neither one was going to change. They shook hands and the director hugged his departing American consultant, encircling him with his huge arms.

Charlie was glad to be leaving Karpaty. He didn't feel that he had accomplished a great deal, and he was anxious to talk to Barry Durand at the American Embassy to make sure that he was aware of the visiting Iranian delegation.

Thirteen:
The Kh55s

The train to Kiev lurched into the station. Charlie waited patiently in his compartment for the aisles to clear before grabbing his bag and heading for the door. He maneuvered carefully through the human mosaic that remained spread over the station's grimy tiled floor. Some of the people looked like the same ones that were in the station two months earlier when he left for Ivano Frankivsk.

Once outside, he grabbed the first cab in line and gave the driver the address to GBC's local office. The cab careened through the early morning traffic before finally entering the general flow of old autos on their way to work. The chestnut trees that lined the avenues were beginning to lose their leaves and they swirled in the air as the taxi sped past. Veering onto Kreshchatyk Avenue, Kiev's central roadway, Charlie was astonished to see that the crowd of protestors gathered on the Maydan had increased considerably since he had previously passed the square on his way to the train station. Where before there formerly had been hundreds of banner-waving demonstrators there were now thousands.

Most of the people were obviously students who had pitched tents and carried rolled up mattresses. It was a peaceful, but highly vocal group. Many of them were standing on empty egg cartons to protect their thinly soled shoes from the cold concrete walkways. The color orange was everywhere; in their clothes, their balloons and particularly in the bright orange banners they were waving in response to the man who was animatedly addressing them.

"Yushchenko," the driver told him pointing to the handsome man on the podium.

The taxi pulled to the curb in front of the Global Bank offices. Charlie dug in his pocket for the large wad of the country's devalued currency he was carrying. Inside the old building a printed sign dangled in front of the elevator door. He couldn't read it, but it was obvious that the elevator had taken a day off. He puffed his way up the staircase to GBC's offices.

"Is Perriman in?" Charlie asked leaning tiredly against the office doorjamb while he caught his breath. Startled, the secretary dropped her nail file and it fell to the desk beside a tall stack of unread magazines. She glanced up, peering with myopic eyes at the blurry figure of a tall man standing in front of her.

"Oh Mr. Connelly," she smiled finally recognizing the visiting American. "Welcome back. How was the closed city? I'm sorry he's not in today. Can I help you?" she asked, not pausing for a reply to her first question.

Charlie searched his briefcase for the stack of expense reports he had prepared before leaving Karpaty. "I wanted to drop these off, and pick up the key to the apartment that Paul told me would be ready when I got back. What's happening out there on Independence Square?" Even inside the office it was possible to hear the repeated chants *of Ya stoyav na Maidani*! It sounded like fans at a football game, beginning softly then slowly building to a thundering crescendo before dying out, and then beginning once again.

"They're yelling I stood on the Maidan," the secretary told him as they walked to the window. Then sometimes they chant *together we are many*! "They call it the Orange Revolution. A couple of weeks ago we had the election, and Kuchma's man won. Now people think that Yushchenko should have won, and they are protesting the election. The court has agreed to review the ballots, and the people don't want to leave the Maidan until they establish a new election. Until then, the government is at a standstill and the demonstrators keep chanting.

"Some mornings the crowd is even larger than today. I have to pass through them to get to work, and it can be a problem. See the men wearing the black coats?" the secretary asked, pointing a group of burly men ringing the demonstrators. "Those are Kuchma's thugs. They'd like to break it up, but they're afraid to try. So far, they just stand and watch. I'm always afraid they'll change their minds and rush the crowd just when I'm passing through."

Charlie returned to the desk and picked up the key, while the secretary wrote out the address. "You're lucky to get the apartment," she told him. The man who had it before you returned to Vienna last week. If he hadn't, you would have to live in a hotel. Apartments are impossible to find. GBC leased it years ago just for this purpose."

She had turned her attention back to her nails, before the rangy American disappeared through the office doorway.

The cab pulled up in front of an old three-story building. At one time it had been a single residence, but long ago the Russians had confiscated it and converted it to small apartments. Charlie's temporary home was on the second floor, and consisted of a living room/kitchen combination, flanked by a tiny bedroom. A few pieces of old overstuffed furniture were haphazardly spread around the main room, and a chipped white-enamel table and three chairs were centered in the tiny kitchen.

A single bulb, dangling at the end of a frayed cord, weakly illuminated each room. An exposed black wire wormed its way along the molding, crawling crazily from room to room. He cracked the window to let in some fresh air and get rid of the musty smell that permeated the bleak apartment. At least there is a window he thought, idly watching the heavy flow of traffic in the street below.

Charlie turned away, and began the tedious job of unpacking. When he finished he took his file folders into the kitchen and carefully stacked them on the table where he planned to work on his report. Afterwards, he was hungry and decided to get something to eat. He recalled the dinner he had at the Dnipro Hotel before leaving on his assignment in Ivano Frankivsk.

He had begun to get an idea on how Kiev was laid out, and recognized that his apartment was within walking distance of the hotel. The evening was crisp and he enjoyed the walk, joining the anonymous flow of people coming from work or going out for the evening. An occasional couple would pass, their arms wrapped affectionately around each other, possibly hoping to find a momentary respite from their cramped living quarters.

Each street corner was home to the makeshift sidewalk stands operated by the old *babushka*, who obtained wares from "suitcase salesmen" who traveled to neighboring countries and returned with their luggage filled with black-market goods. These old ladies with their long coats, colorful shawls, and wrapped legs were unconsciously forming the foundation of a flourishing underground economy in Ukraine.

The beginning of the free-market system Charlie thought, as he bought a Snickers bar from one old woman and stuffed it into his pocket.

The hotel dining room was beginning to fill, and he was shown a small table by the swinging doors to the kitchen. It must be a universal restaurant protocol to assign the single diners the smallest most obscure table, regardless how many larger ones are available. The Chicken Kiev he had ordered during his earlier visit had been good, and he decided to try it again.

Charlie gazed casually around the room, waiting for his order to arrive. A group of Japanese tourists, engulfed in a deepening haze of tobacco smoke, were seated at a long ashtray littered table. The Asian men's eyes would furtively, but frequently stray to a party of young Ukrainian women, accompanied by heavy-set middle aged men, noisily occupying an adjacent table. The lean-limbed ladies of Ukraine had become one of the country's leading export commodities. They were attracting website suitors from around the world who were more than willing to exchange their country entry visas for the anticipated joys of matrimony. "Romance Tours," as they are euphemistically called, offer an added lure to foreign businessmen, and provided the country with an additional source of foreign exchange—as the boisterous men at the nearby table were so abundantly demonstrating.

Four young women, dressed as if they had just come from a sorority soiree, sat by the doorway. They giggled as they appraised each prosperous-looking European businessman entering the dining room. The girls whispered together, behind well-manicured hands, attempting to guess which of the new arrivals might make the most likely customers for their services later that evening.

As Charlie ate, his attention was unconsciously drawn to a raucous group seated in an alcove pouring *Sovietsky* champagne and Georgian wines like beer at a fraternity party. Two of the dark-skinned men wore black and white checked kaffiyehs over their heads, while two others were dressed in tailored business suits; but they all appeared to be from the Mideast. The "suits" looked familiar, and he suddenly realized they were part of the group that visited Karpaty. The fifth man, seemingly the host, was older than the rest. His gray hair was closely cropped, and his pale face was deeply lined, in marked contrast to his swarthy younger companions.

Sipping his coffee and finishing a cherry tart, Charlie's looked again at the men in the alcove. Snatches of conversation floated through the smoky air. The host sounded like an American. There seemed to be something vaguely familiar about the stocky man doing most of the talking, but Charlie rejected the possibility as purely a fantasy born out of the loneliness of eating alone, a long way from home.

The American raised his glass in a toast to his Arab guests. As the man clutched the tapered stem, Charlie noticed that the forefinger on his right hand was missing. That's odd he thought. Good God Almighty he almost blurted, it's Marvin--Marvin the Machinist, his old friend from the CIA. The same man who had recruited him so many years ago. How the hell did he ever get here? Why was he with these swarthy men? A thousand unanswered questions raced through Charlie's mind as he studied Marvin.

The group was rising unsteadily to their feet, and starting on their way to the dining room door while Marvin scattered bills on the bottle-laden table.

The Japanese at the long table had been drinking vodka as if it was sake, and had begun to sing unintelligibly. Everyone's attention was diverted toward the crimson-faced Orientals as their voices grew louder and louder. The Europeans had been winking at the girls at the nearby table, and were arguing among themselves on how best to proposition them.

Charlie covered his own dinner check with a stack of Ukrainian hryvnias, while sliding his chair back preparing to greet his old mentor. He paused briefly as he watched the Mideastern men heading toward the table with the hookers. The young women quickly rose and delightedly joined the men as they left the dining room together. The disappointed Europeans glumly watched in astonishment.

Something wasn't quite right. Not that they were leaving with the women. That was no mystery. But what the hell was Marvin doing with those men in the first place?

Outside the hotel, their host guided his friends into waiting taxis, patted one of the hookers playfully on the behind, and waved as the car pulled away from the curb.

Charlie recalled the Maestro once told him that the Machinist just seemed to disappear, and they were forwarding his pension checks to a Swiss bank account. So, what was he doing in Kiev?

Marvin was drifting away from the hotel, and Charlie decided to follow.

The old spy had obviously become complacent in his new role, whatever it might be. Even Charlie could recognize that he wasn't practicing the most fundamental rules of tradecraft. He didn't stop to see if he was being followed, never crossed to the other side, or doubled back. He didn't even pause to look into store windows, or car rearview mirrors to see if anyone was behind him.

Charlie trailed at a safe distance, occasionally stopping and dodging into a storefront in case Marvin should turn and look behind him. That never happened. He just kept walking, somewhat unsteadily, ahead of him.

He must be very drunk Charlie thought.

Finally Marvin entered the doorway of an old apartment building. Charlie stood, partially hidden behind a street kiosk where he could watch the windows in the converted house. Soon a light went on in a second floor apartment.

Charlie debated going up, but decided against it and walked back to his own apartment. It was late and he was tired and filled with questions. Once inside, he took a bottle of Stolichnaya he had carried with him from Ivano Frankivsk. Sitting at the table he took a drink trying to decide what to do next. Nothing came to mind. He peeled the wrapper off the Snickers bar, poured another vodka, drank it down, replaced the tinfoil cap, finished the candy bar, and went to bed. He'd sleep on it he decided, at a loss for a better idea.

The next morning the sun was struggling to rise in a Pantagonian type gray sky. It was early and Charlie had slept fitfully, but decided he had to find out what Marvin was up to. He dressed quickly and left the apartment. There were only a few workers on the early morning street as he hurried back to Marvin's apartment house. On the way, it began to rain, making the old cobblestone sidewalk slippery underfoot. He pulled up the hood on his heavy duffel-coat to get some protection from the driving rain, coming down so hard it pelted against his face.

An occasional car would pass, its Russian wipers beating an erratic rhythm across the drenched windshield.

He entered a doorway across from the apartment building. It gave him some protection, and kept him out of the view of anyone that might be watching. A chill went down his spine and he shuddered uncontrollably in the dark entryway. He swallowed hard and, in spite of the dampness his mouth and throat were dry; and anxiety tore at his gut.

After watching for what seemed like hours, he noticed a neon sign turning on in the window of small café further down the street. It could provide needed protection from the rain while still being an acceptable observation point.

There was only one other customer in the small diner, and he was paying little attention to anything other than quickly finishing his breakfast before leaving for work. When he rose to leave he tossed his paper disgustedly on the table. Charlie quickly picked it up after the man went out the door. It was a Ukrainian paper, but he thought that it might serve to provide some type of cover in case anyone was curious about a foreigner in a tacky café so early in the morning.

Watching through the diner's window he could see that the streets of Kiev were gradually waking to the stormy morning. An occasional streetcar clattered past as more shops along the soaked sidewalk began to open their tightly shuttered doorways. A scattering of school children, clutching their tattered textbooks underneath hand-me-down raincoats, trailed past. Behind them was a tired babushka, limping along with her scarved head poking defiantly through a plastic garbage bag that protected her tattered sweater.

He was on his second cup of coffee when he saw Marvin standing in the doorway of his apartment house peering impatiently up the street. A large black Zil limousine, with a driver in a Ukrainian military uniform, glided to the curb. Marvin quickly dove through the open car door to avoid the rain. The Zil pulled away with Marvin in the back. He cracked the window and laid his head on the cushioned seat, staring at the car's ceiling. Last evening's champagne had obviously taken its toll.

Charlie stayed in the small diner while the owner brought his order of fried eggs and cold sausage. He ate slowly while closely watching the street to see if Marvin would return. After an hour he paid his bill and left. He crossed the street looking carefully to see if anyone was watching, then dodged into the doorway of the apartment house.

He knew the floor, and the location of Marvin's flat from last night's light in the window. Looking cautiously up and down the dark hallway, Charlie knocked on the apartment door. There was no answer, so he twisted the knob. As he expected, it was locked. He didn't know exactly what he thought he was doing. He rarely acted on impulse, but he certainly had not thought through a plan.

He rattled the door again, and looked around. There was still no sign of life in the hallway, and no one came to the door. He thought for a moment and then took a credit card from his wallet. He had remembered the old Sam Spade private eye movies where the world-weary detective entered the suspect's apartment by quickly sliding a credit card between the door jam and the lock. Perhaps it would work here. It was an old trick, but this was an old apartment.

Charlie selected a credit card from his wallet, and attempted to forcefully slide it through the lock. Damn! The card split in two, one-half falling at his feet and the other half dropping to the floor inside the apartment. Now he really had a problem. Not only had he failed to open the door but, half the plastic card was now inside where Marvin would see it immediately when he returned.

He couldn't give up now. The next time he tried his American Express Card. This time the door opened. *Never leave home without it* he chuckled to himself as he ducked inside, quickly picking up the broken card while he looked cautiously around.

It was dark inside, but he was afraid to turn on the light. He raised the shade slightly to let more light in after first peeking out the window to see if anyone might be passing on the street below.

It was a two-bedroom apartment with the same living room/ kitchen arrangement as his own living quarters. There was more overstuffed furniture, but the air smelled just as musty. Marvin had spread out a large stack of blueprints on the kitchen table. Each print bore the boldly printed designation **Kh55**. The top print was a diagram of a cruise missile. Each subsequent schematic showed a detailed design of an integral missile section. Beside the table was a large stack of documents, with the title of **Kh55 Operating Manual** on the top. Charlie made a note of the title before moving on to one of the bedrooms.

In the first bedroom he entered there was a large chest of draws filled with clothes. Charlie quickly went through each drawer before moving through the bathroom separating the bedrooms. Finding nothing unusual, he moved quickly on to the second bedroom. There was another chest of drawers similar to the one in the first bedroom. He opened the top drawer, and was astonished to find it stuffed with women's lingerie. A faint musky odor filled the room coming from the open drawer. Where had he smelled that scent before? What was it? *Allure*, he decided after a moment's hesitation.

He reached into a drawer and gingerly extracted a pair of sheer lace panties. Holding them up to the light he wondered if they could possibly belong to Marvin? No it can't be, he quickly decided, embarrassed at the thought. Don't be foolish he admonished himself—just before he heard……

"Find anything that fits?"

Startled and ashamed, Charlie began to turn toward the husky voice.

"Don't turn around! Stay where you are! I have a .25-caliber Beretta aimed at the back of your head. It's a small caliber, but at this range it can blow your brains out."

He did what she said. He sure as hell wasn't going to argue with a Beretta of any caliber, particularly while he was holding a pair of lace panties.

"Drop the lingerie, and put your hands behind your head!"

"Intertwine the fingers."

"Now turn around very very slowly."

Charlie turned to see a tall woman in a blue trench coat. She was wearing a scarf covering her hair and forehead.

"Who the hell are you?" the woman demanded. "Who sent you?"

"No one. No one sent me, Charlie stammered. "I was drinking with Marvin last night and just woke up." Not bad he thought.

"Your coat is still wet. I know you didn't spend the night here because I did. Marvin may have been drunk, but I wasn't," she snapped. "You're an American," she waved the gun at him menacingly. "Did the CIA send you? Who do you work for?" The woman fired questions without waiting for an answer.

It was cold in the room, but Charlie could feel sweat rolling down his back.

"Was it the Maestro? Did Emmett Valentine send you after me?" she growled.

The scent in the bedroom. The tall slender woman. The mention of the Maestro, and Marvin. It was finally beginning to make sense to Charlie.

"Karen—Karen Kincaid?" he whispered tentatively.

The woman lowered her gun ever so slightly. "You're-you're Pinstripes aren't you? How did you ever find me?"

"I didn't *find* you. I stumbled on Marvin at the Hotel Dnipro last night. He was entertaining some Arab businessmen, and I followed him home to see what he was up to-and you appeared. Can we sit down?" he asked growing tired of standing with his hands linked behind his head.

Karen approached carefully and frisked him, running her hands underneath his arms and up and down his legs.

"I'm clean. But you can do that again if you like," he told her with a wan smile.

She grimly waved the gun toward the kitchen table. "Ok sit," she ordered, taking a chair across from him, while keeping her pearl handled pistol pointing in his direction.

Charlie thought about the last time they had met in the Chicago CIA office. That was a long time ago. How strange it was to be facing each other once again in a dingy apartment in Kiev.

"How did you get away from them?" he asked, "and how the hell did you get here?"

"It's a long story, and we don't have much time. Marvin could be coming back any minute. Will you promise not to tell Emmett until you have heard my side?"

She had taken off her scarf, and he could see that her long blond hair was now short and dark. How easy it is for a woman to change her appearance he thought. He wouldn't have known her if they passed on the street.

"The CIA needs to know what's going on here, but I can't let them catch me. I was framed, but I really have no way of proving it."

"You have my word," Charlie answered nervously looking towards the door. He had a feeling that if Marvin caught them together he would be a dead man.

"Remember when you were in Lima, we had you go to the Cathedral?" she asked leaning across the table. She had put her Beretta back in her purse. "That was all part of it. It was kind of the beginning I guess."

Charlie nodded. He remembered it very well. He recalled how he had lighted the votive candles to make a cross as identification.

"This afternoon, catch the funicular—do you know where it is?

"I've seen it," he acknowledged.

"All right, ride it down to the Podil area. That way you can easily tell if you are followed. Then walk up Andriyivsky Avenue through the restaurant district," Karen directed, "till you get to St. Andrews. You can't miss it. It's got five domes, and it's green, blue, and white exterior will stand out like a directional beacon. Sit toward the back. Not in the back row, that's too obvious, but toward the back. I'll meet you there at two o'clock. Now leave," she ordered brusquely.

Without a word Charlie rose and left the apartment, much relieved but with his head spinning.

Fourteen:
Karen's Tale

The chain slipped a cog then caught itself, as the antiquated funicular began its jerky descent. Charlie was alone in his car; he had been careful to make sure of that. A drizzle that shrouded the city in fog had now replaced yesterday's rain. He squinted as he peered through the dirty window at the scene below. If the circumstances had been different he might have enjoyed the ride. In the distance he could see the ghostly outline of the tour boats lined up along the bank of the Dnieper, waiting for their next scheduled departure before their brief season drew to an end.

He briefly wondered if the clanking jerking chain, dragging his car downward toward the river, was providing a mechanical metaphor for what was happening to his life. When he first came to Ukraine he thought he was out of the spy business. Now he was being drawn back in once more. First old Marvin appears out of nowhere, and now Karen. Next thing you know we will all be joining hands and singing, *That Old Gang of Mine*. Not very damn likely he thought.

He was curious what he would learn from Karen. Then what? It was obvious that Marvin was dealing missiles to the jihadists and had to be stopped. How could that be done? What about Karen? What was his obligation to her? He knew she was wanted by the FBI—and the CIA, but where did his loyalties lie? Were they to Karen? To Marvin? To Emmett? To himself and Beth? One thing he knew for certain, after his family his loyalty to his country was paramount. But what needed to be done? He knew he would soon have to sort it all out, but not until he had more information than he had now.

Enough of this soul-searching bullshit he decided, as the cable car glided through the leafless trees and came to an abrupt stop. The doors opened automatically and Charlie stepped out. He waited briefly to see if anyone exited the cars behind him, but he was alone. All alone.

Following Karen's directions, Charlie trudged along Andriyivsky Uzviz. The old street was lined with art galleries, shops, and restaurants. The galleries and studios were all closed while their artist proprietors joined the students demonstrating on the Maiden. The bright blue and green spires and domes of St. Andrews shone like the directional beacon Karen described.

Charlie entered through the heavy wooden doors, and peered around the dark interior. It was the middle of the afternoon, and only a few women in their gaudy headscarves were scattered sparingly among the pews. For such an ornate structure the inside was starkly plain. The only decoration was a large painting of St. Andrew hanging above a large unadorned altar.

Under the Russians, St. Andrews was converted to a museum of architecture, to eliminate any semblance of religious influence. Similar conversions were common throughout Ukraine. The old church in Ivano Frankivsk had been converted to a museum of atheism, while the cathedral in Lviv was used to store grain. Hundreds of small village churches had also been closed or destroyed. "This church doesn't work," was the operable phrase of the period.

Charlie peered through the gloom and found Karen seated in one of the rear rows of seats. She was wearing the same scarf she wore in Marvin's apartment. Her eyes were hidden behind a large pair of dark glasses. He sat in the row behind her, and placed his hand gently on her shoulder. She turned awkwardly to face him.

"Thanks for coming Charlie; I really need someone to talk to."

198

Her scarf slipped slightly, and he could see she wore her recently dark hair in a thick braid, Ukrainian style, across the top of her head. She was still astonishingly attractive.

"How have you been Karen?" he asked in a low voice that concealed the extent of his concern.

"I'm OK for now, but I'm in way over my head, and I desperately need your help," she replied brushing a wisp of hair from her forehead before removing her dark glasses. Her normally sparkling eyes were deeply ringed and there were lines beginning to appear across her forehead.

"How's your family Charlie?"

"Their fine--Karen what the hell happened? Why did you betray your country?

"I never did. You have to believe that. I'll tell you, but it's a long story, and I am trying to figure out how it all began. It was the Peruvian project--I guess. The Sendero Luminosa were Maoists and they were raising hell in the mountains. We were afraid that they would eventually take over the country, and we didn't need another Communist takeover in Latin America. Not after we screwed up Cuba so badly.

"The Peruvian government seemed unable to combat them. We thought that many in the government were actually sympathetic to them. There was another group down there that was anti-Communist and anti-government as well. Our management maharajas decided to support them, and they gave Marvin and me the assignment of getting the money down to them. Without any strings to us, of course. That was where you came in. You were what we call a "clean face," and provided the Agency with their desired plausible deniability—so we decided to use you to funnel money to the rebels.

"I think I told you in Chicago that Marvin hoped to get Emmett's job when he retired. I didn't know it at the time-I only found out later that he had heard through the rumor mill—oh yes the CIA has a rumor mill just like any burgeoning bureaucracy—anyway he found out that Stacey Loosetree was going to get Emmett's job."

Once she began to talk it was like a dam breaking, and the words flowed in torrents.

"It made Marvin mad as hell," she continued. "He never got along in the polished WASP world of our Ivy League hierarchy, and now they passed him over in favor of an overweight dolt. Well Marvin hadn't been in the clandestine service all his life without learning how to plan. So he devised a plan to get even, and fund his retirement at the same time."

Karen paused. Charlie looked around to see what she was staring at.

A brown robed, hooded monk had entered the back of the church, and was slowly walking down the center aisle towards the austere altar. He genuflected reverently at the end of the aisle, and prostrated himself in front of the painting of St. Andrew. He stayed that way for several minutes, then rose and exited the way he had come.

"The Maestro had been given $200,000 in unmarked bills to get to the rebels," she continued when the monk went through the wooden doorway. "He gave it to Marvin, and Marvin gave it to me to send to you by an Air Force courier. What I didn't know was that Marvin had taken the money and substituted stacks of worthless Chinese yen. You did as we expected and made the transfer flawlessly.

"How did you know I didn't take the money?" Charlie asked, intrigued to find what had actually happened in Lima.

"We had you thoroughly checked out before we began dealing with you. One word was continually repeated when people described you to our investigators, and that word was integrity. Never the less, I had you followed and the woman reported that she had seen you make the drop just as you were told to do."

"Nice to know I was trusted," Charlie caustically observed.

"Hey my friend, deceit and deception are the bedrock of this dirty business. You can never be too sure, as I found out to my regret.

"Anyway when the rebels got the Chinese yen they were furious. They didn't know if the CIA was jobbing them or you were. That was when they sent someone to check your room to see if the real money was there."

"He damned near killed me," Charlie snorted.

"He was an amateur, and you scared the hell out of him. You had taken off before they figured out what to do next."

"I went to Paraguay. I figured no one would find me there."

"You're right. I've never known anyone who has been to Paraguay," Karen grinned.

"Anyway, I never knew what happened until later, when the rebels finally got word back to us. By that time, Loosetree had been named to replace Marvin, and Marvin had hung up the old jock— so to speak."

"Emmett told me they couldn't even find where to send his pension check," Charlie offered.

"That's right. So now I was the only one around to place the blame on. Marvin was gone. Emmett was gone, and only poor old Karen was around to get hung."

"Tag—you're it, huh?"

"That's it, the next thing I knew the FBI was after me, and I got picked up by a pimply faced novice at a hotel in Santa Fe."

"How did you get away?" Charlie asked glancing at the ornate altar where a young boy in a white cassock had begun lighting two tall candles. As the young man was finishing several old women, their head covered, began filing into the dark church.

"Come on Charlie, let's get out of here. It looks like services are about to begin"

"Where do you want to go? I still want to know how you got here." Charlie told her. He didn't want to lose her before he heard the end of her story.

"I'll tell you. You have a right to know. Besides I need your help. Follow me," Karen whispered.

They began to walk. Some of the restaurants were beginning to open and the street was becoming more crowded. Charlie recognized that they were going back the way he had come. The sun was beginning to set and a definite chill was in the air.

Karen drew the collar of her trench coat up around her neck. We'll go back to the funicular," she told him. "We can talk there."

Charlie inserted two 50 kopeck pieces into the slot of the turnstile, and the doors swung open on an empty car.

"The FBI agent put cuffs on me in my room, and called his office in Washington to see what he was supposed to do with me. They didn't know either, but told him they would get back to him. We waited in the room for hours. The air-conditioning had stopped, and it was hot as hell. Later that night, someone called back and told him that they would let him know in the morning. They couldn't find anyone to make a decision. I was CIA, and the FBI and the CIA never got along so they didn't want to be anymore helpful than they had to be. At the same time, if they were going to turn me over they wanted to be sure that the Bureau got all the credit."

The cable car started up the incline, while Karen continued her tale. "I finally asked him if I could take a shower, and he agreed. The idiot! After I showered, I came out in just a pair of panties, holding my brassiere. You should have seen him. His eyes bugged out like he had never seen a woman before."

"I can believe it," Charlie admitted grudgingly. He had been trying to picture Karen in his mind as she faced the young FBI agent. She was still amply proportioned, and he wondered how he would have reacted given the same set of circumstances.

"Well, I gave him my most engaging smile, and asked him if he could help me with the snaps. He laid down his gun, and I chopped him in the neck like we were taught. The poor kid went out like the proverbial light. I could have killed him if I had wanted to. When we were in training at The Farm we learned how to slit a man's throat with just two credit cards held together, and I had plenty of those. But, I just got dressed and was out there as fast as I could before he woke up. Of course I tied him up so he couldn't follow me for awhile."

"I heard you also took his clothes and left him tied up in only his underwear."

"Well I guess you're right, I had forgotten that. I wanted to slow him down a bit. "He looked pretty funny," she giggled.

"What did you do then?" Charlie asked, now thoroughly engrossed in her story.

"I did what everyone else does when they're trying to get lost. I rented a car and drove south of the border. I had a college chum living in Mexico City, and I bunked with her until I could figure out what to do. My parents came from Poland. I speak Russian and Polish so I decided to try and get there. I got a visa from the Polish consulate in Mexico, and when I got to Warsaw Marvin contacted me."

The lights were beginning to come on in the city below them.

"I don't know how he found me but he did. He wanted me to come to Kiev. He was working for Kuchma's government selling leftover Russian military equipment to anyone he could. He had the Peruvian money in a Swiss bank account, and his pension. He didn't need the money, but he was bitter. He wanted to get even with the CIA and the U.S., and this was his way of doing it.

"He got me a job with Kuchma as a political advisor, helping him run his guy's campaign. I majored in poly sci in college and I know the right words. So that's what I have been doing. It was strange depending on the man that framed me but you know-any port in a storm-that type of thing."

"I have to ask you Karen. You're living with Marvin are you sleeping with him?" Charlie inquired sheepishly looking out the window to conceal his embarrassment.

The cable car came to a stop and the doors opened. The two got out and they stood waiting together to see if anyone would exit any of the cars behind them. No one did. There were benches at the funicular station and they sat to finish their conversation. To the casual passer-by they might have been taken for a pair of middle aged lovers deeply engrossed in each other.

"No Charlie I'm not! Absolutely I am not! I can't stomach what he's doing or what he has done for that matter, but I have nowhere else to go.

"But Charlie, you have to get in touch with Emmett and let him know what is going on here. He has to stop it. He'll listen to you. But first, let me tell you exactly what Marvin is doing."

204

A cable car pulled to a stop at the station platform The two were so absorbed in their conversation they barely noticed a large contingent of young people in orange tee shirts passing them on their way to the evening demonstrations.

Karen related how Marvin, since coming to Ukraine, had become the oligarch of Red army surplus. He successfully sold Russian-made Tupelo aircraft to the Colombian drug cartel, and had recently closed a deal for Ukrainian made Kolchuga radar systems to the Iraqi's. Ukraine had even opened an embassy in Baghdad, and there had been discussion between the two countries on the purchase of airplanes, ships, and missiles.

"Now that Iraq was taken out of play by the Americans," Karen continued "Marvin is negotiating the biggest deal of his career. It involves the sale of 18 Kh55 cruise missiles to Iran. That was why he had the blueprints and operating manuals in his apartment," she explained.

"The pressure is on him to close the deal quickly," she added breathlessly, "because he is afraid the Iraq war will cut off the flow of material through Syria to Iran. If the sale goes through, and the missiles are shipped it will be terrible for the U.S., and even more disastrous for Israel.

"It gets even worse Charlie. Marvin told me one night when he was more drunk than usual that the next thing on his agenda is …." Karen stopped talking as another cable car disgorged its orange clad occupants.

Each of the students carried bulky rolled up mattresses preparing for a long stay. One of them-a young woman-dropped her mattress and watched helplessly as it rolled from the platform and landed on the funicular tracks. One of her companions quickly jumped down to retrieve it before it became caught in the cable. The group cheered enthusiastically as he returned the errant bedding to its attractive blond owner. She smiled her appreciation, and the group continued on its way.

"How could it get any worse Karen? Charlie prompted.

"Poison gas Charlie. Marvin has access to the Central Sanitary and Epidemiological Station. That's Ukraine's equivalent to our own center for Disease Control. Only this place is filled with deadly pathogens like anthrax, diphtheria, and cholera, which were developed under the Russians.

"The Soviets didn't want such toxic material on their soil so they developed it here. Senator Lugar has been negotiating with the Ukrainian authorities for years to dispose of these things, but so far no agreement has been signed. In the meantime the toxins are held in a rickety old building near Kiev that anyone could easily break into. Marvin is working with some of the chemists who are desperate to make a few bucks. As soon as he sells the missiles to Iran, he plans to begin work on selling them the pathogens.

'It's important to him that he gets his hands on them as quickly as possible, before a new government comes in and decides to participate with the United States on its Cooperative Threat Reduction Program. Ukraine is one of the few holdouts. Even Azerbaijan has agreed to participate. But before he can work on that deal, he has to close with Iran on the missiles."

"You're right Karen, it could be worse," he conceded. "And probably will be unless he's stopped."

It was a shocking story, but Charlie had no reason to doubt her. She didn't seem to have anything to gain in lying. In fact, she was obviously putting herself at considerable risk by confiding in him.

Before they parted, Charlie and Karen worked out a way that they could communicate with each other. Charlie began walking away, then paused. "Karen" he called to his departing friend. She turned toward him, her figure partly obscured by the lengthening shadows

"Yes Charlie — what?"

"Karen, what happened to Zhang Zheng? Did you give him up? Why would anyone want to harm such an innocent guy?"

"You have to believe me Charlie. It was Marvin. I never learned about it until I got here. Marvin had decided to peddle his talents to the Chinese. Anyplace that he could make a buck. So in order to provide them with something that would convince them of his value to them he had to dangle a token of his sincerity--so to speak. That's the way the game is played. So Marvin gave them Zhang's name as an agent working for us. And I guess you know the rest.

"The hell of it was Charlie, nothing came of it. Only that Zhang got burned."

That night Charlie slept fitfully. At one time he woke crying Zhang Zheng's name. It was no denying the obvious. It was his fault for trusting Marvin in the first place. If he had been less gullible, his Chinese friend would still be alive.

Early the next morning, Charlie turned up at the American Embassy where he asked the Marine guard for the commercial attaché. This time the only available magazine in the waiting room described the value that Kansas grain provided to the developing world. Not much of a chance selling that concept to Russia's breadbasket he thought.

"Mr. Connelly,"

Charlie looked up to see "Twin Peaks" approaching in a very tight black dress, pearls, and high heeled pumps. "Staff party," she explained as they walked down the dark hallway to the Commercial Office.

"Last night or tonight?" he inquired with feigned innocence.

"Naughty—naughty Mr. Connelly," she laughed shaking a well-manicured finger at him.

Barry Durand motioned Charlie to take a seat, while he finished his telephone call to Washington.

"Well Connelly, how was life in a closed city? Were you greeted warmly? Did they embrace all your ground breaking recommendations?" he chuckled.

Charlie tried to find a comfortable position in a too small government chair. He wanted to get Durand's cooperation in contacting the Agency, but first he had to provide a description of life in Ivano Frankivsk, and the people he had met. He went into particular detail about the Mideasterners visiting the plant, and their interest in Karpaty's radar equipment. While he talked, Eve St. Ives brought in a carafe of coffee, and Durand fished in his desk for clean cups. Both men paused briefly in their conversation to gaze appreciatively at the secretary's exit.

After the door closed, Charlie leaned conspiratorially towards the commercial attaché's desk. "Look Barry," he began. I need a little help."

Barry straightened his bow tie nervously. That kind of opening always meant trouble. He wasn't to be disappointed.

"You know Barry," Charlie began again. "I sometimes have done some part time work for the people at Langley. Purely in an advisory capacity you understand. Well you see—I need to get hold of some people there right away. Do you understand what I'm saying?"

Durand nodded unconvincingly.

"I don't know who the company man is here at the embassy, but I am reasonably sure that you do. I have a number I am going to give you that I want someone here to call on a secured line and get in touch with a man called the Maestro. Tell him Pinstripes has found the Machinist and wants to talk about it. I'll be back tomorrow to discuss it with him."

Barry fidgeted behind his desk while he wrote down the words Maestro, Pinstripes, Machinist. He didn't want to get involved, but he couldn't risk turning down the man's request. Best, he decided to pass the information on and let someone else reach a decision.

"This is pretty confidential stuff," Charlie told him, drumming his pen on the desk for emphasis. "Can you handle it for me?"

Durand looked at his guest in a new light. He really hadn't expected this. Not from a guy who looked every inch the retired businessman. He had known some spooks before, but they didn't look quite like this one.

"I guess I can," he half-heartedly assured him.

"No guessing my friend. You have to be certain. This is serious stuff we are dealing with. It's life and death and all that old crap. Now let's try the question again. Can you handle this for me Barry?" Charlie asked trying to assert some authority that he didn't have.

"I can handle it Mr. Connelly," Durand replied, with more certainty.

"See you tomorrow, I can find my way back. Thanks for the help" Charlie called cheerfully, as he went out the door.

After he left, the commercial attaché nervously flipped a switch on his desk. "Eve, get me Sullivan," he whispered. "Quickly!"

Fifteen:
Dome of Silence

The trolley was almost empty. The decrepit old car usually would be packed at this time of day, but the continuing demonstrations were making the residents of Kiev nervous. The Ukrainian Supreme Court had set a new date for a rerun of the elections, and the demonstrators were continuing to keep up the pressure until they occurred.

Another newspaper editor had been found dead under mysterious circumstances. No mention was ever made of the death of Viktor Ivanov and the destruction of his newspaper office. It was as if they all had disappeared in a puff of smoke; and it would most likely be the same for the latest casualty.

The government also had taken no action to find and prosecute the people responsible for the beheading of Gongadze. Yushchenko, the favorite of the Orange Revolution, had vowed to Gongadze's wife Myroslava that he would seek justice for the murder, if elected.

The lack of street traffic was taking its toll on the sidewalk vendors who were reduced to spending most of their time gossiping among themselves. The economy was slowly improving, but they still had to work at their stands to make ends meet, and the lack of business was cutting into their meager income.

Charlie jumped off the trolley a block after it passed the American Embassy, then waited to see if anyone else got off at the same time. It was doubtful that he was being followed, but there was no harm in making sure. The only other person getting off was an old pensioner, with a string of faded military medals pinned to his tattered lapel. He paused briefly to get his bearings and, after brushing his hand briefly across his forehead, began walking unsteadily in the opposite direction.

Once inside the Embassy he was recognized by the Marine sergeant from his previous visits, but still had to show his passport. "I think I am expected," he told the Marine, and took a chair in the waiting area. He had just begun to leaf through today's supply of Department of Commerce brochures when his name was called. Looking up, Charlie saw a slender middle aged man approaching, walking on the balls of his feet like an athlete, but with a noticeable limp.

"Kevin Sullivan," the man said. You can call me Sully, everyone does. I'm the Agency's station chief here. Durand gave me your message," he told Charlie as they walked down the dim hallway. Stopping in front of an almost concealed elevator, Sullivan punched in a three-digit code, and slid his card through a reader. The elevator rose quickly to the second floor. Once inside his small office the embassy official lowered himself gingerly into an old swivel chair behind a cluttered desk.

"Yesterday, Durand gave me your message, and I sent it off to Langley on a one-time pad," he told Charlie gesturing toward the only other chair in the room.

"One time what?" Charlie inquired, moving the chair closer to the desk as he studied Sullivan.

"Well I guess there is no problem telling you how they work," Sullivan told him leaning across the desk in a manner that implied he was sharing very confidential information. "They operate on the mathematical principal of matching sets of random numbers *once* between the sender and the receiver in small groups in a coded message…"

"Never mind," Charlie interrupted. "I'm sure that it is a very secure process."

"No--no really it's very interesting," Sullivan assured him, obviously pleased he could describe the complicated process. "Once the groups are in the message," he repeated, "they can then be translated into words by referring to a non reusable key. "But they can only be used once. That's the secret of them, and of course the reason they are called one-time pads," he concluded staring at Charlie for a sign of understanding and appreciation. Seeing only a blank stare he went on undeterred. "The message went out immediately after I coded it to the Maestro so that he was the only one who could decipher it. He'll be calling us soon," he advised distractedly searching through his desk drawers.

"I can never find anything," he complained.

While he searched, Charlie more closely studied the man seated across from him. He had a powerful build in spite of his slender frame. His head was shaved so close that it glistened in the reflected fluorescent light above his desk. An old scar ran across his forehead and down his cheek, past his cold gray eyes, and stopping at the man's bushy gray mustache. He was older than he had first thought, Charlie decided. The lack of any eyebrows, combined with the large mustache gave his face a somewhat macbre appearance.

"How do you know the Maestro?" he asked while he continued searching. Unwanted documents fell to the floor. "Are you with the Circus?"

"Nope," Charlie replied. "When I traveled I used to do a few favors for them from time to time."

"You're NOC?

"Operating under non official cover—no nothing so fancy," he replied laughing at the station chief's question. "I'm not a regular, just a volunteer. Over the years, banging around on the international circuit, I have run into some of

212

your guys masquerading as businessmen, or as you say an NOC but they never seemed to stand up under scrutiny.

"The last one I met was in a hotel bar in Arequipa, Peru. I had traveled there with our local licensee who wanted me to see the plant he was building in a new tax-free development zone. I was waiting for him to come down for dinner, and cursing myself for being on time. He was a true South American—always late, and I should have known better than to show up on time.

"While I was nursing my Pisco Sour, a group of young Americans began filing in and filling up the available tables. It was pretty extraordinary to see so many gringos in such an out of the way place in the mountains of Peru. I got to talking to one of the Americans who told me he was with the Helicopter Division of Boeing, and they were there to sell their choppers to the Peruvian Army based on the edge of town. The Army officers wanted to get hold of the Boeing equipment because it was the only type that could carry heavy armament in the thin air at high altitudes. The Peruvians thought that was what they needed to fight the Sendora Luminosa forces hiding in the nearby mountains.

"I ran into him again, several months later, in Montevideo, Uruguay. He was a nice guy, but I had worked at Boeing, and he was definitely not their type. That's what convinced me he was a spook.

"That's why the Maestro likes to use me occasionally. No one ever doubts that I am anything other than a legitimate businessman."

"Where the hell did I put that god-damned file?" Sullivan cursed under his breath, searching through another drawer while only half listening to his visitor.

"What you need is a secretary like Durand's," Charlie suggested.

"Twin Peaks?" he snorted. "What did Durand tell you about her?"

"He told me..."

"That she was dumb as a rock, and the Civil Service made him take her," Sullivan completed the sentence for him.

Charlie shrugged his agreement. "Something like that."

"Durand doesn't know it, but I'm the Civil Service, or at least I had them assign her here. Among other things, I'm responsible for Embassy security and counter-espionage, and I asked Washington to send her. There are people that draw an inverse relationship between breasts and brains. The bigger the boobs the smaller the intellect, they think. I'm not one of them. St. Ives is very bright, and most people don't know that she speaks fluent Russian. She can mingle with the local staff without them ever knowing that she understands what she hears. On top of it, she's so good looking no one believes she can think.

"It's a given, that some of the foreign nationals working here are with the KGB, or the SVR, or whatever the hell they're calling themselves these days. For all we know some of our own people could be moles — weasels are what I call them. In this job ya gotta be a professional paranoid, and I'm perfect for the job.

"Just yesterday, the Ambassador got a new pair of shoes sent from the States. I checked the box after they got here. Whatta ya know, someone had put a bug in one of the heels," he chuckled wryly. "Ya win some and ya lose some. Problem is, sometimes you don't know which is which."

He looked at his watch. "We gotta go."

Crossing the hall, he unlocked the door to a small closet filled with brooms, pails, and assorted housekeeping equipment.

214

"You also do clean-up?" Charlie asked.

"I guess you could say that," Sullivan replied while jerking on a dangling light cord. He paused briefly, and gave the cord two more quick jerks. The back wall slid open, and almost immediately began to close again. Sullivan quickly wedged his body between the wall and the closing door to let Charlie slip past him into the darkened room. "This is our DOS—Dome of Silence," Sullivan said proudly flipping a concealed light switch and quickly stroking a plastic card through a reader on the wall. "I had fifteen seconds to do that before an alarm goes off and the broom closet is filled with security people.

"After we moved into the Embassy we brought over a bunch of Navy Seabees under the cover of being a college glee club from the University of Nebraska. We told everyone they were here on a cultural exchange program. Some of them would tour the area while the others worked on setting this place up so that we could communicate without being overheard. Fortunately, nobody ever asked the boys to sing, and after a month they went back to regular duty with the fleet."

Sullivan took a chair in the center of the tiny room, beside a large communications switchboard. Motioning to Charlie to sit in the only other chair, he flipped a switch on the console, and checked his watch.

Charlie looked around him. The walls looked like they were built of heavy steel sheeting, and were painted a dull battleship gray. Suddenly he looked down as he felt jets of air going up his pants leg.

"Oxygen," Sullivan explained as a large plastic dome descended from the ceiling, completely covering the two men. All of our equipment is cushioned and covered to mute any noise that might be coming from them. They call it a *white sound system* because it masks the incoming and outgoing voices."

A muffled ring startled both men. "It's only our call coming through," Sullivan laughed, while flipping a switch on the small communications console. Immediately afterwards, Charlie heard the familiar voice of the Maestro above the barely perceptible purr of the ubiquitous scrambler.

"Ah my dear Pinstripes, how nice to hear from you again. It seems that you have located our Marvin Brady, after all this time, and he has been up to some mischief I understand. Tell me about him."

Charlie described, as briefly as he could, how he discovered Marvin entertaining a group of Arabs at the Dnipro hotel. Then how he followed him home and later discovered he was dealing missiles to the Iranians. While he talked, he decided to not tell Emmett that he had also found Karen. That could come later.

"So he is peddling Kh55's to our friends in Iran is he?" The old man's voice sounded strained but resolute. We trained him in missile technology and now he is betraying us. How sad. And you think that pathogens may be next. This can't be allowed to happen. He has to be stopped, and Charlie I want you to do it. I want Marvin *clipped,* as your friends in Chicago say."

"Not me," Charlie complained. "I've never done anything like that. I wouldn't know where to start. Let some of your people do it. They do it all the time."

"He's never done wetwork Maestro," Sullivan interjected. "We can find someone here to take care of it."

"We can't risk it Colonel," Emmett's voice faded out and then grew stronger. The crumpet-crunchers at Foggy Bottom would have a fit if they found out that we were in anyway interfering in an election in Ukraine. You know as well as I do that State is calling the shots—at least for the moment--and they think they have it wired there. Still, we can't afford to have rogue nations wandering around selling maverick weapons. The next thing you know the CIA will get the blame.

"Charlie, unfortunately you are our only bet. I don't like it any more than you do, but we can't let Iran get hold of those missiles. They could use them on our troops in Iraq or to eradicate Israel. To say nothing about what they could do if they got hold of Ukraine's supply of poison gas.

"You're a little green I will admit, but the Colonel will help you. Let's face it, if you are caught, or fail to do what you have to do, it will still be hard to trace you back to us. The Global Bank may have a little problem, but not us, and that is essential."

"Fill him in Colonel, I have to go now. Good work Charlie, and keep your head down."

There was a click on the other end of the line, and both men knew their conversation with the Maestro was finished.

Sully threw a switch, and the dome withdrew to the ceiling as quietly as it had descended.

Charlie Connelly, the retired businessman, sat in dazed silence. He had never expected this.

"Let's go," Sullivan ordered firmly. "Sitting here won't solve the problem. We gotta saddle up cowboy."

Back in the station chief's office Charlie still had not regained his composure. "Clipped" — "wetwork," what the hell had he got himself into. All he had wanted to do was alert Emmett so he could handle it. No way was he going to get more involved.

"I think you need to shake hands with my old friend Jack Black," Sully suggested reaching into a desk drawer and withdrawing a half-filled bottle of Jack Daniel's Black Label.

"Did you recognize the music that was playing in the background? Sullivan asked, as he poured himself a drink and waved the bottle at Charlie. "No huh, I didn't either. One time I was talking to the Maestro and he was playing Wagner's Ride of the Valkyries so loud that I couldn't hear what he was saying. After he hung-up I decided he did it intentionally, so I would go ahead and do what I wanted to do without implicating him.

"What kind of music do you like?" he asked Charlie while pouring himself another shot.

"Oh big band, I guess," Charlie offered without much thought. He was still dwelling on what he had just been asked to do.

"You're a damned dinosaur Connelly," Sullivan grinned affably, putting his friend Jack Black back in the drawer.

"Perhaps I am--what kind of music do you prefer Sully?"

"Oh country-western I guess," Sullivan replied.

" I see—so that makes you a Renaissance man I suppose," Charlie laughed.

They were both amused at their own humor, and with each other.

"Sully, when we were talking to the Maestro, he referred to you as Colonel Sullivan. Are you in the military?"

"No—not anymore. I used to be. Emmett and I were in Nam together. I headed up a Green Beret unit, and he was running spooks for the CIA. He was like a goddamned ghost. No one knew where he was, or what he was doing. The Viet Cong couldn't find him, and Washington never knew where he was either. Maybe they didn't want to know. But, Emmett got the job done, and that's all that matters. We were both the same in that regard, and occasionally we would work together when our area of operations overlapped.

"I had a little bad luck," Sully rubbed his finger along his scar-line as he spoke. "I got de-commissioned like an old battleship. Emmett heard about it, and the next thing I knew I was at Langley working for the Agency.

"Eventually I ended up here as station chief. I have sweepers that regularly check the Embassy for bugs. I try and make sure that the nationals we hire aren't working for the Ukies, but I'm never sure. I also check on our own people to try and prevent leaks. Maybe you remember the Marine in Moscow who was sleeping with a Russian agent and told her everything he knew that was going on. Well—I try to prevent that from happening here."

The phone rang, and Sullivan fumbled for the receiver. "Yes Mr. Ambassador, I'll take care of it. I'll get someone over there today." Turning to Charlie once again, he grinned. "And I almost forgot, I also make sure that there are no bugs in the Ambassador's home. I had it swept yesterday when he was out, but I didn't tell him. I'll just have it done again, and then he'll feel better."

"Look Charlie," he squinted across the desk. "I am personally embarrassed that the Maestro has to give you this job. I should be taking care of it, but my cover was blown the day I got here. I just know that it was. It's the same everywhere, but it's even worse here because State won't permit any of our people getting involved in anything approaching these elections. They're afraid that if it's ever found-out that we're meddling it will ruin our relations with Moscow. Can you believe it? We're worried now what the frigging Kremlin thinks. So now I have to spend most of my time sitting in my office waiting for some government official to walk in and volunteer to provide us with information.

While he talked, Sullivan would occasionally, and apparently unconsciously, run his hand over his shiny bald head as if he was running his fingers through a thick growth of hair that was no longer there and now only a memory.

"It's a whole new world for all of us. We're traveling through uncharted waters, and we have lost our compass. Now the CIA has become the CYA organization " he continued ruefully. "When the Agency needs risk takers we're getting bureaucrats at a time when the world is filled with rogue nations buying and selling maverick weapons. Thank God there are still enough of us that believe strongly in what we're doing, and are still willing to take risks to prevent the unthinkable from happening."

Sullivan's office was small and lead sheathed for security. Even though it was cold outside it was warm in the room and stuffy. But, perhaps it was the topics of discussion that made both men sweat.

"I know that you don't want to get involved Charlie, and I can't blame you, but you have to understand what we're dealing with here." Sullivan opened the file that he was searching for before they went into the DOS. "The Kh55 has a range of 1860 miles, which is enough to hit our troops in Iraq, or our friends in Israel. Its 27 feet long, and has a wingspan over 10 feet. It travels at a speed of Mach 0.48 to Mach 0.77, and according to the people at Global Security that compiled these figures, it carries a thermonuclear warhead of 200 kilotons.

"To the best of our knowledge, which has proven to be less than sterling I admit, Iran doesn't operate long-range bombers, but we think that Tehran could adapt its Soviet-built Su-24 strike aircraft to launch the missiles. We believe that the mad mullahs are also making a substantial investment in ballistic missile technology, which contradicts their proclaimed interest in peaceful nuclear energy. Recently they have test fired a bunch of Shahab-2's and Shahab-3's with an approximate ranges of up to 1200 miles. Before that they just had the unreliable Katyushas.

Now if they get hold of the Kh55's it changes the entire geopolitical situation in the Mideast, and they know it has to be done before Kuchma loses control. To make the situation more critical, Marvin knows if he is going to make a deal he has to do it before that happens.

That's why there isn't enough time to bring in the reserves and getting them up to speed. I can't get involved so you're all we got.

"So what are you going to do Charlie?" Sullivan asked pointedly.

"I don't know Sully. I just don't know. Look I'll get back to you."

"Today?"

"Yeah—yeah today."

Charlie walked aimlessly. The street was filled with unemployed workers, who had been either laid off or their factories had nothing for them to do; so they were spending their afternoons walking as aimlessly as he was. He stopped at a food stand for something to eat. The babushka's wrinkled face beamed when he held out a handful of hryvnias for her to take what she needed. She withdrew two bills, and in return handed him two buns wrapped carefully in pages of an old newspaper. *Pirozhkis* she grinned, as he looked at them suspiciously. One had a meat filling he found, while the other was stuffed with a highly seasoned cabbage. He ate them as he walked. And thought.

He wondered how the hell he had got into this. It wasn't supposed to be this way. Now he found himself involved with international arms dealers, and he was in a center of a circle of betrayal. Marvin had betrayed Karen, and the CIA. Karen was betraying Marvin, and Charlie had betrayed Emmett by not telling him that he had also found Karen. One thing he was certain of, and that was that Marvin had to be stopped. But how, and by whom?

Kiev is an ancient city that just grew through the ages without the benefit of any form of central planning. The streets resemble a crazy quilt of intersecting angles wandering through the city without a recognizable pattern. In other words it fit Charlie's mood perfectly.

After some time, he found himself in front of the Chernobyl Museum. Inside there were photographs of the devastated area alongside graphs of the resulting radiation and contamination that occurred when reactor number 4 blew. There was also a room containing pictures and identity cards of the people who had died as a result of the explosion. On a far wall there were frightening photos of the deformities in animals and humans the accident caused. Over the doorway was a sign in bold letters saying "Never Again."

After leaving the museum, Charlie found himself at the city's old funicular. He fished into his pocket for a 50-kopeck coin, which he slipped into the rusty slot and climbed aboard a vacant car. As he rode he looked down on the city below. The tranquil scene was in marked contrast to the pictures he had just seen.

As he rode, he wondered what the ethical and moral consequences were of what he had been asked to do. Surely Marvin had to be stopped from selling the missiles to the Iranians, but did the end justify the means? If they didn't, what were the consequences of inaction? If you agree to work in intelligence, and your life is based on deception, can you deceive ethically?

The cable car ride finished sooner than he would have liked, and before he had arrived at an acceptable answer, but he had reached his decision and knew what he must do and how it could be done.

A single taxi was waiting at the station. The driver immediately pulled alongside the curb while quickly reaching back to open the door for the welcome customer. "American Embassy" Charlie ordered curtly, before settling back on the worn plastic seat.

As the cab pulled away from the curb the engine coughed and died. The driver cursed under his breath and ground the starter before the old engine leapt back to life and the taxi headed in the right direction.

For the second time that day Charlie approached the Marine sergeant. "Connelly for Sullivan," he told him sliding his passport over the tile counter. The sergeant smiled and slid it back, then pressed a key on his communications console. The station chief appeared in the hallway almost immediately, motioning Charlie to follow him.

Back in his office, Sullivan looked quizzically at the man facing him across the desk. "Well?" he asked.

"Does your DOS operate this late in the day?" Charlie inquired noncommittally.

"Depends on where you want to call," Sullivan replied. "Let's find out."

This time Charlie dodged through the sliding door without Sullivan having to hold it for him. The station chief quickly followed him. Once inside the secure room the dome began its silent decent while Charlie fished the address book he always carried from his suitcoat pocket. After quickly paging through the alphabetical list of names he gave Sullivan the telephone number he wanted to call.

A few moments later he heard, "Shalom--Aaron Greenfield here."

It had been several years since they last met in Tel Aviv, and after bringing each other up to date on their families and mutual friends Charlie asked Aaron, "Do you remember the night you introduced me to the man with the eye patch?"

Aaron confirmed that he did, as a matter of fact he recalled it clearly.

Charlie proceeded to tell him he had become aware that a man he once knew was now working for the Ukrainian government and was involved in selling cruise missiles to the Iranians. He added he thought that if the sale went through there would be dreadful consequences for both the United States and Israel. Aaron understood the urgency of the situation and the potential consequences. The two men had known each other long enough to be able to talk together while leaving many things unsaid.

"I'll see that our friend gets this information right away," he told Charlie, then he asked how he could be reached with his answer.

After the call to Tel Aviv was completed they returned to Sully's office. "Look," Sullivan told Charlie as he settled into his chair and shifted his position to better accommodate his aching leg, "there are a few things I can do to help you, but there is a lot that I can't, unless you're really in a jam. Then call me immediately.

"When you leave here I'll assign one of my men to make a surveillance detection run on you. He'll be on your tail to see if you're followed. If you aren't, you won't hear from me. If you are, someone will get in touch with you. In this case, no news is good news."

Sullivan adjusted his position once more, appearing ill at ease. It had been a long day. His leg ached, and he was angry that he couldn't get more involved. "Another thing," he continued more sharply than he intended, "tomorrow I'll send some of my sweepers to your place to make sure that no one has planted bugs there. It's not uncommon for them to plant listening devices in the living quarters of our people, and probably in the apartments of some of the NGOs like GBC."

"And one more thing," he added pointedly. "I don't think it's a good idea for you to come here anymore. I don't know what you're going to do, and I guess I don't want to, but the less connection you have to the embassy the better it will be for both of us. But..." he flipped a switch on his desk, "St. Ives can I see you for a few minutes."

After entering Sully's office, Eve smiled at Charlie and positioned herself on the edge of the desk. Both men watched as her short tight skirt crept up her long legs, while she maintained the casual nonchalance of an attractive woman, used to being stared at by men.

Sullivan got up from behind his desk. As the day had progressed his scar had become more evident; turning from pale pink to red, and by now it was a bright crimson. "It turns out Eve that old Charlie here is a friend of a friend of ours, and may need our help. I've given him your phone number at our funny farm, and at your apartment. If he wants to contact me, or needs our help he'll contact you, and you're to do whatever's needed."

"OK Sully," Eve smiled, "whatever is needed. I understand."

"If he is able to do what he has been asked to do he may have a little problem getting out of here without attracting too much attention."

Charlie was shocked to hear what Sullivan was saying. He had not thought the problem through enough to be concerned about how he could get out of Ukraine. Sullivan obviously had. That's probably the difference between an amateur and a professional he decided.

Sullivan returned to his chair and moved it to the side of the desk where he could sit and face his audience. Pointing his finger at Eve he continued, "You need to begin thinking about what he might need for him, and whoever may be with him, to get out of here quickly and quietly. But above all, safely and secretly.

"Yes sir, Colonel Sir," Eve grinned impishly, making a mock salute.

Sullivan ignored Eve's sarcasm. "We need an extraction plan. That's what we used for our agents in Nam when their job was finished and their cover was blown. They'll have watchers at the airport and train station, and we need to figure out how to get him out without them seeing him. Our boy here will let you know when things will be coming down, but you should be thinking about what type of an extraction process will be the most effective. If things go sideways on him he may have to leave damn fast. *Comprende' amiga?*"

"Si Senior," I understand. I'll think of something," she acknowledged, languidly sliding to her feet.

Charlie liked her confidence, and hoped profoundly that it wasn't misplaced.

Leaving the embassy, he wondered if he was being followed. He paused occasionally and glanced at anything that might reflect an image. Once he even ducked into a store and spent a few minutes looking at the belts and wallets that were displayed behind the counter. He left again as quickly as he had entered, but he couldn't identify anyone that might have been waiting for him.

He decided to have dinner before going back to his apartment, and hailed a passing taxi. "Sam's Steakhouse," he told the driver who flashed a broad grin of acknowledgement. The old auto lurched from the curb in a cloud of blue smoke, and swerved dangerously into an open path in the evening traffic. As the driver passed the golden domes of St. Sophia he blessed himself and turned to wink at his passenger.

The bar at Sam's was filled, and the dining room crowded. The restaurant was a favorite of American's assigned to Kiev who longed for a taste of home. Pictures of American cities hung on the wall and American music played in the background. A small table in a corner of the dining room opened up, and Charlie wedged himself through the crowd to get to it before another customer could. Once he was safely seated he turned to look around the room.

Sam's customers were internationally eclectic. There were Russian oligarchs and blackmarketeers, accompanied by flashy female companions. Their black Mercedes' and bulky drivers were left idling at the curb. Their white-linen tables were loaded with bottles of vodka and champagne scattered among the now empty plates, which were liberally littered with smashed cigarette butts.

European businessmen were drinking French wine to wash down their thick hamburgers. At a nearby table an attractive Ukrainian woman in a low-cut peasant blouse and tight jeans was finishing her meal with a huge chocolate sundae. Her American boyfriend had ordered bourbon and branch water for his dessert.

After finishing a watery martini, Charlie ate his overcooked filet and thought about Beth and his family. An old Glen Miller record played in the background. He seemed to be the only person eating alone. A lump began to rise in his throat. Suddenly he felt he was smothering in the smoky atmosphere of the restaurant. He hurriedly paid his check and stumbled through the crowded room to the anonymous refuge of the descending night.

Sixteen:
The Man from Mossad

It was raining again in Kiev. In Charlie's Midwest, fall is a transitional season filled with football games and vivid colors. In Ukraine it was the season for demonstrations and preparation for a bitter winter ahead. The political protests had intensified, and most of the government buildings and their respective agencies closed until the new election was over. Never the less, life went on and people still hurried along the slick sidewalks, attempting to avoid the chilly drizzle while continuing their daily routine.

Connelly turned away from the apartment's grimy window and returned to work. It was slow going. It was difficult to concentrate on what he was doing. Every few minutes his mind would wander to Marvin and the missiles. He could still remember when they had first met, and how impressed he was with the man. Time brings change to all of us he thought, but the change in Marvin had been extraordinary. At one time he had been a war hero dedicated to his country and to the CIA. Now his only allegiance was to himself and to amassing a fortune as quickly as he could, regardless of what the consequences might be.

Returning to the kitchen, he heard a loud knock on the door. "Who's there?" he asked tentatively, and was relieved to hear an answering "Global Bank Corp." Slitting the door slightly, he peered into the hallway and saw two well-dressed young men wearing business suits and ties, carrying large black briefcases. Once inside the apartment, the taller of the two explained in a loud voice that they were sent by GBC to inspect the premises for any repairs that were needed before the next occupant was assigned.

Setting down his briefcase, the other man handed Charlie a note on an Embassy letterhead, with the words "Sullivan's sweepers" scrawled across it in pencil. He smiled, and put a finger to his lips while making a circular motion above his head with his other hand. It was the same gesture the Apex men had used on their trip to Tianjin when they had wanted to alert others their hotel room might be bugged.

"Take your time," Charlie said loudly as the men quickly unpacked a variety of electronic devices, and mysterious gauges. Afterwards they carefully spread their equipment in a row on the carpeted floor.

Tuning the radio to a local station to muffle their conversation, the men quickly went to work adjusting their dials, then passing their electronic wands with triangulated antennas back and forth over the telephone, television, radio, light fixtures, and plumbing outlets in each room of the small apartment.

The taller of the two men searched through his tools until he found a telescoped extender that he quickly attached to the handle of his wand. Once it was securely in place, he began running the wand along the molding in the living room, and then repeated the routine in each of the adjoining rooms. While he was doing this, the other sweeper concentrated on the kitchen; first checking the refrigerator, and then the stove, and eventually passing the wand over each small appliance looking for any concealed devices.

After the electronic phase of their search was completed, the men methodically began to look behind, under, or overturn, each item of furniture to see if a listening device was installed in a way that would possibly mask its signal from detection by their electronic surveillance equipment.

The two sweepers worked quietly and efficiently with minimum communication between each other. They soon finished their search and began replacing each item of furniture to its original position. "Your place is in good shape," the taller of the two reassured Charlie with a broad wink before carefully returning the electronic equipment to its proper role in his briefcase. After they finished packing their devices, the two snapped the locks on their briefcases with a click of finality. "I'll tell the Bank they don't have any problems here," the tall man promised. "They'll be glad to hear they don't have to do nothin' to fix up the place for the new occupants. They hate to spend money, as you probably already know," he observed caustically, keeping up the verbal charade.

"Glad to hear it--give them my regards," Charlie called as they went out the door and down the hallway to the stairwell.

That evening Charlie had returned from dinner and was preparing for bed when a light tapping on his door startled him. He quickly turned out the light so he wouldn't be outlined in its glare, then cautiously slipped the chain and cracked the door only to stare in astonishment at a tall powerfully built black man outlined in the dim hallway light.

"Shalom. The one-eyed man said you needed to see me," he offered cheerfully.

"But—but—you don't look....", Charlie sputtered.

"Jewish?" the man finished his sentence for him. "I know, but, believe me I am," he laughed congenially. "Can I come in?"

Blushing with embarrassment, Charlie stood aside to let his visitor pass. Once inside the apartment, the man removed his wet slicker, letting it drop nonchalantly on the worn carpet. Quickly moving to the window, he peered carefully through the rain soaked pane. Apparently satisfied he turned, "I'm sorry to shock you, but our mutual friend said you needed help, and needed it quickly. He and I have known each other for a long time and he thought that, under the circumstances, I would be the best man for the job." His eyes darted around the room, as he placed one hand over his ear while waving the other in a circular motion.

"It's clean," Charlie assured him. "It was swept this morning. But I don't understand, I never knew there were black Jews in Israel."

"Not many people do. Even those who have lived there for years are surprised to hear we exist. Very few had ever heard about us until Whitney Houston came to Israel-- to bond with her people she told the press. That's just our luck. The Kabbalahists get Madonna, and all we get is Whitney Houston and her husband floating over the countryside," he chuckled, shaking his gray head in mock dismay.

"Let me give you a little background on us since you seem so surprised to see me," Ben offered straddling a kitchen chair. "Most people call us the Black Hebrews. It is our belief that we are directly descended from the ten lost tribes of Israel who were expelled from Jerusalem by the Romans in 70 AD. They say our ancestors migrated for over 1000 years before reaching West Africa, and then later on to the United States as slaves. Eventually we were able to get back to Israel, and now there are more than 2500 of us living in a kibbutz near the desert town of Dimona. For a long time, the Israeli Government didn't want to recognize us as Jewish citizens, but that's gradually changing."

As he talked, Ben kept adjusting the steel rimmed bifocals on his slender nose, while Charlie leaned forward to better hear the soft-spoken black man. Outside, the rain had increased to a downpour and was steadily beating against the apartment window.

Charlie went to the refrigerator and removed a half-full bottle of vodka. Ben waved it away. "Don't drink," he grinned "but I may have to if I want to blend in here."

Charlie poured himself a glass. "No problem with me on that score," he assured him, "but how the hell did you end up with the Mossad?"

"I didn't say that I was with the Mossad — but I am. Some time ago, as part of the Israeli Government's liberalization process we were allowed to serve in the Army. I was pretty strong, and quick too, and I ended up in a Jewish Commando unit that was part of the raid on Entebbe."

"Yeah I remember that," Charlie told him. "I was doing a lot of traveling then, and when they hijacked an Air France flight and took it to Uganda it really caught my attention."

"Then you'll remember," Ben continued pressing his glasses further up on his nose, "the hijackers demanded the release of 50 militants held in jails around the world, as well as in Israel. It was an impossible request. No one can give in to terrorists and survive for very long. When they didn't get the response they wanted they released most of the passengers but hung on to only those who were Jewish — about 100 of them.

"After alerting his local press, old Idi Amin came to the airport to make speeches, and to provide the hijackers with extra troops and more weapons. He demanded that Israel release all their prisoners or the hijackers would kill the Jewish passengers."

Ben paused a moment and rose to peer out the window once again. Standing in the shadows, he put a finger on the pane and absently followed a trickle of moisture till it finally reached the bottom sill. Assured that no one was watching from the street he returned to the table. "I needed to stretch," he explained in response to Charlie's quizzical stare. "The damn dampness always makes me stiff," he added lamely.

"Well," he continued "they loaded 250 of us commandos onto three Hercules transport planes for a 2500 mile trip from a secret base in Israel to Uganda. We got there in the middle of the night, and took them by surprise. We stormed the airport building and the hijacked plane, and ended up killing all of the hijackers and 20 Ugandan military men. As long as we were there, we also blew up 11 of their MIG fighters for the hell of it, and that pretty much destroyed their Air Force.

"We lost our commander, but we completed our mission and rescued all of the hostages.

"I guess someone liked how I performed, because a little while after that I was asked to join the Mossad, and I've been part of the Special Operations Division ever since. Now I'm *alt* and ready for retirement. Each time I go out on a job I think it will be my last one, but when they ask me again I always go. My boss understood that this job involved undercover work that couldn't be traced back to either your country or mine. He thought that I would be perfect for the assignment, so here I am.

"Now tell me about yourself Mr. Connelly."

"Call me Charlie, and I agree with your boss. You should fit into this situation very nicely. Every one involved is over-due for retirement."

"OK Charlie then, the man with the eye patch told me that you were a corporate guy who once did a favor for some friends of his in Tel Aviv. What brought someone like you to this dingy apartment in Kiev, trying to stop missile sales to Iran?"

"That's a good question Ben," he replied thoughtfully as if he had been wondering that himself. "It all began when I was at the university." Charlie related how, after his initial contact with the CIA, he was later re-contacted while working in the private sector. He described how he agreed to help the Agency, but with each of their requests he was asked to take a more active role, and eventually was drawn more deeply into the Agency's bureaucratic intrigue.

Charlie paused momentarily to gather his thoughts before plowing forward, and recounting his experiences in China, and how Marvin had later burned his friend by turning him over to the communist government just to gain favor. He heatedly related how Marvin sold him—and the CIA—out in Lima in order to get his hands on the cash that was intended for a dissident group fighting the Sendora Luminosa; and afterwards took the money and disappeared.

For Charlie it was like reliving his experiences over again. For Ben it was an opportunity to study the man's expressions to determine if he was providing a plausible explanation for the sequence of events; as well as gaining a better understanding of why his boss in Tel Aviv assigned him to help. It wasn't that he lacked confidence in his people at the Mossad, but he had lived long enough in the shadow world to know that things are rarely what they seem to be on the surface. After all, he was going to be the man on the spot in Ukraine, and he had learned long ago to trust no one.

Charlie confided that after he retired, he thought all of his espionage activity was behind him until he accidentally ran across Marvin in Kiev and later learned that the former spy had now become an international arms dealer.

As the two men talked, the small-screen black and white television in the living room flickered and faded in reaction to the storm outside, casting erratic shadows on the anxious American and the black Hebrew agent in the adjoining room.

"So then," Charlie continued, "my contact at Langley explained that Marvin had to be stopped. He had to be *clipped* I was told. And, because of the current political situation here, I would have to take care of it myself." Charlie paused, and then added in a hushed voice, "that was when I decided to contact your people in Tel Aviv for help."

Ben Silver cleared his throat and stared at the man across the table from him. He thoughtfully cleaned his glasses with the tail of his tie as he considered what he had just learned. "Well you did the right thing," he began. "Of course you realize that bringing a person gradually into covert service, as you just described, is a typical method all intelligence agencies use to recruit people who might otherwise be reluctant to get involved."

From the perplexed expression on Charlie's face, Ben realized immediately that the tall American seated across from him had never considered that his participation might have been more choreographed than he had first thought.

"I really don't think that was the case," Charlie replied with conviction.

Ben shrugged and continued, "Your man at Langley was certainly right about one thing. Your friend Marvin definitely has to be stopped. As soon as possible!" he exclaimed slapping the table with the palm of his hand. He then continued more calmly, "the Iranians have a visceral hatred of Israel, and the Untied States because of your unyielding support of my country. If the Iranians get their hands on those Russian missiles, and combine them with an atomic warhead, they could wipe Israel off the map. They could also use them to blackmail the United States, and the rest of the non-Islamic world into doing whatever they want without ever firing a shot.

"I can also sympathize with your Agency people. The Mossad is acutely aware that any intelligence organization sometimes has to govern its actions not only on what they think is the best thing to do, but what the government will permit them to do. We have had our own problems with that issue, just as the CIA has.

"Now the problem is—how do we get to Marvin?" he asked leaning forward, "and can we do it without the Ukrainians knowing who did it."

Charlie stood and began pacing back and forth in the small kitchen. Glancing out the window he noticed that the rain had stopped and a slender moon was trying to shine through the rapidly thinning clouds. He had to decide how much he should confide in the man from the Mossad. "I have a friend here," he told him speaking as he thought, "Whom I have known for some time. She works for the Ukrainian Government, and can help us get to Marvin," he explained before describing how Karen had a job as a political advisor and was familiar with Marvin's schedule.

He decided it was better not to tell Ben that she was also wanted in the U.S. by the FBI, and was presently living in the same apartment as Marvin. He had learned from working with the Agency that it was better to reveal only as much as you had to, and only when you had to, and that was exactly what he decided to do.

"We can meet with her here tomorrow afternoon" Charlie suggested. "Do you have a place to stay?"

When Ben learned he was coming to Kiev he had contacted a local group that had been keeping the Mossad informed of Russian's activity in Ukraine. After the massacre at Babyn Yar, the Jewish population of Kiev had sadly learned they had to constantly be aware of the prevailing political climate if they were to continue living in safety.

Because the Kremlin continued to wield an influence on the local Government, even after independence, the local Jews were worried they might eventually have to flee to Israel. They were more than happy to provide a member of the Mossad with whatever support he might need during his stay.

236

After agreeing to meet the next day, Ben went to the window and waved. In the street below, a driver hidden in the shadows flicked his car lights on, then quickly off, in apparent response. Ben Silver left the apartment as quietly as he had come.

After his visitor left, Charlie went to his phone and dialed the number Karen had given him at their last meeting. According to her instructions, he let the phone only ring twice before hanging up. He waited two minutes before he called again. This time the phone on the other end of the line rang once before he hung up. It was a standard routine for contacting another agent and he recognized that if Marvin was in the apartment he might recognize the calls as tradecraft rather than coincidence. When they had discussed this, Karen assured him that Marvin usually spent his nights at the bars, and if he happened to be home he would probably be too drunk to think anything about it.

He waited by his phone for a confirming call. It came exactly at the end of thirty minutes — ringing twice and then going dead.

Karen had told him that the simplest tradecraft was often the best. After a call from him she was to come to his apartment at two o'clock in the afternoon the following day. If the window shade was drawn to the three-quarter point it would be safe for her to come in. If it was pulled all the way down it would signify a "wave-off," and they would try again the next day. This was the same set of signals he and Ben Silver had agreed on before he left.

Karen's pleasant scent mingled with the musty odor that normally filled the apartment; while she, the man from the Mossad, and Charlie huddled together over the small kitchen table. A single naked bulb, hanging precariously from the soiled ceiling, cast a pale yellow light over the odd group, as Karen began to describe what was happening inside the embattled Ukrainian Government.

"The Kuchma people are getting desperate," she told them nervously after meeting Ben. "Now that a new election has been called they believe there is a good chance they will lose. I see them huddled together with the KGB men trying to figure how to nullify Yuchenko and the demonstrators. They don't take me into their confidence any longer—I've really got to get out of here," she added with undisguised concern.

"They have given up on the normal methods of campaigning, and now only rely on issuing *temniks*. That's what they call secret orders they give to the journalists telling them what to say on the air, or in print," Karen explained turning to Ben. "I believe they're going to resort to some type of violence. I really think they are going to do something desperate to get rid of Yuchenko before the election takes place. They have been reluctant to try anything in the past, but the way things are now--all bets are off.

"Yesterday, I heard they were bringing in a specialist from Moscow. I think he's a chemist, so they may be trying to poison someone in the Yuchenko group before the election." She looked around the table to see if they fully understood how serious things had become. "They will stop at nothing!" she added with finality.

"You don't think you may be getting a little paranoid, do you Karen?" Charlie asked.

"Perhaps a little. God knows I have been through enough to make anyone paranoid, but not about this," she countered, rubbing her temples as she spoke. "The CIA has known for a long time that the KGB has been using exotic poisons to get rid of their enemies. They work with the "Kamera," which is part of an old Cheka organization that, ever since Lenin's time has been housed in their top-secret

"Laboratory Number 12". That's where they specialize in developing biological and chemical agents that can kill quickly, while at the same time producing symptoms that will baffle their local doctors and eliminate the possibility of tracing it back to the KGB.

"The people at the Agency believe that Trotsky's secretary Wolfgang Salus was done away with that way, and just recently the Chechen rebel Khattab was poisoned in an identical manner. I'm sure that the specialist they brought in is from the Kamera, and his target is very likely Yuchenko."

"What about Marvin?" Charlie asked. "How is he taking all of this?

"He's frantic," Karen replied, shaking her head. "The technicians have been ordered to begin preparing the missiles for shipment, and the crates have already been camouflaged so they can't be detected on the rail cars that will transport them to the sea. Marvin is already packed and plans to accompany the shipment to Tehran so he can teach them how the missiles are used.

"He has to close the deal with the Iranians next week, or they'll leave Kiev and try someplace else for missile technology. He told me they are driving him crazy. The Ukrainians want more money, and they want it immediately. The Iranians on the other hand are master bargainers and want more technical support and better payment terms."

"I can sympathize with your Marvin," Ben told her. The Persian's principal method of bargaining is delay. They'll delay till you get desperate to close the deal and eventually agree to give them anything they want. Israel has had considerable experience with them, and we know you can't give in or they'll walk away from the table with your head in their satchel."

"Marvin understands that Ben," Karen assured him. "He's taken all the prints and manuals up to his dacha to prepare for one last session. He has to close the deal in two days or everything goes down the drain."

Karen took a piece of paper from her purse, and began drawing a rough map of the road into the exclusionary zone.

"He thought that he was getting a wonderful perk when the government people gave him his own dacha," she told them as she continued to draw. "Turns out it was in the dead zone--close to Chernobyl, and no one else wanted it," she laughed sardonically.

Frustrated, Karen wadded up the paper, and dropped it on the floor. "I was never very good at art," she blushed and began again.

"He doesn't care. He says that he has enough alcohol in him to protect him from any pansy-ass radiation," she related mimicking Marvin's gruff voice. "He may very well be right," she continued more seriously. "He's drinking more than ever now. He hates himself for what he's doing, but his desire for revenge against the Agency exceeds his self-loathing. He anesthetizes his conscience with vodka, but his drinking will give us a better chance to take him out before he can close a deal with the Islamists."

"Will he be alone, or will he have other people with him?" Ben asked studying the map.

"Alone. He says that's the beauty of his place. No one else wants to be there, but don't ever underestimate him. He's an expert in all kinds of combat, and everything he has is riding on closing this deal," she told them tapping her pen on the table for emphasis. "He knows more ways to kill a person than you can imagine. If he thinks that you are interfering with the missile sales he will take you out in an instant---drunk or sober."

The three plotters pored over the makeshift map, and finally developed a plan. Ben could get a car from his people, and early the next day he and Charlie would drive to the dacha. The two of them would first try to convince Marvin that he should leave Ukraine, and give up on the sale of the Kh55's. If that didn't work they would have to do what the Maestro wanted. They would take him out and destroy the documents. When it was over, all three of them, Karen, Ben, and Charlie would get the hell out of Dodge, as fast and as secretively as they could.

When his visitors left, Charlie picked-up the crumpled paper that contained Karen's first attempt at drawing the route to Marvin's dacha. Then he went into the bathroom and tore it into small pieces before flushing them down the toilet.

Afterwards, he picked up the phone and dialed the number that Colonel Sullivan had given him. "Hi Eve," he said in his most seductive voice. "Look baby, my job here is finishing up and I sure would like a chance to see you before I go."

It had been a long time since he had asked anyone for a date and he had almost forgotten how it was done, but he thought his awkward approach would at least convince anyone listening on the line.

Eve St. Ives immediately understood what was happening. She had been working on an extraction plan and now knew that she would need to have something ready very quickly.

"Why Charlie—you old fox. Sure I'd like to see you," Eve chuckled, picking up the theme. "This is a pretty boring job in a boring town and I could use a little diversion. How about us meeting tonight at the *Za Dvoma Zaytsamy*? The taxi driver will know where it is."

"Za Dvoma what?" Charlie sputtered.

"*Zaytsamy*—oh never mind, if he speaks English tell the driver to take you to *Chasing Two Hares*," Eve translated impatiently. The name comes from a Ukrainian proverb that say's *if you chase two hares, you will lose them both*. It may be a good lesson for us," she giggled, then added as an afterthought "of course they have rabbit on the menu."

The doorman was dressed as a Cossack, and the interior was replete with old movie posters—as well as being desirably dark. Eve was dressed more demurely than usual, with her highly noticeable charms hidden underneath a heavy peasant sweater. The mournful strains of the *bandura*, strummed by a young woman in a bright peasant costume, floated through the smoky restaurant, all but ignored by the noisy diners. It was just the type of atmosphere where two Americans could meet unnoticed by the other customers.

"I like to come here," Eve commented as they sat down, "to get in touch with my Ukrainian roots. My family came from a farming community near Lviv. They fled Ukraine, many years ago, because of the famine.

"Have you ever heard of the famine Charlie?" Eve asked distractedly gazing around the crowd for any potential threat.

He shrugged, and she continued her story. "I'm not surprised—not many people have. The potato famine in Ireland is widely known, but Stalin managed to keep a tight lid on what was going on in Ukraine. In a land that was once called the breadbasket of Europe, over ten million people starved to death in the early 1930's. The irony of it was that they died surrounded by fields of wheat, and tons of food in locked government warehouses. Old *Uncle Joe* wanted to collectivize the people's farms and figured that the best way of doing it was to starve the peasants off their land.

"Most of the world's press ignored the plight of the Ukrainians, and either swept the evidence under the rug or denied it ever existed. A New York Times reporter even won a Pulitzer for soft peddling the story," she added bitterly.

Charlie watched her closely as she spoke emotionally about the tragedy. Her voice was so low that it was difficult to hear above the noisy crowd. "My family made it to the United States, and settled in Brighton Beach along with other Russian expatriates. They worked hard and became reasonably successful. I graduated from NYU at the height of the Cold War. The CIA recruited me because I could speak Russian--and my profound hatred of Communism," she whispered vehemently.

"When I was in training at The Farm, I met Colonel Sullivan who was an instructor there. When he eventually was posted to Kiev he remembered me, and here I am. End of story," She finished sheepishly before adding, "He wanted me because he believed I could easily pass as a Ukrainian."

"Not as easily as you may think," Charlie told her. I'm just an amateur at this, but I could immediately tell you were not originally from here."

"How in the world could you do that?" she asked him thinking it was a joke.

"No joke," he told her seriously. "It's your teeth."

"My teeth are perfect," she snapped

"Exactly, Eve. They are perfect. Look around you. All of the Ukrainian women have a jaw full of gold teeth—either out of necessity or design."

Eve studied the tall blond woman drinking vodka at the next table. Each time she smiled at her companion she unintentionally exhibited a dazzling array of gold inlays.

"You know you're right. Maybe you're not such an amateur after all Charlie Connelly."

"I'm learning. Now tell me how you plan to get us out of here. We need to leave tomorrow night. There will be three of us, a black Israeli—don't ask," he cut her off before she could form the question, "and a woman friend of mine from who has been helping me here."

"Hey Charlie—you are a sly fox after all," Eve giggled with renewed respect, wagging a well-manicured finger in his face.

She understood that it wasn't her place to inquire too deeply into the plan, or for that matter, the plan's participants. If Charlie wanted to take a woman with him that wasn't her concern. Sullivan asked her to come up with an extrication plan and that was what she was doing.

"Once Kuchma's people learn that you have put a hit on Marvin, and the arms deal can't go through they going to put a lid on this town like you can't believe," Eve told him over coffee. The airport and the train depot are both small and they can easily zip them up so tightly that no one can move. So you can't even try to get out that way."

"Then how the hell will we get out," Charlie exclaimed more loudly than he intended. "If we stick around here it won't take long for them to figure out what happened, and we will be rounded up in less than a day."

"Yes, you are right there," Eve assured him, her eyes flashing. Brushing aside the crumbs of her Kievsky Tort she leaned across the table conspiratorially and whispered, "you'll get out all right. All of you. Don't worry about that. Meet me at the funicular station at five o'clock tomorrow night. If you are there it will be a piece of cake. If you're not, I'll say a prayer for your souls."

"I like your confidence Eve," Charlie told her as they were leaving. See you tomorrow… I hope."

After returning to the embassy, Eve continued working on the final details of her plan. It was late, and none of the other staffers were around. There were a few more calls to make, and Sullivan's office was a good place to do it. She had hoped to have more time to assemble her alternatives and print their travel documents, but Charlie had told her tomorrow night, and tomorrow night it would have to be. He also told her that he liked her confidence. She hoped his faith in her wasn't misplaced.

Back in his apartment, Charlie sat on the edge of his bed and tiredly rubbed his eyes. It had been a long day, and he didn't know what would happen tomorrow—but he was certain that it would be worse. There was so much depending on how it would come out, and he worried if he would be up to what he and Ben would have to do.

He rose stiffly, and walked on his bare feet across the cold floor to the refrigerator. It wasn't hard to find his remaining bottle of vodka. It was the only thing in there. He had to get up early for the drive to Marvin's dacha, and he wanted to be sure to get some sleep. He took the bottle with him back to the bed, turning off the lights on his way.

Seventeen:
Devil's Playground

A glimmer of dawn sliced the eastern sky, casting a pale light on the nearly empty streets. The city of Kiev had completed its seasonal transformation from vibrant green to somber gray. The tree-lined avenues were now devoid of leaves, and the remaining bare branches were starkly outlined in the colorless early morning sky.

Ben Silver's people had provided an ancient red Moskva automobile that Charlie drove while Ben studied the map of the exclusionary zone Karen had drawn for them the night before. A large X indicated where Marvin's dacha was located, tucked away in a secluded portion on the far edge of the contaminated area.

The sidewalk vendors were rolling back the canvas tarps on their small stalls, in preparation for their early morning customers. The beer trucks, with their large tanks and small individual spigots, had not yet seen fit to begin dispensing their sudsy beverage to passing drinkers.

On the Maydan, some of the student demonstrators could be seen emerging from their tents and rolling up their mattresses; while others were busy unfurling their orange banners in preparation for the day's speeches. The bright colors of their streamers were in marked contrast to the sunless winter sky. It was apparently too early for the black-coated KGB "watchers" to assume their daily vigil on the park's periphery

Traffic thinned as the Moskva reached the outskirts of the city. Even with fewer cars it was apparent the Ukrainian drivers were quickly adopting the European style of relying more heavily on their horns than their brakes, maneuvering for an improved position among the steady flow of old autos.

In spite of the cold air seeping through the Russian-made car's ill fitting frame Charlie's palms, tightly gripping the steering wheel, remained damp and he grew more nervous each time he glanced at the battered leather bag tucked unobtrusively between Ben's feet.

Once outside the city, they began to pass through a series of small villages with neat wooden houses. Every modest home had its own window box and well-tended garden. In each town, all of the houses were painted the same color, depending on which shade was being produced in the paint factory when their particular village's order was ultimately processed. As a result, the two travelers first passed through a white town, which was a few miles away from the brown town, before reaching a tiny hamlet composed entirely of green colored houses.

While Charlie drove, Ben dozed peacefully. His gray head bobbed in rhythm with the swaying auto. He had fallen asleep almost as soon as he had got in the car. Automobiles did that to him. As he slept he dreamed of the citrus groves outside of Netanya, where he hoped to buy some land when he eventually retired from the Mossad.

Charlie marveled at his passenger's ability to relax in spite of what lay ahead of them. His own thoughts were filled with Beth and the children. It had been a long time since he had called them, and he was sure they were wondering when he would return home. He didn't know himself so he hadn't called. It seemed better to avoid the question than to attempt to provide an answer that was untrue.

He also wondered what was going to happen to Karen. It was obvious that the Ukrainian Security Service would immediately pick her up for questioning after Marvin had been taken care of. He knew that she would refuse to provide the kind of answers they would demand, and it wasn't hard to imagine what they would do to her.

She must leave with him and Ben, but where could she go? He might be able to convince the Maestro and the Agency people that it was Marvin not Karen who had betrayed them, but he could never convince the FBI that she was innocent. Particularly after Karen had tied-up one of their agents, and embarrassed the entire Federal Bureau with her escape. They would be relentless in tracking her down once there was even a faint whiff of her being in the United States.

There were too many questions and too few answers that gray morning. There was a more immediate problem, however, and that was eliminating Marvin and stopping the sale of the missiles.

Eventually the two men drove through the deserted streets of Pripyat, which was once a thriving city inhabited by families of workers at Chernobyl. Now, there were only ghostly rows of white and pastel apartment-blocks with their charred windows resting on rotted frames; their few surviving occupants long ago moved to areas with a more benign environment.

Outside of the abandoned city, the kaleidoscopic imagery continued as the two men passed through an area that the remaining peasants cynically referred to as the Red Forest. Following the Chernobyl explosion, a drifting radioactive cloud killed a large swath of tall pine trees turning their formerly green needles into an eerie shade of red. The dead trees were surrounded by new growth, but the lingering radioactivity had shaped them into grotesque patterns of permanently deformed life.

Occasionally, the two men sighted packs of wild wolves that were slowly reclaiming the deserted forests. Once a large flock of low flying black storks soared over the old car. "A bad omen," Ben observed ominously.

They had little to say to each other as they drove, thinking about what might lie ahead of them. Their immediate surroundings gave grim evidence of the potential consequences of their possible failure.

At one point in their apocalyptic journey, Ben reached into his bag and withdrew a small envelope and a bottle of Moldavian brandy. "The Rabbi that loaned me the car told me there were two antidotes for radiation. He said one of them is brandy, and the other is iodine tablets." Charlie looked at him to see if he was serious, then took a deep swallow from the opened bottle. Ben did the same and, wiping his mouth with the back of his hand, muttered something about "medicinal purposes only," before returning the bottle and unopened envelope of pills to his black leather bag.

By now, the asphalt road had turned into a narrow rutted dirt path. Even here, however, the two men occasionally saw a few old peasants who had returned to reclaim their former homes in decaying villages. Either because of their age or their health, they were unable to take adequate care of their cottages. The paint was faded and peeling while the doors and shutters hung at odd angles on their loose hinges providing a macabre appearance to the crumbling communities.

Snow was beginning to fall as they passed a rusting graveyard of old trucks and helicopters once in fighting Chernobyl's fires. The white mantle on their corroded iron frames gave the discarded vehicles a ghost-like appearance. This place is *khitsoynim* Ben observed grimly as they passed the last truck partially covered in its white shroud.

"What?" Charlie grunted as he attempted to keep the car from falling into a deep rut.

"This whole damned area is haunted," Ben told him turning away from the window. "It's filled with demons and evil spirits--*khitsoynim* we call them in Yiddish. No wonder the peasants call it the devil's playground."

Passing through the deserted village of Opachichi they were startled to see a tall man dressed in gray corduroy trousers wearing a red plaid lumberjack shirt underneath and old bomber jacket, striding alongside the road intently studying a device that was hung on a large leather strap around his neck.

"Geiger counter," Ben guessed.

Looking in his rearview mirror after they passed, Charlie saw the man give a friendly wave. It was the English academic whom he had met in the airport when he first arrived in Kiev.

"We should be getting close," Ben finally told Charlie as he put away the map and reached once again into the bag between his feet. "They gave me a Glock 23," he said proudly, slamming a 15 unit clip into the gun's butt and working the action to put a .40 caliber shell in the chamber. This model was made originally for the Austrian Army, but now even your FBI is using it. They said it has a hair trigger and no safety so I have to be a little careful not to spray my shots." He stroked the blue-steel barrel with the affection that men have for their weapons when they are used to depending on them for their own survival.

" I got a 9mm Beretta for you, it's a little lighter, but it has less recoil and it's just as accurate," Ben assured him placing the smaller gun on the seat between them.

Charlie's face turned ashen as he glanced at the lethal looking weapon he was supposed to use, and then quickly returned his attention to steering the car over the narrow dirt path.

Ben, on the other hand, again removed the clip from his gun to make sure that it was full, before professionally palming the magazine back into the handle. Afterwards, he searched in his bag once more for two extra clips, putting one in his pant's pocket and stuffing the other in the pocket of his borrowed parka.

"I'll check the Beretta for you," he offered with a grim smile on his wrinkled face as he effortlessly removed the pistol's clip and replaced it in the gun's handle with a jarring click. "You can never be too well prepared," he commented absently, replacing the gun on the seat between them.

Charlie grudgingly conceded he had a point. Without Ben he would have been poorly prepared to confront Marvin.

"Slow down," Ben cautioned, nudging him in the ribs. "According to the map Marvin's dacha is just past this grove of birches." As they rounded the curve they could see a lone cabin at the foot of a hill almost hidden by a dense grove of trees.

Charlie pulled the car to the side of the road, while Ben once again checked the action on his Glock. They could barely see the nose of Marvin's black Zill, parked behind the small house, partially obscured by the falling snow.

"It will be hard for him to see us from the inside," Ben told him. "I'll go in while you keep the motor running. If you see anyone else coming, honk the horn. If you hear shots, come on in firing. If not, be ready to get the hell out of here as quickly as we can. We can't tell if there are other people in there with him--or nearby-- so we have to be very careful," Ben warned as he got out of the car.

Charlie watched as the Israeli zigzagged through the birch trees. His ebony features and dark clothing weren't the most effective camouflage among the stark white trunks and fallen snow, but he managed to get to the dacha without being seen. After peering through the window to assure himself that no one else was there, Ben put his shoulder to the doorway and shoved it open before quickly disappearing inside.

Charlie held the Beretta tightly in his hand, and watched intently through the grimy windshield to see any signs of activity that would require him to move. His nervous breathing had calmed as he became caught up in the necessities of the moment. His only thought now was following Ben's instructions and getting to him if he was needed.

The wintry silence was suddenly shattered by a jarring exchange of shots coming from the dacha. Immediately afterwards, Marvin emerged through the small doorway running toward the Zill, and firing blindly behind him. As Charlie watched, he saw Ben emerge aiming his pistol at Marvin while groping desperately for the extra clip in his coat pocket.

Charlie stuffed the gun into his pocket, then threw the old car into gear and stomped on the gas pedal. He was filled with a seething rage watching Ben crumple to the ground.

Marvin saw the car for the first time as the Moskva lurched forward. As the car hurtled toward him, Marvin spread his legs slightly apart to steady his aim and, holding the gun tightly in both hands, began firing rapidly at the approaching vehicle. A bullet impacted the side of the car with a frightening thud, quickly followed by another that pierced the windshield by Charlie's head. It was the last shot Marvin was able to get off.

The car sped forward and Marvin stared in horror, until he was violently thrown into the air landing spread-eagled across the Moskva's hood. His sightless eyes stared through the windshield as Charlie stomped on the brake. Once the car skidded to a stop, Marvin's body slid slowly to the ground, and Charlie began to breathe again.

Getting out of the car, he looked down impassively at Marvin's lifeless body. The head rested grotesquely on the shoulder and his eyes stared blindly at the gray winter sky. Ejected cartridge casings littered the snow nearby.

Ben was searching for his glasses and trying to rise to his knees as Charlie ran toward him. Once on his feet he pressed a handkerchief to his bleeding shoulder, while Charlie helped him to the car. "Burn the prints," Ben whispered hoarsely in his ear. "He has them spread all over the dacha. Without Marvin, and without the documents, the Ku55 deal is dead."

"What happened in there?" Charlie asked helping Ben lay down on the back seat

"Tell you later," he wheezed. "Take the brandy. Light a fire, then let's get out here before someone comes, or we get snowed in."

Charlie covered Ben with his duffel-coat before leaving the car. He had started the engine to try to get some warmth, but the ancient heater was not up to the task.

Once inside the dacha, he was astonished at the number of prints and operating manuals that Marvin had scattered around the sparsely furnished room. In order to more effectively bargain with the Iranians, he had apparently assembled every piece of documentation that even remotely related to the missiles.

Charlie hurriedly poured the brandy on the largest piles, after attempting to spread them out as much as possible. There were some old stick matches by the wood stove that, when ignited and combined with the liquor, provided an effective accelerant to the stacks of blueprints. The fire was spreading quickly through the cabin as Charlie returned to the car and his wounded friend.

He trembled violently as he drove. Without his coat he was colder than before, and his nerves were beginning to kick in so that it took all the control he could muster to keep the ancient auto from sliding off the rutted road.

It was hard to realize that he had just killed someone — and intentionally at that. It was even more difficult to comprehend that the person he had killed was Marvin-- the man who had recruited him so many years before. It made no difference to him now that it had to be done — or that Marvin would have most assuredly killed him if he hadn't first hit him with the car. His mind filled with wildly racing thoughts, and his body racked by conflicting emotions as he headed the car back toward Kiev.

From the rearview mirror he could begin to see a thin plume of white smoke rising above the top of the spindly birch trees. He knew that it meant the end of the dacha, and Marvin, and the pending deal with the Islamists.

In the back seat Ben drifted in and out of consciousness. "Take me to my people" he moaned at one point. "They'll take care of me."

As they drew closer to the city, Ben grew gradually stronger and was eventually able to tell Charlie what had happened when he first burst into the dacha. It seems that Marvin had been concentrating on arranging his documents and was shocked at the unexpected intrusion. Before a word was said, he had grabbed the gun lying on his desk, and immediately began wildly blasting away.

Ben dove for cover and returned the fire as he was rolling over. At that point, Marvin dashed outside with Ben following close behind. In the doorway he lost his footing in the new snow, and as he attempted to regain his balance and take aim, he was knocked to the ground by a slug tearing into his shoulder. Before Marvin could fire-off another round he saw the Moskva bearing down on him, and decided it presented the greater threat — "until he was spread across its hood," Ben chortled grimly before fading out of consciousness once again.

Charlie pulled the car into a slot in front of the Podil Synagogue, which was the address Ben had given him. Before he could get out of the car, it was surrounded by six tall men with faces framed in dangling black ringlets, and dressed entirely in black from the top of their flat hats to the bottoms of their ankle-length coats. "We'll take him," the youngest of the group told Charlie, gently helping Ben out of the back seat.

"Fix him good," Charlie told him. "We have to leave soon."

Shouldering him aside, a young Hasidic told him brusquely, "He'll be ready, we've done this before."

Charlie was glad that no one asked about the dented hood or the flecks of blood on the front bumper of the borrowed car. Ben could explain to his friends how that had happened he decided, hailing a taxi.

Eighteen:
Extraction Plan

After leaving Ben with his friends at the synagogue, Charlie stopped at his apartment to collect the bag and briefcase he packed the night before. He looked around the drab rooms one final time to make sure he hadn't left anything that was traceable to his work with the embassy. He grinned broadly as he carefully locked the door. It was like shutting off a brief phase of his life that he wasn't eager to repeat, and he was happy to be finally leaving Kiev.

His next stop was at the GBC offices to drop off the apartment key. Everyone had gone for the day and the office was locked. He slid the key through the letter drop in the center of the office door. It was fortunate that he could avoid answering any questions regarding the details of his report. He didn't have much time, and any discussion would be better left for Vienna. Assuming he was able to get there at all, he thought sardonically.

Going-home traffic was flooding the streets, and dusk was beginning to fall by the time he got to the funicular station. After paying the driver he looked cautiously along the station platform. At first it looked as if he was alone, but as he drew closer he saw the slim figure of Eve St. Ives standing with her back to him as she stared at the lights along the river bank below. She whirled defensively at the hollow sound of his footsteps echoing along the wooden platform. Recognizing that it was Charlie, her face broke into a broad smile. "I'm getting a little jumpy," she admitted sheepishly, "but I'm glad to see your safe. How did it go?"

"OK," he replied grimly. "We're alive—he isn't."

An empty cable car screeched to a jerking stop at the station's platform, and the automatic door glided open. "Let's get on," Eve suggested taking him by the arm. "We can talk without being overheard." As they entered a lone figure of a woman darted from the shadows of the dilapidated wooden shelter, joining them just before the door slid shut.

"I wanted to make sure you weren't being followed," she explained crisply.

"Karen Kincaid meet Eve St. Ives," Charlie grinned, as he introduced the two women while concealing his surprise. Karen was blond once again, reminding him more of the woman he used to know so very long ago. She was still strikingly attractive, with a few more lines accentuating her dark eyes than he had noticed in the pale light of his apartment, but they only made her appear more urbane. Karen was dressed for travel, wearing a dark blue trench coat over her black blazer and gray flannel slacks; the only thing she carried was a small brightly patterned travel satchel.

"Nice bag," Eve offered admiringly.

"It's a Ferragamo. The thing is too damned colorful, but it was all I had," Karen explained dismissively.

They appraised each other, the way beautiful woman invariably do. Someone who was unfamiliar with the two female spies could have easily mistaken them for sisters. They were close to the same height, and both had blond hair and dark brown eyes as evidence of their East European heritage. Karen was definitely older than Eve, but that's not necessarily uncommon for sisters.

Eve was curious who Charlie's attractive friend was, and how she fit into the picture. Outside of an expensive travel bag, it didn't appear that she had much in the way of possessions. From what little she had learned about Charlie, it didn't seem that he would be going to all this trouble just to take a girl friend with him, but she thought that this was not the time—nor the place to inquire. She would wait to discuss it with Sullivan when she got back to the Embassy she concluded, as she carefully committed Karen's features to her memory.

While the ancient funicular strained against its taut cable Charlie stared enviously at the peaceful panorama passing below him. The lights of the city were just beginning to come on, and from the tram's window he could see the five steeples of St. Andrews where he and Karen had met to discuss what was to be done with Marvin, such a very short time ago.

Both women were curious and becoming impatient to learn what had happened on his trip to the exclusion zone. Charlie reluctantly turned away from the window to fill them in as best he could. He could tell Karen more later, but for now he wanted Eve to know enough to assure Sullivan that the threat of Ukrainian missiles going to the Islamists was definitely over. If he wished, Sully then could use his beloved one-time pads to pass-on the encrypted information to the Maestro.

As he finished his story the cable car reached its destination, and its three passengers got off to a vacant platform. "Do you have an extraction plan for us?" Charlie asked Eve anxiously "Now that Marvin has been taken care of, how the hell are we going to get out of Kiev without being picked up?"

"We don't have much time," Karen warned. "Before I left, people around the government building were already wondering what had happened to Marvin. He told them he would return this afternoon to brief them for tomorrow morning's meeting with the Iranians. They've already sent a couple of their goons up to his dacha to see if they can find him."

"You're going to leave from down there," Eve pointed to the muddy Dnieper flowing below them. A light fog was rolling up the river, but they could still see several large boats tied along the bank. "I've booked a passage for the three of you on the MS General Valeriy. It's a tour boat that's leaving for Odessa tonight on its last cruise of the season.

"The boat has been booked by a group that handles alumni travel, and it will be filled with Americans from several different universities. Try to look happy and relaxed and you should all fit in without anyone questioning who you are or why you are there.

"It may be slower than a plane, but the best thing is," she added smugly, "the black coats will never think that you might be leaving on a river cruise. They'll all be too busy covering the obvious exits like the airport, highways, and train station to think about boats. When you arrive in Odessa you can figure out how to get to wherever you want to go next."

Charlie thought for a minute, and then faced Eve, "that's a hell of a good plan. It sounds like it might work."

"What about tickets and travel documents?" Karen asked, guardedly. "I can't use the passport I have. If I do, it will set off an alert all over Ukraine." And in the US she was about to add, but stopped herself in time.

"I've had the wizards at the Embassy working on that," Eve told her. "Sullivan was a big help. He's an expert at phony documents, and he was glad for a chance to use his skill again. He hates to be playing such a passive role.

"They fogged up one of my pictures for Karen's passport, and Ben's and Charlie's documents should still be good. Just in case, they made an extra Latvian passport for you Charlie. No one ever knows what a Latvian is supposed to look like anyway," she giggled, "so you should be safe. We didn't have time to establish a new "myth" for you so you'll just have to stick to the story that you're a traveling businessman. I guess that's really what you are, so it should work all right," she assured him confidently.

"After I had the documents, I had to call in some old markers with the booking agent for the cruise line to get all of you on board. She and my parents are from the same area around Lviv. Our mothers used to go to school together, and she was willing to help.

"Unfortunately, there are three people from the University of Minnesota that will have to miss their cruise....... Maybe I can fix another tour for them when I have more time," Eve added unconvincingly.

"Before I left the embassy I also checked with the listeners in the com-room. So far, they haven't noticed any increased "chatter" so it looks like no one has found your friend Marvin. So Far!" she added pointedly tapping Charlie on his chest.

"Sullivan also assured me that no one else at our Embassy even knows that you are here, so the geeks at State won't be able to connect you to Marvin's death — if they ever figure out that he's gone."

"You do good work Eve," Charlie complimented her. Twin Peaks indeed he thought fondly. She was a lot more than that. Her plan had taken considerable initiative to create--and work out. He never thought when he first met her in the Embassy lobby that one day his life might depend on her ingenuity.

She gave Charlie a hug, then stepped back and put her finger to his lips. "You're a good man Charlie Connelly," she told him affectionately, waving impatiently for a cab.

As the taxi pulled away from the tram station she leaned out the window, "take care you old fox. I'll tell Sullivan what happened. Have a good trip home."

"We have to pick up Ben," Charlie told Karen waving for another cab in the waiting queue.

"Podil Synagogue," he told the driver, while Karen looked at him inquiringly.

"Ben took a slug in the shoulder," he explained. "His people at the synagogue are fixing him up."

Apparently someone at the temple had been watching for his return. As soon as the cab pulled to the curb, two black-garbed Hassidics came through the large wooden doors, flanking Ben unsteadily between them. Before helping him into the back seat each hugged him, and patted him affectionately on the back. "Shalom" they called as the old taxi pulled from the curb. The taller of the two men smiled and yelled after them, "have a safe journey."

"From your lips to God's ear," Ben replied weakly resting his head against the back of the seat.

On the way to the river, Charlie explained to Ben the arrangements that Eve had made for them. The man was obviously in pain, but he listened intently. When Charlie finished, he nodded approvingly.

Karen began telling them what had happened to the opposition candidate while they were searching for Marvin. The night before, Viktor Yuchenko had become deathly ill and his wife rushed him to the hospital. She then stationed their bodyguards outside the hospital room. The rumor was that the Kuchma people had decided that they would not be able to defeat him in the polls, and had resorted to putting a form of dioxin in his food.

"I told you they had brought in a chemist from the Kremlin," she reminded them as they rode. "Apparently that is why they brought him here.

"If they would risk poisoning Yuchenko, you can imagine what they might do to us when they find Marvin," she warned. "They were desperate for the money they were going to receive from the missiles—they considered it to be their Swiss pension. Also, once the Iranians find out they've lost out on getting the prints and the manuals, the missiles won't be any help to them. At that point, they may take out after us to get even."

Nineteen:
Cruise to Odessa

The taxi pulled into the River Terminal, and dropped its passengers alongside the General Valeriy. They were relieved to see there were no signs of the Ukrainian Security Service checking the travelers going on-board. The three of them hurried to report-in with the dockside purser and, after showing their tickets and passports, they were assigned to their cabins. Their travel documents received only a cursory inspection. The boat staff assumed that they were merely some late arriving alumni whose presence would now allow the cruise to get underway on schedule. As soon as the late arrivals were on board the crew raised the gangplank and heaved off the heavy lines that held the old boat to the dock. The large diesel engine coughed, sputtered, and eventually chugged into life as the General Valeriy finally pulled away from its moorings on its journey down the Dnieper River to Odessa.

Charlie and Ben shared a cabin, while Karen stowed her belongings in an adjoining room. Before going to his cabin, Charlie turned to take a last look at the lights of Kiev that were rapidly dissolving into the thickening fog. It had been a relief to him that they had been able to get underway without incident. Walking to his room he felt as if the haze was forming a protective envelope around the old craft, shielding it from the chaos that had become Kiev. For the first time it seemed there was now a good chance they would get out of Ukraine safely.

Before independence, the MS General Valeriy had been operated by the Russian Intourist organization. The government tourist agency had used the excursion line to reward loyal members of the Russian *nomenklatura* or, when there were not enough of the party bosses available, the remaining cabins were given to loyal *apparatchiks* working for the myriad Ukrainian bureaucracies. Over years of indifferent neglect, the boat had fallen into a sad state of disrepair, but it recently had undergone a complete renovation in order to attract foreign tourists and their much-needed hard currency. The cabins were clean and comfortable and the boat provided its passengers with a pleasant, if not swift, passage to the Black Sea.

The Jewish doctor at the synagogue who had removed the bullet from Ben's shoulder had provided medication that helped ease the pain. Once he was able to lie down in the cabin the gentle movement of the boat lulled him into a fitful sleep.

Seeing that his partner was resting comfortably, Charlie began unpacking. He removed his pinstripe suits from his bag and carefully hung them in the cabin's small closet. As he picked up his duffel-coat from the chair, the Beretta fell from its pocket with an alarming thud on the newly carpeted floor. Ben stirred slightly at the sound, but didn't wake. Fortunately the gun's safety was still on.

Suddenly it occurred to Charlie that if he had wanted to use the gun on Marvin he would have never been able to fire it in time. The realization of how close he and Ben had actually come to failure — and possibly death caused him to blanch and break into a cold sweat.

Putting his concern aside he decided to return the 9mm to Ben when he woke, and stuffed it back into his coat pocket for the time being. Ben continued to sleep soundly. The medication, combined with the gentle undulation of the boat was proving to be a powerful sedative.

After he finished unpacking, Charlie decided to stroll around the boat. The walls of the cabin were thin, and earlier he could hear Karen stirring in her cabin getting settled for the trip. It was quiet in her room now, and he assumed she was resting. Anyway, it might not be such a good idea for them to be always seen together. If Kuchma's people were looking for anyone in connection with Marvin's death the chances were good that they would be searching for her.

The General Valeriy was a large craft—130 foot long with four decks, a barbershop, lounge, and a restaurant with a large stage for evening entertainment. Charlie ended up in the lounge where a "happy-hour" get together of the participating alumni groups was already in progress. The couples moved around the room in a display of collegial affability. They obviously had been looking forward to this excursion, and intended to take full advantage of every opportunity.

He elbowed his way through the milling crowd of name-plated passengers until he found an empty seat at the bar. "Bombay Martini if you please my friend," he ordered from the busy Filipino bartender in a stiffly starched white jacket. "Extra dry," he added as an afterthought. It had been a long time, in the land of vodka drinkers, since he had a chance to enjoy the pleasures of a good gin drink. The first sip scorched his throat. The second one went down more smoothly.

He turned on his barstool, scanning the crowd to see if there was anyone who might pose a potential threat. The only thing that he saw was a vast sea of blue blazers and bobbing gray heads connected to aging bodies swaying gently with the motion of the boat; while their individual owners mingled congenially with fellow tour travelers. The alumni had paid a considerable amount of money and they were eager to make new acquaintances. Charlie on the other hand, was just as interested in keeping his identity to himself. Introductions are invariably followed by questions and, he would have found it difficult to provide acceptable answers.

In the far corner of the lounge, a black piano player energetically worked on a medley of 40's tunes for the appreciation of the AARP oriented crowd. The nostalgic melodies floated above the room with the old-style grace of a beautiful woman gliding across a crowded dance floor.

On his way to the dining room Charlie paused to place a folded dollar bill in the empty glass sitting on the drink ringed top of the piano. The man smiled his appreciation while the plaintive strains of "Stardust" vainly competed with the cocktail-fueled conversations of the passengers.

The boat's buffet was filled with dishes from Ukraine, along with more traditional American dishes. The main courses were book-ended by a large cauldron of aromatic borscht, and on the other end with plates of caloric loaded cakes and pies. There would be plenty of roast beef and pork chops when he got home, so Charlie concentrated on the Ukrainian dishes he would probably never see again. He passed the chicken Kiev in favor of meat dumplings, then added a sampling of *holubtsi* with its stuffed cabbage leaves. He turned to leave the buffet, then returned to take a few of the meat filled ravioli's the Ukrainians called *plemeny*, topped-off with a small slice of smoked pork tenderloin, locally referred to as *balyk*. He grudgingly passed by the desserts, and took his plate to an empty table where he ate quickly. After finishing, he returned to the buffet, and filled another plate for Ben.

He wondered what food might not conform to his friend's religious beliefs, and decided that beef and potatoes must be universally acceptable—along with a couple of slices of great looking Ukrainian bread. Turning to leave, he almost bumped into a white-jacketed waiter carrying a large silver tray heading for the desert table.

"What are those funny looking things?" Charlie asked as the young man carefully positioned the tray where it would be most obvious to the diners.

"We call them *metiors*," he answered with a broad grin."
They're the chef's specialty. He makes them by combining
nuts and honey and then covers them with melted black
chocolate." After finishing his explanation, he glanced
around the dining room to make sure that none of the staff
were watching before slipping several of the sweets into his
jacket pocket.

It seemed like a good recommendation, and Charlie put
two candies on Ben's plate for dessert. If he can't eat any of
those, I'll take care of them myself, he decided.

The piano player interrupted his rendition of "Laura"
long enough to wave as Charlie squeezed through the
crowded lounge, precariously balancing the plate containing
Ben's dinner. Nearing the large wood-paneled doorway he
encountered an impromptu quartet of alums attempting a
boozy rendition of "The Sweetheart of Sigma Chi." He
passed unnoticed on his way back to the cabin.

The next morning broke clear and cold. After a good
meal and a nights sleep, Ben felt considerably better, and
was able to walk around the cabin without assistance.

"I'm not sure I thanked you yesterday for getting us out
of there," Ben told Charlie who was busily shaving off his
beard. "I was the one that was sent to scrub your friend
Marvin, and the way it played out you had to take care of
me."

"That's OK," Charlie assured him. "I could never have
handled it without you. Anyway that's behind us, and we
can forget it. Now we can relax and enjoy our trip to
Odessa, and figure out how we get home from there."

"Don't worry, I have connections there," Ben grinned.
"In the old days, I used to run a gun smuggling route from
Europe to the Black Sea and then into Tel Aviv. As a matter
of fact, I used to bump into your friend Sackman when he

was working the same circuit. I'm sure some of the old network is still around."

As Charlie was going out the door, Ben took him by the arm. "I don't know what your friend Karen plans to do. She's a good-looking *shiksa*, and if she would like to come to Israel with me, it would be a big help to us. I believe she is familiar with the people Marvin was dealing with. My people were convinced that they were with the Iranian MOIS, and it would be helpful to the Mossad if she could identify them for us. Once the Iranian agents find out that Marvin's dead, they will go some place else for their missiles. They're religious fanatics who will never give up until they are dead, or we are wiped off the face of the earth."

Ben started to run hot water for his bath. "Tell her that afterwards we will be able to fix her documents up so that she can go anyplace else she wants. And I mean anyplace," he emphasized pointedly.

On his way to the lounge for breakfast, Charlie stopped to pick-up Karen. A bright morning sun had dispersed the dense fog of the night before. There were a few white caps on the river but the old boat, with its four heavy decks, settled low enough in the water to plough through the chop without annoying the passengers.

The alumni had gathered in the lounge for their lecture on the history of Ukraine. They were listening intently, and some were taking notes. The bespectacled history professor from the University of Kiev was graphically describing the tremendous suffering of the 1930's famine, which he referred to as the *Holdomor*. His topic reminded Charlie of the night he and Eve met at the restaurant when she told him the famine was the cause of her family fleeing Ukraine.

As Charlie and Karen passed the seated group, there were a few veiled glances at the pair who apparently slept too late to attend the early morning lecture. One man nudged his wife and winked as the couple passed on their way to the breakfast buffet. The wife smiled knowingly then returned her attention to the professor.

A Ukrainian breakfast essentially contains the same heavy food as lunch, and the lunch bears a strong resemblance to dinner. The General Valeriy's staff had made a concession to the dining tastes of their American tour group by setting the buffet table with platters of eggs, sausages, bacon, and toast; along with varieties of the American breakfast staple--cold cereal and milk. Hopefully pasteurized Charlie thought as he concentrated on the cooked foods.

Karen and Charlie found a table by the window, and watched the small villages and fields of grain gliding past along the river's muddy bank.

Relaxing over their coffee, Charlie considered a question that had haunted him since the day they met in Marvin's apartment. After the waiter had refilled their cups he asked, "What was it like living with Marvin and working for someone like Kuchma? How could you live with yourself?"

Karen slowly stirred her coffee, averting his gaze. Finally she told him, "It was awful—I felt terrible, but I did what I had to do," she said sadly. "I didn't feel I had a lot of options. I just moved where the momentum took me. It was like being caught in a rip tide. All you can do is try and keep your head out of the water until you can find something to hang on to—and you gave me that chance.

"Now I'm really homesick. I want to get back to the States and see what might be left of my family—and the few friends I may still have. "As she spoke her eyes filled with tears, "but not enough to go to prison for something I didn't do. Maybe some day," she told him wistfully.

"I guess you haven't told the Maestro that I was in Ukraine?" Karen asked more as a statement than a question, while she dabbed her eyes with a tiny handkerchief.

Charlie took a swallow of coffee before he replied. "No you're right. I haven't told anyone who you are — or where you are from for that matter. I'm not sure why, but I guess I didn't see how it would help anything, and I felt that I owed you a level of personal loyalty that was stronger than what I might owe to the Agency.

"I'm probably wrong — I usually am, but that's just the way it is," his voice trailed off as he stared out the window.

"Now it's my turn to ask questions," Karen told him as they were leaving the dining room. "How do you feel about killing Marvin? Any regrets?"

"Perhaps I should," he replied earnestly. "But I don't. The son of a bitch had already shot Ben, and he was doing his best to kill me. The picture of him lying there dead will probably haunt me the rest of my life but, at the time, all I could think of was what would happen if the Islamists ever got their hands on those Kh55's.

"Am I sorry I killed him? No — not a bit," he answered adamantly, as much to himself as to Karen. "In the words of that great philosopher John Wayne," he smiled wryly, "*a man's gotta do what a man's gotta do*. And, I had to stop Marvin from selling those missiles."

In the lounge, the professor was droning on, tediously describing how resilient the Ukrainians were to withstand the various foreign groups that had historically dominated their homeland. His knowledge of history exceeded his language ability, and a few of the "golden agers" were beginning to nod, while several others were quietly gathering their things together, eager to return to their cabin to prepare for the scheduled excursion ashore.

270

Later in the day, the alumni tour was planning a trip to the town of Zaporizhia where they would visit the Cossack Glory Museum and attend a Cossack Horse Show. A group of Russian dancers would then accompany the tourists back on board, and provide after-dinner entertainment while the boat continued its journey down the Dnieper.

Karen wanted to stop at the dispensary and pick up a roll of gauze so they could replace the dressing on Ben's wound. Afterwards the three of them spent the time relaxing in his cabin and reminiscing about their former lives. Charlie told about his family. Karen described her experiences working in the Kuchma government, and Ben entertained his two friends by describing some of his less secret, but never-the-less exciting assignments with the Mossad.

Ben also offered Karen the proposal he had previously mentioned to Charlie about her accompanying him to Tel Aviv.

"It's the best offer I've had today," she replied, patting him gently on the hand. "I was wondering what I would do in Odessa." Later, she returned to her cabin so Ben could rest.

Charlie spent his time making a few changes in his GBC report before deciding to get some fresh air. Putting on his coat, he took a last check of the slumbering Ben before leaving the cabin for a walk around the deck.

On his second pass, he paused to watch the tired American travelers straggling up the narrow wooden gangplank returning from their visit to the land of Ukraine's famous warrior horsemen.

It was a strange looking group. The happy but tired tourists were dressed sensibly in their drab flannel traveling clothes and comfortable white athletic shoes. Mingled liberally among the returning crowd were grim-faced

Russian dancers wearing gaudy gold-braided Cossack uniforms and tall lambs-wool hats, while sporting knee-length boots partially obscuring their bright blue trousers. Each of them carried a theatrical looking leather horsewhip clutched tightly in their hand. It was sad to see how the one-time protector of the czars and wild riders of the steppes were now reduced to a parody of their former selves.

The contrast in the appearance between the tourists and their entertainers couldn't have been greater, and Charlie chuckled as he headed to the lounge for a cold beer. Tourism is thirsty business, and the bar was already crowded. He found a seat, and ordered a Pilsner Urquell from the harried Filipino bartender. Relaxing, he sipped the dark amber colored Czech beer, oblivious to the idle conversation of his fellow travelers that flowed around him until the words "black-coated man" pierced his consciousness. Scanning the crowd, he quickly identified the source as a shrill voiced woman who was precariously perched on a tall stool at the far end of the bar.

He sidled closer to the woman who had now captured the rapt attention of her companions. She continued her breathless description of the "ominous" looking man, with bad breath, speaking broken English, and wearing a long black leather coat who was canvassing the crowd getting-off the tour bus. According to her, the "horrible" man was showing a faded photo of a woman, and wondering—she thought he had asked—if anyone on board knew her. Everyone she knew was too tired to pay much attention to him. The last she saw, he was trailing the tour guide onto the boat just before the mooring lines were cast from the dock. The focus of the ladies' conversation swiftly turned to the pleasant smile of their handsome tour guide, and Charlie put down his drink and quickly headed for the door.

As he approached Karen's cabin he heard a muffled scream, followed by the sickening sound of a body violently thrown against the wall.

The entertainment in the lounge had begun, and the stomping boots of the crouching Ukrainian Cossacks punctuated the wild folk music.

Charlie jammed his shoulder against the slightly cracked cabin door and shoved, while at the same time reaching into his coat pocket and thumbing off the safety on the Beretta. Stepping inside, he confronted the back of a hulking heavy-set man in a black leather coat who was strangling Karen with ham like hands as he crushed her against the cabin's wall.

Hearing a sudden noise, the man whirled. His hand fell from Karen's throat as he reached for the butt of the Glock protruding from his KGB shoulder holster. Charlie could see a crooked grin on the man's pockmarked face as he drew his gun and crouching took aim. Before he could fire the Glock, Charlie instinctively jerked the trigger on his pocketed Beretta. The small-bored gun gave a muffled bark, as its lethal projectile ripped through the lining of his pocket, racing toward the broad chest of the still crouching thug. The man's grin dissolved into a grimace of pain and he pivoted against the wall, then slid slowly to the cabin floor. A crumpled woman's photo fluttered slowly to the floor beside him.

Karen sobbing uncontrollably ran into Charlie's arms. "I didn't hear him come in. I couldn't get to my gun. I was lying on the bed, and when I jumped up…"

"That's all right, don't worry," he tried to calm her. "I didn't even have time to take my gun from my pocket"

"… When I got up he threw me against the wall," she sobbed. "He was trying to choke me when you came in."

"Someone may have heard the shot," he warned. "But I doubt it. The crazy Cossacks are kicking up a hell of a storm in the lounge."

Karen was quickly regaining her composure. "We'll have to figure out how to get rid of the body before someone finds him."

"Or learns he's gone," Charlie cautioned.

A crimson stain on the dead man's shirt grew larger as they watched. Collecting the towels from the bathroom they quickly wrapped them around his chest to absorb the bleeding, and prevent any telltale stains on the newly carpeted floor. When they finished cleaning-up, they cautiously peered outside before hanging a "Do Not Disturb" tag on Karen's door.

They told Ben what had happened. He thought he may have heard the body fall against the wall; but he was sure he hadn't heard the shot, which was comforting.

The three of them spent an anxious evening in the cabin, listening to the sounds of the Russian Chorus energetically entertaining the crowd in the lounge. As Charlie had predicted, between the loud singing and the Cossack's tumultuous dance routines, no one heard any of the violent struggle that took place in Karen's cabin.

Late that night, after the passengers and crew had gone to bed, Charlie and Karen dragged the heavy body of the Ukrainian agent to the boat's side. A full moon lighted their way. Charlie propped the dead man against the rail while Karen lifted his feet as they slid his body silently into the murky Dnieper. His black hat floated on the surface in the moonlight, giving the only grim evidence that he had been onboard. It too, soon disappeared in the tour boat's wake.

Charlie paused to watch the hat sink slowly from sight before pulling out the Beretta. He carefully wiped it clean of any fingerprints before wrapping the weapon in the blood-soaked towels from Karen's cabin. When he finished, he quickly dropped the grim bundle over the side.

The two of them turned to look at each other. Words couldn't express their feelings. Charlie comfortingly put his arm over her shoulders, and slowly guided her back to the cabin.

Following the professor's morning lecture on 15th century *Kyiv Rus* history, the alumni group was scheduled to leave the boat and travel by bus to the town of Kherson in the Ukrainian region of Tavria. They then planned to tour the town's ornamental gardens and vineyards. After the traditional wine tasting, the tour group would be taken by small boats up the river's delta where they were to visit a remote fishing village, before finally returning to the General Valeriy.

Karen, Charlie, and Ben knew that their fragile cover as tourists was blown, and would no longer provide them with the anomalous protection they needed to travel safely the rest of the way to Odessa. Once the black-coated man didn't return to his base, it wouldn't take his companions long to retrace his steps, and discover what had become of him.

As the cruise passengers gathered by the rail to watch the Valeriy pull alongside the dock, none of them noticed that the three people who previously had kept to themselves now mingled among them.

There was very little conversation on the bus trip to Kherson. The seniors were beginning to tire from the tour's pace, and many gray heads nodded as the bus navigated the narrow roads.

After the wine tasting, the alumni boarded the small boats taking them up-river without anyone noticing that three of their fellow passengers were no longer with them.

When the opportunity presented itself, Karen, Charlie, and Ben separated from the group and headed for the town's small train station. The depot was empty. The manager came only when a train was passing through Kherson, and that happened just once a day. On even days the train stopped in the afternoon on its way from Kiev to Odessa. The following day it stopped at Kherson in the morning as it retraced its route north.

The chalkboard schedule indicated they would have to wait only two more hours before the afternoon train arrived. The government goons seemed to be looking for Karen more than they were for Charlie and Ben so, once the station agent arrived, she and Ben waited outside. Charlie purchased three second-class tickets in a *kupe*-- a sleeper compartment for 3-4 people. His experience traveling by train to Ivano Frankivsk was helpful, and he managed to make the Russian speaking agent understand what he wanted. He had to show his travel documents before getting the tickets, and decided to use the Latvian passport Eve had given him. The station manager only glanced at it, and had no interest in looking at documents of the other two ticket holders.

The old steam train was part passenger and part freight, hauling grain and produce from the fields of the north to the Black Sea where the cargo would then be shipped around the world.

Their compartment was dirty and the train was slow, but Charlie and his companions didn't care as long as they got to Odessa without incident. The gentle motion of the passenger car, accompanied by the rhythmic clicking of the rails, soon lulled them to sleep; awakening only for the intrusion of the gray uniformed *providnik* whose responsibility apparently was to punch their tickets on an hourly basis.

276

The three travelers were awakened abruptly as the engine jerked to a grinding halt in Odessa's station. The narrow isle outside their compartment quickly filled with passengers elbowing their way to the exit. Charlie and his companions gathered their few possessions before squeezing into the slowly moving line.

The railroad station was old and badly in need of repair. Wooden scaffolding covered one of the walls where workmen had once attempted to replace a line of mosaic tiles. The laborers apparently gave up before the job was finished, and only the scaffolding remained as evidence of their failed effort. Ben leaned tiredly against one of the wooden supports while removing a small red notebook from his inside coat pocket. He quickly thumbed through the pages to assure himself that his Odessa numbers were still there.

"I know a place we can stay safely till I can find a way out of here," he assured them as he slid the notebook back in his pocket.

Outside, they were greeted by a blast of warm damp air that was difficult to adjust to after the dry cold climate of Kiev. Ben hailed a taxi, while Karen and Charlie removed their coats. While they waited, Charlie noticed a large singed hole in his duffel coat's pocket. Amused, he stuck a wiggling finger through it, then laughingly stuffed the old coat into a large refuse can next to the station's marble doorway.

Ben ushered them hurriedly into the waiting cab, ordering the driver to take them to the Black Star Hotel. The battered old Skoda struggled to maneuver the city's narrow streets that led downward toward the town's sprawling waterfront. As they rode, it was becoming obvious that the climate wasn't the only difference between Kiev and Odessa. The port city appeared more cosmopolitan and the people along the street looked happier and more prosperous than the usual grim-faced Kievians. As they drove it occurred to Charlie that he had handkerchiefs larger than most of the woman's skirts that he saw along the busy streets. Both he and Ben furtively glanced admiringly in their direction.

There was a noticeable difference in the Mossad agent since they arrived in Odessa. He seemed more relaxed than he had since he and Charlie first met. While they drove through town he amiably pointed to familiar sights, like a traveler returning home.

Karen, on the other hand, had become more melancholy as they rode through town. While Ben was headed home she no longer had a home to return to. She stared dejectedly out of the window, as if she was trying to dull her memory with the details of the Byzantine architecture that provided a surreal character to the old city.

Ben winced momentarily as he turned from his position next to the driver. "You know," he began "this place used to have one of the largest Jewish populations in Eastern Europe. They were people who, over the years, were fleeing persecution in other parts of the world. At one time, almost one-third of Odessa was Jewish. Then, after the pogroms, a majority of them fled to other countries. But I still have good connections here," he concluded proudly.

Karen continued to stare out the window, lost in her own thoughts.

Ben grinned broadly as he continued his impromptu travelogue, while Charlie studied Karen.

The cab pulled to a stop in front of small hotel in a seedy section of town. "Don't worry how this place looks," Be assured them. "We'll be safe until I'm able to arrange for our passage out."

The hotel appeared to be a cut-rate haven for Odessa's underworld. Walking through the lobby Ben continued acting like a guide pointing to some of the city's more illustrious drug dealers, gunrunners, and the two Mafia bosses huddled in a corner discussing, in hushed tones, their lucrative international flesh trade

The Pakistani desk clerk seemed to recognize Ben, and smiled as he casually flipped three keys on the stained lobby counter. Ben scooped them up tossing one to Karen and the other to Charlie. Before going to their rooms they agreed to meet in the bar later that afternoon.

Charlie tossed his bag on the sagging brass bed. The depressing room gave stark evidence to generations of "quick-time" visitors. The carpeting design was worn past recognition, and the finishes on the bureau and night table were badly marred with years of careless cigarette burns. Staring out the window, he watched the setting sun cast long shadows over the dockworkers hustling heavy bales into the hold of a waiting freighter.

He shoved his bag to the side of the bed and dialed a call to Austrian Airlines. After a long wait on hold he was able to make a reservation for an aisle seat in Business Class on an early morning flight leaving the next day for Vienna.

After hanging-up he lay back on the stained coverlet and gently massaged his temples. His head ached badly, and he felt exhausted from his experiences the last few days. Perhaps Ben was right. They may both be getting too old for this miserable business.

A soft sea breeze fluttered the faded curtains on his open window, and finally a wave of sleep washed over him. It was a troubled slumber, filled with dreams of being chased and falling down, then getting up and falling down once again.

A farewell blast from a ship heading out of the harbor wakened him abruptly. For a few minutes he tried to recall exactly where he was, and eventually decided get out of the dreary room and go to the lobby.

Karen was sitting alone, dejectedly stirring a cup coffee. She looked up with a pained smile as Charlie joined her. He looked away when he saw that her eyes were rimmed with red. She must have been crying in her room and decided to go where there was at least some semblance of life.

"Well old friend," she smiled sadly, "this looks like the end of the line for us. Tomorrow you head home to your family, and I go to Tel Aviv for only God knows what.

"Oh Charlie—whatever is going to happen to me?" she blurted. I'm caught in a warp where I can't go forward, and I can't go back. I'm going to have to create a whole new myth for myself when I get to Tel Aviv. I've had so many phony histories that I soon will have forgotten who I really am.

"When we first met in your office in Chicago, who would have thought that we would end up in a dingy bar on the edge of the Black Sea," she sobbed forlornly dabbing her eyes with a hotel napkin. .

He reached out, covering her small hand with his. "It's incredible Karen. I can't really believe what's happened to us. In just a few days I've killed two men, and now we're sitting together in this dive, and I can't find the words to console you.

"I'll talk to Emmett when I get back. I'll explain how Marvin set you up. I'm sure he'll understand, but I don't know what he can do about the Feds. Maybe, after awhile, they will be so busy chasing terrorists that they will have forgotten all about you. Then perhaps you can come home," he added feebly.

Ben pulled up a chair and joined them, breaking the tension. "My contacts came through," he beamed. "Karen and I are booked on a tramp freighter out of here tonight. It stops in Istanbul and then on to Tel Aviv from there. I had to call the one-eyed man before the Captain would let us on board. Apparently, the old rust-bucket is flying a Liberian flag and has its hold filled with black market armaments. The skipper wasn't going to take any chances with the people that he was letting join his happy cruise until we had clearance from his contractor. As it turns out, his contractor is my boss.

"By the way Charlie, he says to tell you that you do good work, and you can get a job with the Mossad anytime," Ben told him, with a broad grin spreading across his wrinkled face.

The three of them had a final dinner together at the Shanghai Chef, a decrepit Chinese restaurant next to the hotel.

The last Charlie saw of Karen she was resolutely trudging up the gangplank, trailing behind Ben, and carrying the old blue trench coat and her Ferragamo bag. Halfway up she paused and turning blew Charlie a farewell kiss. He waved, and she disappeared on-board.

Charlie remained on the dock until the lights of the outbound freighter faded from view, then returned dejectedly to his room.

Twenty: Reprise

Odessa airport was filling with tourists and business travelers. It was also very hot, and the humid air was heavy with the smell of sweat mixed with tobacco smoke. Charlie's check-in counter was at the far end of the crowded terminal. After walking only halfway his shirt was sticky from perspiration.

Passing the Delta counter, he thought that he recognized some of the people waiting to check-in. Drawing closer he was shocked to see that the group huddled tightly together at the end of a long line were the same alumni travelers that were on the General Valeriy. Picking up his pace, he averted his face hoping not to be recognized.

A graying, heavy-set man smoking a cigar at the end of the check-in line elbowed his wife. "Look Dora. That tall fella walking past. Isn't he the one that was with that good-looking blond on the Valeriy?"

Distracted, his wife looked-up from searching through her purse, and glanced briefly at the back of the man walking hurriedly past them. His face seemed to be permanently turned away from them. "No of course not—don't be ridiculous," she sharply admonished her husband, while continuing to hunt for her missing passport.

"I wonder where his blond tootsie is?" the heavy-set man mused to himself. "She was one hell of a looker," he grinned approvingly while moving forward in the slow moving line.

The 737 banked sharply to get on course to Vienna. As the plane gained its desired altitude the wheels thudded into the fuselage, and Charlie released a deep sigh of relief. The passenger sitting next to him looked quizzically out of the corner of his eye, but Charlie didn't care. He was just happy to be finally headed home. Below, the flat steppes of Ukraine melted into the high peaks of the rugged Carpathians. Charlie watched until the clouds shielded his view of the ground.

Reclining his seat he thought about his trip to Ukraine. It had turned out much different than he expected. Originally, he had hoped for a challenging reprieve from the grinding routines of retirement. Perhaps, he had thought, there might even be a taste of the adventure that his former life provided. But, certainly not to the extent of being involved with clandestine missile sales, and the eventual elimination of two people who wanted to kill him. Still, he remained conflicted with a sense of grudging gratitude toward the Agency for inadvertently providing a missing feeling of exhilaration he had unconsciously missed, and had previously come to accept.

It had always been important for him to be a contributor. It was also critical that, if required, he would be able to help his country, particularly now that America was involved in an asymmetrical war with Muslim Jihadists. If that effort meant working undercover to provide the Agency with a level of plausible deniability—then so be it. Perhaps it was better that way for everyone involved, including his family. But this had gone too far. The next time Emmett, or anyone else at Langley, wanted his services they could damn well find someone else.

The man seated next to him had already dozed off, and Charlie pulled down his window shade and closed his eyes. Soon, he too was asleep.

He was awakened by the flight attendants scurrying around the cabin as they prepared for landing in Vienna. He rubbed his eyes, and decided to head up the aisle for the toilets before the red seatbelt sign flashed its warning.

The air over the Alps had become turbulent with an approaching winter storm. After crawling awkwardly over the man in the aisle-seat next to him, he headed toward the forward lavatory. The little 37 bucked, and he steadied himself against the reclining backs of the forward seated passengers. Inside the tiny john he quickly threw the lock, and braced himself against the curved bulkhead. Assured that the door was secure, he quickly removed the phony Latvian passport from his suit pocket and began ripping out the identifying pages before shredding them into tiny pieces and flushing them down the plane's toilet. When he finished, he took the empty passport cover and shoved it, as far as he could, into the wastepaper bin. On arrival at Schwechat Airport he wanted to use his American passport and didn't need the Custom Agents finding a second travel document.

There was no need to be concerned. Both Customs and Security ignored the arriving passengers; perhaps lulled into complacency by the strains of Mozart's Piano concerto piped over the airport's sound system.

Afternoon traffic was light as his taxi passed over the Danube Canal, and sped along the Ringstrasse. Soon, Charlie was inside the marble-lined lobby of the General Bank Corporation. The empty elevator swiftly deposited him at the fifth-floor office of the Assistant Director of Foreign Affairs.

"Ah my dear Mr. Connelly. How good it is to see you once again. Please sit down." Helmut Mueller obviously hadn't lost any weight since Charlie had seen him last. He was as corpulent as ever, and his greeting just as cordial.

"I've heard good things about you from our man in Kiev. They tell me that you scrupulously followed our instructions of maintaining a low profile."

"I did my best," Charlie smiled circumspectly while searching in his briefcase for the finished report.

"We had expected you a little earlier, however. I had planned a small celebratory luncheon for you. Ahh— actually it was several days ago." Herr Mueller observed, while flipping the pages of his gilded desk calendar. "I heard that you dropped off the key to the apartment some time ago and we wondered what had happened to you."

"Well I decided to spend a few days in the south of Ukraine. Doing a little sightseeing before I left for home. I paid my own expenses," Charlie assured him handing over his report and a sheath of expense accounts.

"That's quite alright. It is a beautiful country, so I am told, but so troubled. Did you know that Viktor Yuchenko is with us here in Vienna? His wife, a beautiful woman by the way, brought him to one of our hospitals for treatment. It is clear he was poisoned with dioxin, and it is gradually leaving his system through his skin. Right now his face looks like holy hell, but they think he will recover, but probably will remain terribly disfigured.

"What isn't clear at this time," Herr Mueller added absently scanning the bulky report, " if he will be able to continue campaigning. The US and the EU have spent a lot of money in Ukraine in hopes that it stays independent. If Yuchenko loses, it will no doubt revert back to Russian domination. But, my dear Mr. Connelly, you and I have done all we can to prevent that. Your report seems thorough, and my staff can digest your recommendations at their leisure."

Before leaving the office, Charlie shook the fat man's sweaty hand, and thanked the Assistant Director for the opportunity of working for GBC.

Once he was alone, Herr Mueller quickly buzzed his secretary. "Get me Washington," he ordered impatiently.

On the way to his hotel Charlie stopped at Café Central, a Viennese coffeehouse. It was a pleasure to be in public without the threat of being followed--or worse. Once he caught himself, out of habit, looking into a store window to see if someone was trailing behind. Then he remembered what it was called — "a wilderness of mirrors" someone had told him. They described it as a state of extreme paranoia sometimes experienced by agents who had been in the field too long, and lost their grasp on reality. Well that wasn't going to happen to him. He was done with all of that.

Inside the Central the air was heavy with the pungent aroma of strong coffee, and the acrid odor of stale tobacco smoke. On his way to an empty table, Charlie paused at the newspaper rack and removed the decades-worn rod containing the day's edition of the "International Herald" from among the many German language dailies.

Seated at the faded leather banquette he relaxed, stretching his long legs under the marble-topped table before ordering a cup of rich strong coffee and one of the city's famous strudels from an elderly, immaculately clad waiter. After the old man shuffled back to his station, Charlie brought himself up-to-date on the world's news he had missed in communications deprived Ukraine.

Motioning for a second cup of coffee, he gazed absently out the restaurant's large glass window at the rapidly gathering throng of happy well-dressed tourists across the street who were lining up in front of the Chapel for the afternoon performance of the Vienna Boys Choir. In spite of a bitter chill in the air, the crowd waited patiently for the scheduled opening of the heavy wooden doors. Charlie basked in the orderly scene that was so unlike the dreary streets of Ukraine.

Still, he recalled, Vienna was not always like this. Once the Allies had secured the city after the war, it had been divided into separate zones under the control of the individual commands. At that time, it became a Mecca for black marketers and a haven for clandestine agents representing the major competing powers. The Marshall Plan helped rebuild Vienna, and eventually the magic old city had become a center for international commerce, culturally rivaling anything the more established economies could offer. Hopefully, under the proper political guidance, the same thing could happen in Ukraine.

Instead of staying where he had before, he decided to check into a small hotel overlooking the Danube. He knew the hotel was out of the way, but the rooms were clean and comfortable. By the time he got to where he was staying and checked into his room night had already fallen. He preferred not to turn on the lights so that his room was lighted only by the blinking neon lights outside his window. In the distance he could hear an ambulance racing through town with its claxon caroling its eerie two-tone melody that was all too familiar to Europeans, but always unnerving to Americans such as himself.

He immediately dialed the overseas operator, anxious to let Beth know that he was safe and finally on his way home. Due to considerable trans-Atlantic traffic he was told he would have to wait for an open line.

While he waited, he kept his room dark on the theory that the lack of light would allow time to pass more rapidly. As time passed without hearing from the operator, he began to lose confidence in the validity of his rationale.

Gazing out the window he could barely make out the dimly glowing lights of the slowly revolving giant Ferris wheel that had come to symbolize Vienna's past, as well as its future. Turning stiffly away from the window and his thoughts, he bent over the small room's single bed and fumbled with the clasp on his worn suitcase.

Tucked discretely among his carefully folded clothes was a still unopened bottle of Stolichnaya that he had purchased at Odessa's duty-free shop. Certainly the vodka would make the time pass more quickly and, if nothing else, perhaps tonight it would bring a less troubled sleep. He broke the seal and poured an ample amount into the room's only glass, before returning once again to the frosted window.

By now the Ferris wheel had stopped operating for the night. Vienna was almost entirely dark, and only a few faint lights flickered in the distance. He raised his glass in a silent toast to old times and old friends.

The discordant sound of the hotel phone suddenly interrupted his reflections. Anticipating his wife on the line, he ran to grab the receiver before the circuit was lost.

In place of Beth's voice he heard instead, "hello Pinstripes?" spoken more in question than a greeting.

"Maestro?" He had long ago given up wondering how they were always able to find him.

"The wizards at NSA just picked up an intercept. It's over. They have found the Machinist. Now everyone believes that the other people did it so we are in the clear. Now you can come home knowing it was a job well done."

Charlie noticed for the first time how the Maestro's voice had become fogged with age. "That's what I am planning to do Emmett, I already have a reservation out of here in the morning, and I was waiting for a line to Beth to let her know I'm on my way."

"Just one more thing old boy. I would really like you to stop by Langley on the way. A bit of a debriefing."

"Go to hell Emmett. I've had enough."

"I know—I know, you really have done a bang-up job for us, but it's most important that I see you." With that there was a distinct click on the line, and the connection went dead.

He knew, and they knew, that regardless what he said he would do as the Maestro asked. He always did. As he thought about the conversation, it occurred to him that there was something slightly odd about it. Not about the context. That was predictable but, for the first time, he had not heard music playing in the background.

He replaced the phone carefully in its cradle. Then once again called the overseas operator. After what seemed an interminable wait he heard a muffled response on the other end of the line.

"Hello hon," he offered tentatively.

"Hello dear, do you know what time it is here? After all of the time I haven't heard from you, you could have waited at least until the alarm went off," she joked lovingly."

Of course she was right, and like a dutiful but errant husband, once he found out that everything was alright at home, he was quick to apologize;

"Terribly sorry dear, but I just got a call from Washington. They heard about the results of my project in Ukraine and wanted to compliment me on my work. They also asked me to drop by their office for a little chat on my way home. There may be an opportunity for other projects. I wanted to let you know that I will be home soon. Go back to sleep. Love you."

"Can't wait to see you. Good night," came the drowsy but affectionate reply.

Turning down the bed, Charlie returned for the last time to the window. Taking one last look at the sleeping city he emptied his glass, and noticed that it had begun to snow. The snowfall was growing heavier as he returned to bed.

The flight over the Atlantic was uneventful, but there was a heavy cloud cover hanging over Dulles, and Charlie's flight had to become a part of a circling queue. After the second pass, his flight was granted permission to land and the 757 sliced through the dispersing clouds, landing on the grease-stained tarmac with a slight bounce. Even with the increased surveillance following 9/11, the line for US citizens moved rapidly and their passports received only a casual examination. The line for foreign nationals seeking entry moved more slowly.

At the baggage carousel, Charlie recognized Frick and Frack; the two joy boys the CIA had sent for him before who were now waiting by the exit door impatiently scanning the new arrivals. Their tinted aviator style sunglasses allowed them to opaquely scrutinize the passing travelers, but also made them more conspicuous in the crowded terminal. He waved cheerfully to them before they focused on him, and a slight smile of recognition crossed the taller man's boxer-scarred face. After Charlie reclaimed his luggage and was waved through Customs, the two men led him to an awaiting gray Olds for the drive to Langley.

The Marine Guard waved them through the checkpoint, and while one man stayed in the parked car the other led Charlie to the elevator at the far end of the lobby. Once there, he quickly inserted and removed his card, and keyed a three-digit recognition code. When the elevator door slid open, Charlie felt a gentle nudge and found himself alone inside the rapidly descending elevator.

In seconds the door slid open again, and he tentatively entered the amber-lighted room he recalled from his last visit. The Maestro sat behind a large desk, his patrician features engulfed in a cloud of aromatic tobacco smoke rising from the bowl of his battered meerschaum. The pale yellow light accentuated the old man's wrinkled countenance.

As Charlie approached, Emmett slowly uncoiled and, leaning rigidly on his cane, nonchalantly waved to a nearby chair. "Good to see you Pinstripes. I hear you did a fine job in Ukraine. I know it was difficult for you to have to clip Marvin, but unfortunately it had to be done. It could have been disastrous if the Iranians got their hands on the Kh55's. Tell me all about it," Emmett requested, wincing as he resumed his former position behind the desk

Charlie tried to decide what to include and what to leave out. He should have thought this all out before he got to Langley, but he had not.

He hesitantly began by describing in some detail how he had contacted the Mossad through a friend in Israel; and as he talked he mentally backed and filled his account to avoid any reference to Karen. He continued by relating the details of his trip to Marvin's dacha in the exclusionary zone, while Emmett listened attentively. From there he progressed to the fateful shootout, and finally concluded with the Machinist's ultimate death.

The Maestro listened intently, vigorously nodding his approval when Charlie animatedly described how he had used the old auto to take out Marvin.

"I also heard from Colonel Sullivan that they provided you with a novel way out of the country. How was your trip home?" Emmett inquired when Charlie finished.

"Actually, it was Eve St. Ives that made the arrangements and….."

"Oh yes I've heard a lot about her," Emmett grinned.

….and the trip out of there went fine."

"Sullivan also mentioned that there was a young woman accompanying you. Was she anyone I know?" Emmett inquired, as he absently tamped down the remaining tobacco in the bowl of his pipe.

"She was just someone I met in Kiev who needed a way out, but I left her in Odessa," Charlie answered dismissively.

While they were talking, Mary Kool would occasionally dart in, pick up a stack of boxes behind the Maestro's' desk and, with a hacking cough, dart out as quickly as she had entered.

Noticing that there was not the usual sound of music playing in the background while they talked Charlie finally asked, "what's happening Maestro? There's no music, and it looks as if Mary Kool is cleaning out your office."

"That is correct my boy. The music has ended and this is our last dance. It's now time to sheathe the dagger and fold the tattered cloak. In a few days I am out of here. Going into retirement again. This time for good."

"I'm sorry to hear that Emmett," Charlie offered sympathetically. I've always had a great deal of respect for you, and what you were trying to do at the Agency. You will be badly missed."

"Perhaps," Emmett replied morosely. "Actually my time was up long ago. The Agency is changing, and it is difficult for an old man to change with it. In my heyday we lived our creed. We were loyal to our country, and our friends. Our work was based on deceit but we never deceived ourselves. There is a new matrix of morality operating here now. The old CIA orthodoxy is changing. We are getting too many gray men in jobs with black and white responsibilities, and the result is ambiguity replacing certainty, along with an increasing aversion to risk.

"The Agency will prevail, however, because we are essential to the well-being of our country. We are, after all, the bearers of the torch and the keepers of the flame. The tip of the god-damned spear so to speak," he concluded resolutely.

"Which brings me to the main reason I wanted to talk to you."

"I've been wondering about that," Charlie told him as Mary Kool picked up another stack of recordings before heading out the door. In the amber light her complexion looked even more wan than he recalled, and her cough more corrosive.

"The agency still needs men like you," Emmett resumed. "You have always done a good job for us. The embers of the Cold War continue to smolder, requiring only a hot breath to rekindle the flame. Islamofascism is spreading throughout the world, and if it ever combines with the disgruntled remnants of Communism it can become even more deadly to peace loving nations.

"Once again we have problems in the Southern Hemisphere, and South America could erupt to distract us from fighting the jihadists. That is where you could help. You are an expert in the economies of those Latin countries. We can set you up with a position in one of our cover companies. That way we can keep our silhouette to a minimum while maintaining our much-desired aura of plausible deniability. You, on the other hand, can travel there under your usual cover as an innocent businessman, and accomplish whatever we might like you to do for us — on a salary this time — of course."

"That's kind of you to suggest Maestro, but no thanks.

"Pity," Emmett exclaimed, not giving up. You are a perfect spy. You're dedicated, resourceful, and understand that sometimes the end does justify the means. You also have an impenetrable cover — because it's true."

Charlie waved the suggestion away with a faint smile, and a flick of his hand.

"But since you are not interested in continuing to work for us there are a few things that you are entitled to know. I can tell you now because I am leaving, and I believe I have the responsibility to tell you the truth after all you have done for us. I should have told you before but, at the time, it seemed better not to, and everything worked out all right in the end. Didn't it?" Emmett asked looking for reassurance.

Charlie only shrugged, baffled by what the maestro was saying.

Emmett paused, and painfully shifted his position in his large chair. "You see," he began again nervously. "When you first interviewed with us we were all very impressed with you, your background, your attitude, and your integrity. I was convinced that you were just the type of man the Agency needed, but....well, the word came down from the bureaucracy that there was a hiring freeze, and we had to cut you loose. We didn't want to but, as you say in Chicago, you can't fight City Hall.

"However, ah....would you like some coffee?" Emmett asked. "This isn't easy you understand."

Charlie shook his head no. He was eager to hear what would come next. So far, what he was being told was nothing he had not heard before, and he was perplexed why the usually articulate maestro now seemed so uncomfortable.

"Well," Emmett cleared his throat. "As I told you, we were impressed and, even though we were unable to bring you aboard at the time we flagged your file, and decided to keep track of you in case something might pop-up in the future.

"When you rose through the corporate ranks and eventually got into the international business, and started travelling around the world, we decided to activate your file to see if you could be of some help to us. As you recall, our budget was being cut once more, and we needed all of the help we could get.

294

"That's when Marvin and Karen contacted you in Chicago. The plan was to gradually bring you into the fold...so to speak," he added lamely.

As Emmett talked, Charlie's mind went back to the conversation he had with Ben Silver on the General Valeriy when Ben observed that Charlie's past experiences were typical of how intelligence agencies sometimes recruited new agents. At that time, Charlie rejected the idea as preposterous, but now he wasn't so sure.

"We gradually began feeding you assignments. They were all valid you understand, and you performed wonderfully, but they also gave us an opportunity to evaluate how you performed under pressure.

"Then all hell broke loose!" Emmett exclaimed throwing up his hands in consternation. "Karen was implicated in the Peruvian plot, Marvin was incensed that he wasn't promoted to my position and disappeared. At the same time your job at Apex evaporated."

Emmett calmly re-lighted his pipe. Soon his gray head was once more ringed with an aromatic cloud. It reminded Charlie of an ethereal halo, but he knew too well that the old man was no angel.

"After I was brought back to the Agency," Emmett continued, "we cleared you of any involvement with our beautiful Karen. Then I heard from Colonel Sullivan in Kiev that there was an American woman who was working as a political advisor to the Ukrainian Government. He suspected that it might be Karen, and wanted to check it out. We decided that his position at the embassy was too sensitive. He was also aware that he was constantly under surveillance by the Ukrainian Secret Service.

"The solution I came up with was to activate you," Emmett grinned broadly. "Who better?" he asked, not expecting a reply. "You were retired and looking around for something to do. So I found it for you," he smiled benignly.

"Why the hell didn't you tell me what you were doing, and just send me over there under cover?" Charlie asked angrily. "I would have gone willingly if you asked."

"Ah yes, I guess we could have done that. It just never occurred to us to be that straightforward. You see old boy, after you have been in this business as long as I have, you find that the direct approach is usually not the best. We spend our lives being devious---actually we really prefer to refer to it as disingenuous---and it just never occurs to us that the old geometric axiom of a straight line being the shortest route could apply to anything outside of a high school textbook."

Perplexed, Charlie shook his head in astonishment.

"Anyway," Emmett continued drawing on his pipe. "An old friend of mine—I believe you know him as Helmet Mueller—was now head of the General Bank Corporation in Vienna. He had told me that he was always looking for qualified international advisors and voila! I gave him your name, and suggested that you could be most helpful to him in Ukraine," Emmett chuckled.

"The problem was that Sullivan and I couldn't figure out how to get you headed toward the American advisor without letting you know, or tipping off the Ukrainian Government. While we were trying to set that up, you surprised us by independently discovering Marvin and his missile sales to the Iranians. At that point we forgot about the woman, and you were off and running on your own.

"Isn't it wonderful when a plan comes together?" Emmett asked delightedly. "But, I guess we will never know who the American woman was," he added pointedly.

Charlie sat in stunned silence, more confused than caring about being used by the Agency. "I guess not," he mumbled. "But—but," he stammered," why couldn't you have at least sent someone to help me? Someone with more experience in wet-work than I had."

"Didn't need to, old boy. There wasn't time, and besides we really didn't want to get involved. Also, we wanted to keep you at arms length so we could deny everything if it all fell apart.

"By the way, bringing in that colored fellow from the Mossad was brilliant. I couldn't have done better myself," Emmett exclaimed with unconcealed pride.

"The whole situation was handled very resourcefully my friend. "You understand that you can always work with us again whenever you might want to reconsider our offer."

"Do you think that I would work for you after learning how you used me all these years? You must be crazy!" Charlie exclaimed indignantly.

"Of course I am. If I weren't I would never have been able to handle this job. If I were sane," Emmett chortled, "I would have been out of here long ago."

Charlie laughed at Emmett's candor. "Well I guess that, if the truth be told, I did find the work challenging. It gave me an opportunity to make a difference. But, like St. Francis of Assisi, I just want to tend my garden.

"Anyway how can you offer me a job if you're leaving?"

"Actually, the offer is coming from my successor, who you already know. Colonel Sullivan is going to replace me."

"He's a damned good man," Charlie agreed. Who will replace Sully in Kiev?

"Eve St. Ives. Colonel Sullivan assures me that she will be a most competent replacement."

"I'm sure she will be," Charlie agreed rising from his chair to leave. "Have a good retirement," he offered shaking the old man's hand. "And you too Mary," he called to the woman disappearing once again with a heavy load of classical records.

Emmett struggled to his feet and called after him, "oh forgive me Pinstripes. I almost forgot to congratulate you on the success of your daughter."

Charlie paused. "My daughter. What about my daughter?"

"Well I thought you would like to know that she graduated at the top of her training class at The Farm."

"At—at The Farm at Camp Peary?" he stammered. "But she told us that she had taken a job with the Commerce Department."

As the heavy door slid open, Charlie heard a dry chuckle cascading into a hearty laugh, immediately followed by, "*Vaya con Dios* my dear friend." The door slid silently closed behind him.

Author's Notes

Although still bearing the scars from dioxin poisoning, Viktor Yuchenko recovered sufficiently to return to Ukraine, and continue his campaign. With the strong support of his "Orange Revolutionaries" he was ultimately able to force Leonard Kuchma, the authoritarian former President, and Viktor Yanukovich, Mr. Kuchma's Russian backed would-be successor, to concede defeat.

Russia's President Vladimir Putin viewed the success of the Orange Revolution as his country's biggest defeat since the collapse of the Soviet Union. After Yuchenko's administration rejuvenated its ties with the United States and the European Union, the Kremlin blamed them for supporting the Orange Revolution. As a result, Putin subsequently tightened the screws inside his own country on foreign non-governmental organizations (NGOs), which he believes were partially responsible for the loss of Ukraine; and concurrently rebuilt Russia's espionage capabilities against the U.S. to former Cold War levels.

The victory in Ukraine initially gave renewed hope to opposition parties challenging authoritative rulers throughout the former Soviet Union. In addition to cementing closer ties with the EU and the US, Ukraine and the United States have signed a joint agreement designed to curtail and control the threat of bioterrorism by placing modern safeguards on the supply of deadly pathogens left over from Soviet-era biological weapons programs.

However, many other things have not gone smoothly for Yuchenko and his party. They inherited a country with a failing industrial infrastructure in which everything from roads and train lines to water, sewage, and gas pipelines had been completely neglected. In the years following the election, the excitement and ideals that brought thousands of demonstrators to the Maydan (the capital's main square) have turned into an orange- tinged nostalgia as a result of the slow progress in enacting reforms.

There has been considerable bickering among his advisers that has sparked resignations of integral members of his cabinet. The economy is slowly improving, but too slowly for many impatient Ukrainians. The decapitation of the journalist Georgy Congadze is still unsolved, and even more frustrating the investigation appears to have stalled. In addition, the investigation into the poisoning of Yuchenko seems to have ended without any assignment of responsibility.

Because of the slow progress on multiple fronts and dissention among his supporters, a widening ideological divide between the pro-Russian eastern part of the country and the nationalistic west has strengthened the Russian supported opposition.

The long-term outcome in Ukraine remains uncertain.

As Emmett Valentine predicted, the political picture in Latin America has become considerably more problematical. The democratically elected Venezuelan President Hugo Chavez has emerged as the most formidable adversary to the United States since Fidel Castro seized power in Cuba some 45 years ago. The two men have formed a strong alliance based on the free-flow of oil money from Venezuela to Cuba. Chavez has also formed close political ties with the leaders of Iran and Syria and could potentially provide a base for Iranian missiles aimed at the United States.

The Venezuelan President is advocating what he describes as "a multipolar world, free of Yankee imperialism" for the region. His dreams of controlling Latin America are supported by his ability to provide neighboring countries with billions of dollars worth of discounted oil. So far, his efforts have acquired only limited traction among the neighboring countries; with the exception of the newly elected Bolivian President Evo Morales.

Chavez's hand is strengthened with the continuing rise in the price of oil. At the same time, as oil rises America is placed in a weakened position since Venezuela is one of this country's principal suppliers of crude.

President Chavez has not limited his efforts to political intrigue. In the middle of 2006 he signed a deal with Russia, valued at more than $1 billion, for a receipt of 100,000 Kalashnikov assault rifles, 30 helicopters, and 30 Sukhoi Su-30 advanced fighter aircraft to replace the country's aging US F-16 fighters. Chavez then plans to sell Venezuela's older U.S. jet aircraft inventory to Iran. At the same time, the Russian oil companies Gazprom and Lukoil were granted rights to participate in Venezuelan oil ventures.

Charlie Connolly was seen recently at the Venezuelan Consulate Office in Chicago applying for a Business Visa for entry to that country.

Russell R. Miller

Russ Miller has traveled to well over 100 countries as an international executive, and on NGO projects for the Vienna-based UNIDO, UNDP, The World Bank, and the IESC. *The Spy with a Clean Face* is his fourth book focusing on the East-European Region including *Journey to a Closed City* recently published by Science and Humanities Press. Miller and his wife live in the Chicago suburb of La Grange, Illinois.

Other Books from Science & Humanities Press

HOW TO TRAVEL — A Guidebook for Persons with a Disability – Fred Rosen (1997) ISBN 1-888725-05-2, 5½ X 8¼, 120 pp, $9.95 18-point large print edition (1998) ISBN 1-888725-17-6 7X8, 120 pp, $19.95

HOW TO TRAVEL in Canada — A Guidebook for A Visitor with a Disability – Fred Rosen (2000) ISBN 1-888725-26-5, 5½X8¼, 180 pp, $14.95 MacroPrintBooks™ edition (2001) ISBN 1-888725-30-3 7X8, 16 pt, 200 pp, $19.95

AVOIDING Attendants from HELL: A Practical Guide to Finding, Hiring & Keeping Personal Care Attendants 2nd Edn — June Price, (2002), accessible plastic spiral bind, ISBN 1-888725-72-9 8¼X10½, 125 pp, $16.95, School/library edition (2002) ISBN 1-888725-60-5, 8¼X6½, 200 pp, $18.95

The Bridge Never Crossed — A Survivor's Search for Meaning. Captain George A. Burk (1999) The inspiring story of George Burk, lone survivor of a military plane crash, who overcame extensive burn injuries to earn a presidential award and become a highly successful motivational speaker. ISBN 1-888725-16-8, 5½X8¼, 170 pp, illustrated. $16.95 MacroPrintBooks™ Edition (1999) ISBN 1-888725-28-1 $24.95

Value Centered Leadership — A Survivor's Strategy for Personal and Professional Growth — Captain George A. Burk (2004) Principles of Leadership & Total Quality Management applied to all aspects of living. ISBN 1-888725-59-1, 5½X8¼, 120 pp, $16.95

Sexually Transmitted Diseases — Symptoms, Diagnosis, Treatment, Prevention-2nd Edition – NIAID Staff,

Assembled and Edited by R.J.Banis, PhD, (2006) Teacher friendly — free to copy for education. Illustrated with more than 70 illustrations and photographs of lesions, ISBN 1-888725-58-3, 8¼X6½, 200 pp, $18.95

The Stress Myth -Serge Doublet, PhD (2000) A thorough examination of the concept that 'stress' is the source of unexplained afflictions. Debunking mysticism, psychologist Serge Doublet reviews the history of other concepts such as 'demons', 'humors', 'hysteria' and 'neurasthenia' that had been placed in this role in the past, and provides an alternative approach for more success in coping with life's challenges. ISBN 1-888725-36-2, 5½X8¼, 280 pp, $24.95

The Way It Was-- Nostalgic Tales of Hotrods and Romance Chuck Klein (2003) Series of hotrod stories by author of Circa 1957 in collaboration with noted illustrator Bill Lutz BeachHouse Books edition 5½ X 8¼, 200 pp ISBN: 1-888725-86-9 $14.95

The Way It Was
Nostalgic Tales of
HotRods and
Romance

Chuck Klein

MacroPrintBooks™ edition (2003) 16 pt. 8¼X6½, 350pp ISBN: 1-888725-87-7 $24.95

50 Things You Didn't Learn in School–But Should Have: Little known facts that still affect our world today (2004) by John Naese, . ISBN 1-888725-49-4, 5½X8¼, 200 pp, illustrated. $16.95

Republican or Democrat? (2005) Moses Sanchez, who describes himself as "a Black Hispanic" thinks for himself, questions the stereotypes, examines the facts and makes his own decision. Early Editions Books ISBN 1-888725-32-X 5½X8¼, 176pp pp, $14.95

Journey to a Closed City with the International Executive Service Corps

describes the adventures of a retired executive volunteering with the senior citizens' equivalent of the Peace Corp as he applies his professional skills in a former Iron Curtain city emerging into the dawn of a new economy.

Before this adventure, Russ Miller spent 20 years traveling to over 100 countries as Sr. Vice President of International Development.

Since retiring, he has served as an advisor with the World Bank, United Nations Development Program, and the Vienna-based United Nations Industrial Development Organization, as well as the International Executive Service Corps.

This book is essential reading for anyone approaching retirement who is interested in opportunities to exercise skills to "do good" during expense-paid travel to intriguing locations.

Journey to A Closed City should also appeal to armchair travelers eager to explore far-off corners of the world in our rapidly-evolving global community.

Journey to a Closed City with the International Executive Service Corps — Russell R. Miller (2004) ISBN 1-888725-94-X, Describes the adventures of a retired executive volunteering with the senior citizens' equivalent of the Peace Corp as he applies his professional skills in a former Iron Curtain city emerging into the dawn of a new economy. This book is essential reading for anyone approaching retirement who is interested in opportunities to exercise skills to "do good" during expense-paid travel to intriguing locations. Journey to A Closed City should also appeal to armchair travelers eager to explore far-off corners of the world in our rapidly-evolving global community. paperback, 5½X8¼,270pp,$16.95 **MacroPrintBooks**™ edition (2004) ISBN 1-888725-94-8, 8¼X6½, 18 pt, 150 pp, $24.95

Science & Humanities Press

Publishes fine books under the imprints:

- Science & Humanities Press
- BeachHouse Books
- MacroPrint Books
- Heuristic Books
- Early Editions Books

Educators Discount Policy

To encourage use of our books for education, educators can purchase three or more books (mixed titles) on our standard discount schedule for resellers. See **sciencehumanitiespress.com/educator/educator.html** for more detail or call

Science & Humanities Press,

PO Box 7151,

Chesterfield MO 63006-7151

636-394-4950

Books by Russell Miller

Journey to a Closed City with the International Executive Service Corps — Russell R. Miller (2004) Experiences in Ukraine ISBN 1-888725-94-X, paperback, 5½X8¼,270pp, $16.95 **MacroPrintBooks**™ edition (2004) ISBN 1-888725-94-8, 8¼X6½, 18 pt, 150 pp, $24.95

The Spy with a Clean Face (2008) ISBN 978-1-59630-031-6 paperback, 5½X8¼, 300pp, $18.95

ISBN 978-1-59630-032-3 **MacroPrintBooks**™ Edition (16pt) paperback, 6½X8¼, 350pp, $28.95

Order Form

Item	Each	Quantity	Amount
Missouri (only) sales tax 6.325%			
Priority Shipping			$5.00
	Total		
Name			
Address			

Science & Humanities Press

PO Box 7151
Chesterfield, MO 63006-7151
(636) 394-4950
Sciencehumanitiespress.com